STUDENT OF DEATH

FLESCH & STONE
BOOK 1

IAIN ROB WRIGHT

ULCERATED PRESS

WANT FREE BOOKS?

Don't miss out on your FREE Iain Rob Wright horror starter pack. Five free bestselling horror novels sent straight to your inbox. No strings attached.

VISIT THE BACK OF THE BOOK FOR DETAILS.

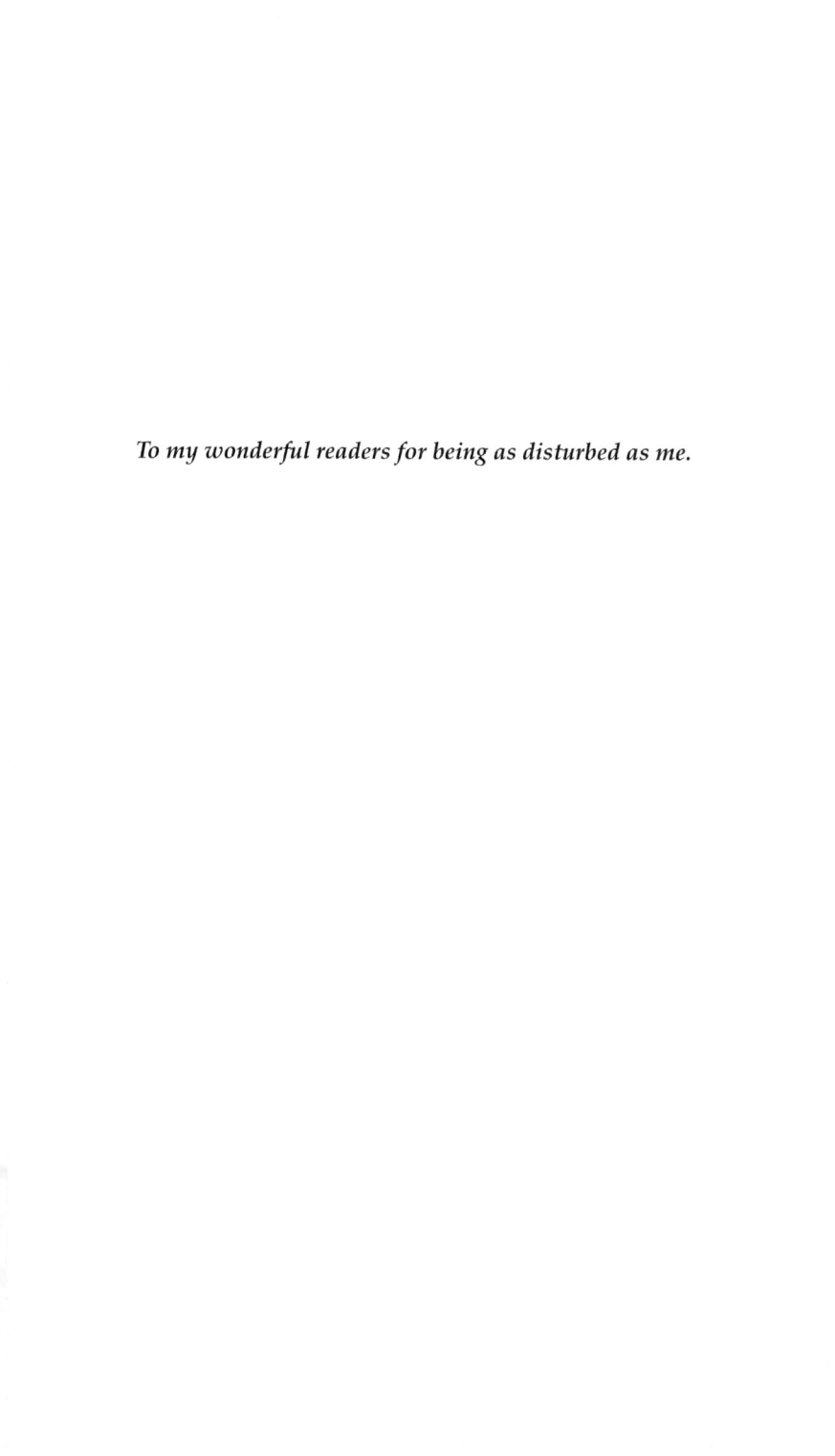

To my wonderful readers for being as disturbed as me.

With my greatest thanks to the following:
Suzy Tadlock
Marie Warnquist
Anthony Wilkins
Paula Bruce
Murder Shrimp
Ruth Witcomb
Andrea Oakes
Francis Keenan
Michael Greer
Angela Rees
Philip Clements
Elaine Anderson
KT Morrison
Trudy Meiser
Tracy Burrows
Steph Brown
Julie Adams
Richard Keeble
Sue Jones
Bridgett Duffus
RynoTheAlbinoRhyno
Susan Hall
Marci J Green
Julie McWhorter
Julian White

Wendy Daniel
Fear kitty
Renee Master
Mike Waldinger
Lola Wayne
Sarah Crossland
Lanie Evans
Lorraine Wilson
Sue Newhouse
Dominic Harris
Lindsay Carter
Rach Kinsella Chippendale
Leonard Ducharme
Jonathan & Tonia Cornell
Rigby Jackson
Carmen Hammond
Katrice Tuck
Minnis Hendricks
Kelli Herrera
Terrie-Ann Thulborn
Darrion Mika
Suzy Tadlock
Gillian Moon
Armando Llerena
Stephanie Everett
Ali Black
Angela Richards
Adrianne Yang
Angelica Maria
Kristina Goeke
Andrew Moss
Emma Bailey
Xya Marie
Leona Overton
Susan Hayden

Jennifer Holston
Roy Oswald
Chris Aitchison
Catherine Healy
Carol Wicklund
Lawrence Clamons
Mark Pearson
Dabney Arch
Tracy Putland
Tracey Newman
David Greer
Sandra Lewis
Windi LaBounta
Stephanie Hardy
Janet Carter
Lauren Brigham
Clare Lanes
Cindy Ahlgren
John Best

PROLOGUE

SHE BLED FROM EVERY ORIFICE, her legs so bruised they were swollen to twice their normal size.

But she was free.

The cold night air kissed her face like a mother offering safety. Behind her lay hell, a temple of decaying flesh and evil biting monsters. Teeth marks punctured her flesh in the most intimate of places.

But she was free.

She had survived.

She had escaped.

The knee-height, wet grass tried to bring her down, but she wouldn't let it as she picked up more and more speed. Her body was desperate, her spirit broken, but her will to survive was intact.

Panting, her tongue darted in and out of the gaps between her splintered teeth. Moaning, she found herself hoarse and without a voice.

But she was free.

Only darkness and isolation lay ahead, but it was a blinding, sun-drenched paradise compared to what she had just endured.

The monsters were sleeping, and by the time they awoke, she would be gone. All she had to do was find help. Find rescue.

She was free.

But not yet saved.

CHAPTER ONE

THE AIRWAVE RADIO on the dashboard squawked to life, jolting Detective Richard Mullins from his thoughts. "DI Mullins, requesting ETA. Over."

Mullins leant forward and thumbed the transmit button. "Arriving at scene. ETA two minutes. Over."

"All received. Thank you. Out."

Truthfully, Richard's driver had parked their silver Ford Fiesta outside the derelict train station twenty minutes ago at 14:03, but Richard had just been sitting there ever since, trying to calm his nerves. Blood, death, murder – these were the things that ignited his synapses and sent his mind spiralling. He needed to keep control of himself. Stepping into a murder scene could be overwhelming.

Overexciting.

Intoxicating.

"You can do this, Richard," he told himself, his voice barely a whisper. He was alone in the car, his driver having gone to stretch his legs. Tony was a civilian, and he would be left with nothing to do for the next few hours while Richard did his job. The man had chosen to go for a walk rather than sit in the car.

From inside his trouser pocket, Richard retrieved a weathered brown auger shell. He had stumbled upon it eighteen years ago at a beach in Saltburn, and he had kept the tiny item ever since. Gripping it now, he drove the sharp point of the spiral shell into the base of his thumb and focused on the pain, using it to block out everything else. It pushed aside the approaching brain fog that had been threatening to occlude his thinking.

There was one final ritual that would help him prepare his mind for the grim task ahead, and then he would get out of the car. He opened the glove box and retrieved a crossword book, quickly flipping to the most recent puzzle he'd been working on. With a Staedtler ballpoint pen taken from his blazer's inside pocket, he started to fill in the answers with lightning speed.

Retire from a job? Six letters… Resign.
On drugs? Five letters… Using.
Statement of beliefs? Five letters… Credo.
Montenegro's capital city? Nine letters… Podgorica.

"Okay, I'm ready." Richard slid the crossword book back inside the glove compartment and repocketed the pen. Then he climbed out of the car and shut the door gently behind him. Loud noises bothered him, even ones he made himself. Fortunately, the surrounding area was almost completely silent.

No traffic.

No bystanders.

Only the raspy chatter of a disapproving magpie spying him from the branches of an elm tree.

In front of Richard, the dilapidated train station stood like an ancient ruin. Nestled in the run-down ex-mining village of Pit Dean, County Durham, the station had been a victim of Beeching's axe – a series of profit reforms in the sixties that had stripped back the nation's railways substantially. The building only remained standing because of its unique Parisian architecture and its Grade 2 listed status.

From what Richard's initial research had told him on the

drive over, a local pit owner and native Frenchman named Hugo Alisander had wanted to import a piece of his homeland, while also increasing his standing with the local community. So, at the turn of the last century, he had paid for a flamboyant train station to be erected, designed and built by skilled Parisian architects. The station had immediately become a regional landmark, famed for its audaciousness, and yet, a hundred years later, its white facades were now mouldy and its sculpted ornaments had all but crumbled. The weeds, bushes, and trees grew so wildly that the building was barely even visible from the road.

Richard left the car, leaving it unlocked as Tony had the keys.

A liveried squad car and forensics van were both parked up ahead, blocking the narrow access road that led to the train station. A separate footpath snaked alongside the road, but it was barred by a rusty metal gate and a uniformed police officer who was currently yawning and checking his watch.

"Can I help you, sir?" the officer asked Richard when he noticed him approaching.

Richard pulled his badge and ID. "DI Mullins. I've been called up from Darlington. Have we locked down the scene yet?"

"Aye, sir. Forensics arrived an hour ago to secure the location, but it's…" He sucked in a deep breath and let it out through his nostrils. He couldn't have been much older than twenty-five. "It's pretty grim down there."

"Death is rarely anything other than grim, officer. Who found the body?"

"An anonymous tip-off came in at eight AM. The responding officers found the body at around zero nine hundred hours, but they're no longer at the scene. DCI Flannigan told 'em to go take a break and calm their nerves. They'll be giving statements later."

Richard would have preferred to speak with the responding

officers right away, but there was little to be gained from complaining. "Thank you for the update, officer. May I enter?"

"Aye, sir. We, um, cannit get hold of a key for the padlock, so you'll 'ave to climb over."

Richard glanced at his polished brown lace-up shoes and tailored black trousers. "I'm not really dressed for it, but if needs must."

The officer stood aside, and Richard climbed the gate's horizontal bars, slender fingers clamping around the cold steel. The fishy tang of rust filled his nostrils, and he knew the odour would cling to his hands until he washed them.

Don't fret. And don't slip.

Fortunately, it was an easy enough traversal to reach the other side of the gate, and he avoided embarrassing himself. Not that he ever felt anything so mundane as embarrassment.

"Watch yersel' around the side cut, sir. It's a right jungle, it is."

"I'll employ caution. Thank you again, officer."

Richard edged down the uneven path towards the train station. The front entryway was boarded up, but the mascaron above it – a sculpture of an inscrutable female face – was remarkably intact. Had this silent, stone-faced lady been gazing upon this patch of desolate wasteland for decades, with nothing and no one to entertain her? Had she seen those responsible for the grisly scene he was about to encounter?

The snaking path lived up to the beat officer's cautionary words, and with every step, Richard had to fight to keep his balance as a vast tangle of ivy reached out from the station's foundations and tried to trip him. The sprawling roots of more voracious elm trees made the ground ever harder and more uneven. Thick brambles tugged at his trousers like the fingernails of grasping corpses.

He eventually made it to the back of the station, where he found a graffiti-covered platform where passengers had once stood waiting for trains to take them to Peterlee and Durham.

At the far end of the platform, rusted gantry cranes stood like silent sentinels, their colossal bulk the only thing keeping them from being pilfered for scrap. A substantial section of the station's overhanging roof had collapsed, and it was clear that the building had been left to rot.

Richard heard the rhythmic *ka-chick-ka-chick* of a digital camera shutter.

Ka-chick-ka-chick.

Stop it!

Richard reached into his pocket and squeezed his auger shell. Then, taking a deep breath, he approached a small group of people clustered around a pile of debris in the centre of the platform. The photographer's shutter continued to click-click-click, but Richard remained composed and responded with a polite nod when the man looked his way.

Please stop the clicking.

The next person Richard made eye contact with was Detective Chief Inspector Flannigan, a woman he had dealt with many times before. Her expression, as she looked at him, was less than welcoming. "Ah, DI Mullins," she said. "Splendid you could join us. Are things a little busy at the murder university today?"

Richard attempted a smile but found it difficult. He disliked the morbid nickname commonly associated with his place of work, but he understood it wasn't far from the truth. As part of a specialised task force, dedicated to catching serial murderers and sex offenders, he knew it took a certain kind of person to do what he did.

"I apologise for my tardiness, ma'am. How can I be of use?"

DCI Flannigan was a woman in her fifties who had probably never been feminine or attractive, nor likely ever cared about such things. Her black hair was cropped to her square shoulders, and she wore no make-up at all. The only jewellery she wore was a simple gold watch. Richard felt ill at ease around most women, but Flannigan didn't have that effect on him. She was strictly business and spoke plainly, which he found comforting.

Flannigan scrunched up her nose as if she had smelled something bad. "I want you to do your... thing. Tell me, what kind of animal would do something like this?"

Richard frowned, but when she stepped aside, his focus fell upon the crime scene. A monster indeed had visited this place. His mouth immediately went dry.

This is a work of art.

A trio of forensic technicians in white polythene suits were currently cataloguing the scene, but they scurried aside as Mullins stepped forward. They had either worked with him before or knew of his reputation.

Macabre Mullins.

The weird guy from the murder university.

Detective Ghoul.

Richard got to work.

The victim, a barefooted young woman wearing indigo jeans and a bloodstained lavender blouse, had been silenced with a black ball gag. He judged her to be around twenty years of age, but her sagging grey cheeks pulled away from her eye sockets and made her look older in death. Someone had tied her hands behind her back and hoisted her upwards by the wrists, wrapping the rope around an exposed rafter in the collapsed ceiling and tying it off around a concrete support pillar. The over-rotation of her shoulders had caused her head to hang lifelessly in front of her and her bare feet to dangle. To add even more suffering, it appeared the killer had torn out her fingernails, leaving behind bright red, bloody beds.

I can hear her screams.

She would have begged for her life and then, eventually, for her death.

Blood caked the girl's golden hair, having leaked from a section of scalp missing from the top of her head. A translucent layer of yellowing flesh clung to her exposed skull, surrounded by some kind of cruddy black substance. Dried blood stained the rubble beneath her bare feet.

This was a bad ending.

You poor thing.

Richard closed his eyes and inhaled the metallic scent of blood and the fruity stench of human decay. The silence was unsettling, devoid now even of the magpie's irritable birdsong. This was a quiet place, a lonely place. A place that stunk of death and echoed with memories of the past.

The perfect spot for a monster to play its games.

"I don't think this was personal," Richard muttered.

Flannigan's voice carried a hint of repulsion as she regarded the dead girl hanging from the rafters. "It seems highly personal to me, Mullins."

Richard reluctantly met Flannigan's gaze. "This wasn't about the girl. It was about the suffering. The killer tied her hands behind her back and strung her up by her wrists, a method of torture called *strappado* – or reverse hanging. It exerts agonising pressure on the shoulder blades by over-rotating them and causing them to gradually tear. The victim would have suffered over several hours as she tried to lift herself up on her tiptoes to ease the pressure on her joints, but eventually exhaustion would have caused her to collapse and most likely asphyxiate."

"And what about her head? Is that part of it?" Flannigan was a smart woman, and likely had theories of her own, but Richard was there to give his opinion, so she wanted to hear it.

He pointed to the victim's exposed skull. "Do you see that black substance around the edges of her scalp?"

"Yes. We don't know what that is yet."

"Likely tar or some kind of oil, which suggests the killer performed an additional method of torture called pitchcapping."

"Pitchcapping?"

"Yes. It involves pouring tar or molten metal onto a victim's head and allowing it to cool before ripping it free. It was used several times throughout history, dating back to even before the Roman Republic."

One of the forensics grimaced, likely unsettled by Mullins' knowledge of torture, and the enthusiasm with which he shared it.

The suffering must have been immense. I can almost smell it. The air is charged.

Flannigan was staring at Richard. She wasn't wearing her dress hat, so she ran a hand over her short black hair to flatten it. "How do you know these things, Mullins?"

"I read a lot."

"You read a lot about obscure torture methods?"

"It's my job."

Flannigan nodded slowly. "I suppose it is. Anything else you see here?"

"Like I said, this was about inflicting pain. The victim remained alive for several hours, maybe even a full day, before her lungs finally gave out. While the pain in her scalp would have been severe, it was probably minor compared to the mounting pressure on her shoulders and chest."

"You're sure this wasn't personal? This girl might have pissed someone off, someone who wanted revenge. An ex-boyfriend, perhaps?"

Richard shook his head. "The killer planned and researched this. The torture methods, the location…" He turned and looked around at the overgrowing elms and drooping willow trees casting shadows over the abandoned train tracks. "This station has been abandoned for decades, and the entire area has been completely neglected. It's the perfect spot for a monster to play. The killer might have known the victim, but it wasn't about her. Any young female would presumably have done."

"Wonderful." Flannigan closed her eyes and let out a sigh before opening them again. "She's fully clothed, so we're uncertain about any sexual element to the crime. I'm assuming the ball gag was only to silence her."

"There's always the possibility of an intimate assault," Mullins said, knowing a high percentage of ritualistic and pattern killings were at least partly sexual in nature. "I wouldn't hazard a guess without forensics."

"Fair enough." Flannigan folded her arms and shivered slightly. "There's one more piece of the puzzle I need to show you."

He raised an eyebrow. "I'm waiting."

"Okay, don't get excited. Follow me."

Flannigan led him around the pile of debris with the dead girl hanging at its centre to a place several metres further down the platform. Beside a spattering of what seemed to be blood, the only thing of note was a rusty oil drum. The acrid reek of burnt chemicals sullied the air, and a glistening black stain marred the concrete.

"This must be where our killer heated the tar," Flannigan surmised. "If it's like you said."

Richard nodded, pleased to see that his theory was panning out. He always liked to be right. The victim had been hung from the rafters, begging for her life while the killer heated a shallow bowl of pitch in this nearby oil drum. It had probably delighted him to spend time alone with his terrified prey, breathing in her futile screams and exerting complete control over her life.

Richard turned back to Flannigan and tried to look her in the eye as he spoke. "The killer would have scouted this place before bringing his victim here. We need to check CCTV for the past two weeks."

Flannigan grunted. "Have you seen the area we're in? Most of the factories have been condemned for over a decade. There are no houses for half a mile. The entire area is neglected, just like you said. The chances of getting camera footage are slim."

"Still worth checking. You never know."

"I agree, but there's more. You need to look at this." She

moved past the oil drum and pointed to something behind it on the ground.

Richard stepped around the drum to see.

Curious.

A pale blue pillowcase had been spread flat on the concrete, with a strange object placed on top of it: a pitted grey bowl matted with clumps of blonde hair and stained with black tar. Inside the shallow bowl was a delicate fillet of pink and white meat infested with maggots.

Richard shook his head. "What's this?"

"We found a small piece of flesh missing from the victim's lower back," Flannigan informed him. "I'm guessing this is it."

Richard agreed that the chunk of meat could have been human flesh, but that wasn't what had captured his attention. One additional item had been set up on the pillowcase, placed just above the blackened skull cap – a scrap of cardboard with three words scrawled in blood:

EAT UP FLESCH.

Flannigan straightened her uniform and cleared her throat. "I've been rolling it over in my mind, but I don't understand what it means. Is it a misspelling?"

The word transfixed Richard. He knew it well. "It's not a misspelling. It's a surname. Austrian."

"Okay. So what the bloody hell does it mean?"

"It's a message."

"For whom?"

Richard walked to the edge of the concrete platform and squeezed the auger shell inside his pocket. Under his breath, so that Flannigan wouldn't hear him, he muttered to himself. "It's for me."

The killer knows my real name.

———

It was a bright sunny day in Wolverhampton; the kind of day that made you feel guilty for not having plans. This being Britain – and specifically the Midlands – the local populace was in full summer mode, ready to make the most out of the decent, yet undoubtedly fleeting weather. Young men shuffled up and down the high street with their tops off, putting their tattooed chests and gold chains on full display. Meanwhile, women of all shapes and sizes strutted about in tiny shorts and strappy vests.

Sarah wore jeans and the black Guns N' Roses T-shirt she'd found at a charity shop last week. She wasn't one for showing flesh; men only ever looked at her face anyway.

And then they run away.

Sarah was currently between gigs. Her one-person security firm earned enough to keep her alive – and mostly sane – but the work arrived inconsistently. At the start of the year she'd been managing a team of bodyguards for a Saudi businessman visiting the UK. Last week, she'd been giving self-defence lessons to the employees of an inner-city taxi firm. The tasks – and the money – varied, but truthfully the only thing that mattered was that she worked for herself. No obligations. No emotional dependencies. No unexpected thrills.

Just me, myself, and I. The way I like it. Although the company sucks.

Sarah had driven into Wolverhampton's city centre that afternoon to drop off some files for her accountant, but now that she'd done that, she had the rest of the day to herself. The sunshine lifted her mood after a seemingly endless winter, and she knew she'd regret it if she didn't enjoy it.

"I'll go have a pint," she told herself, ignoring the old woman staring at her as she hobbled past on a crutch. Sarah was so used to people staring that she barely noticed any more.

It had been fifteen years since she'd lost half her face in Afghanistan.

She went inside the Royal London, a small pub that filled up with students at night but was quieter during the day. In fact, right now it was completely empty. She had to wait at the bar until a young barman appeared from a side room. He only flinched a little at the sight of her, which meant he'd probably served her before.

She ordered a pint of Fosters from on draught.

"Lovely day," the lad commented as he poured the chilled lager into an overly tall glass. He had a streak of red in his tousled brown hair and a silver stud piercing in his bottom lip.

Sarah glanced out through one of the pub's floor-to-ceiling plate-glass windows. She saw more topless men and scantily clad women passing by, dressed more for Ibiza than the Black Country. "People are really making the most of the weather, huh? I've never seen so much flesh on display."

"Ha! You wouldn't believe the things I see in here some nights." The lad topped off the pint and slid it towards her. "Everything hanging out, I can tell you."

"I'll bet." She paid him in change and thanked him, grateful when he looked her in the eye and smiled. The younger generation weren't so bad, even with their stupid hair and piercings.

The Royal London didn't have a beer garden, so Sarah chose a table next to one of the tall windows, sitting with her good side facing the sunny street. At forty-four, she was curvy and athletic, with long blonde hair and even longer legs. She could catch a man's eye easily enough, but it always played out like a practical joke. As soon as they saw the scars on the left side of her face, their flirtatious glances turned to awkward exits.

I just remembered I need to be somewhere.
I left my wallet in the car.
I-I-I'm married.

For a while, Sarah sat and watched the world go by. Pensioners pushing little tartan shopping trolleys. Students rushing to lectures. A fluorescent-jacketed council worker emptying a bin. Everyone just getting on with their day, the centre of their own little universe.

A scraping of chair legs caused Sarah to look away from the

window and cease her people-watching. A slim, suited gentleman in his early fifties stood at her table, and he was staring at her. "Do you mind if I take a seat?" he asked with an American accent. Possibly from New York

Sarah didn't know if he was asking to take a chair away, or if he wanted to sit down at her table, but when she realised there were empty chairs everywhere, she knew he was asking to join her.

She scooped back her hair and exposed the left side of her face. "I don't think you want to do that, buddy."

He whistled. "Afghanistan, right? IED?"

Under the table, Sarah's fists clenched. She tensed up in her seat. "Who are you?"

"A friend, I promise."

"I asked who you are," she growled. Her default position on strangers was not to trust them.

The man took a seat without her permission, causing her to slide back from the table and give herself more room to manoeuvre. Her precaution didn't go unnoticed, and the stranger shook his head and chuckled. Waving a hand dismissively, he finally told her his name. "James Westerly. I'm the Chief Superintendent at the Institute of Pathological Crime in Darlington. You're Captain Sarah Stone, right? Retired, of course."

Sarah shrugged.

"You might have heard the IPC referred to as the murder university." He grimaced. "Although we're not fond of the nickname."

"Jim, I'm really not—"

"James."

"Whatever. Look, I'm just trying to enjoy my day here. I don't know what you want or why you're interested in me, but I'm pretty sure you're going to annoy me. Maybe save your breath and just leave me be, yeah?"

That was met by another chuckle, and the persistent

stranger leant forward on one elbow. He studied Sarah a moment before grinning. "You're gonna want to hear this, I assure you."

She picked up her pint and supped at the head before taking a deeper swig and enjoying the chill at the back of her throat. "Fine, let's have it then. What do you want?"

"To offer you a job."

She rolled her eyes and placed her pint back down. "Not interested."

"I'm here to persuade you."

"Good luck. I'm too old for a career change. Also, I don't want one."

"You mean your security business?" He smirked, a little deridingly for her taste. "How long until you climb the walls with boredom? I know all about you, Sarah. You're meant for more than protecting pampered CEOs and corrupt politicians."

"You can just say politician. The word corrupt is superfluous."

"Indeed."

"You don't know anything about me," she said, supping her pint again. "Probably better to leave it that way."

James leant back in his chair and took in a breath before speaking again. "I know you worked as a regimental liaison in Afghanistan, tasked with local diplomacy and co-ordination. You were a highly trained soldier with a lot of combat experience, but you excelled at keeping the peace."

"I was pretty good at killing too, to be fair."

"Perhaps. But then you were injured." His brown eyes focused on her scars for a split second, but he didn't stare. "After your discharge, an agent from the Major Crimes Unit approached you and recruited you into its antiterrorism task force. Your work there was instrumental in taking down several terrorist cells and stopping attacks on the United Kingdom. You were exemplary. You thrived."

"If you think that, then you really haven't done your

research. Don't you think I'd still be on the job if it was such a bloody good time, you idiot?"

He flinched at her sudden outburst, clearly not expecting it. She had warned him he was going to end up annoying her. She had kept her word. For a moment, he just sat there, so she took the opportunity to study him. His slender frame and open-collared shirt screamed pencil pusher.

I could snap him like a twig if I felt like it.

"Sarah, I know that you—"

A group of teenagers barged through the doors and entered the pub, laughing and giggling and staggering towards the bar. It was a little past three on a Tuesday afternoon, but they were clearly drunk.

The sudden ruckus caused Sarah to flinch, and while James continued to speak, she was no longer listening. She didn't like the noise the youths were making. There was too much of it.

Calm down, Sarah. No one is after you.

You're retired.

And you're going to stay that way.

"I'm not interested, James," she said, interrupting whatever he'd been saying. "I gave up on chasing bad guys for good reasons."

"What reasons?"

"My reasons."

"That's vague."

She smashed her palm down on the table, almost knocking over her pint. "Fine. How about the fact evil isn't finite? You can't stop it. It's a great big gushing geyser, spewing bile into the ocean while the innocent little fishes swim around without a clue about how poisonous the water is. You can try to plug the hole, but every time you do, more cracks open up and the gushing only gets worse."

James gave her a lopsided grin. "That's quite the metaphor. A tad dramatic for my liking, but impressive nonetheless."

She shrugged. "War makes poets of men and women."

"I suppose it does."

The teens continued making a racket at the bar – shrill female voices joined by foul-mouthed male bravado. The young barman did his best to serve them, but he appeared anxious, probably having a sixth sense for impending aggro.

"Sarah, listen to me for just a—"

Sarah bashed her fist on the table and yelled towards the bar. "Oi, kids! Let's turn the volume down a bit, yeah?"

A knee-high-booted girl in the group turned to her and glared. "You what?"

"I said keep it down. It's the middle of the afternoon and not everyone's in the mood for a rave."

"A rave? God, how old are you?" The girl flicked her bleach blonde hair over her bare shoulder and tutted in disgust.

"I'm old enough to come over there and shove my fist in your mouth, so keep it down or else."

James cleared his throat and put his hand on the table. "Um, Sarah…?"

The girl chuckled dismissively, a hand on her hip. "Or else what?"

"I think I just covered that with my fist in your mouth," Sarah said. "You're not very bright, are you?"

"I go to university. I'm smarter than you."

"I doubt it, sweetheart."

James put his hand out to touch Sarah's arm, but she pulled away. Her eyes fixated on the blonde girl at the bar, a girl who knew nothing about anything but acted like an entitled brat anyway.

A wiry lad stepped to the front of the group to join the blonde girl, flexing some very average muscles beneath his T-shirt. Students could rarely back up their fighting talk, but this lad seemed willing to give it a go. "Mind your business," he said, "and we'll mind ours, yeah?"

"I'll mind my business if you keep the noise down, yeah?"

"It's a pub, ain't it? People come here to have fun. Leave if you don't like it."

"There are different kinds of fun, buddy. You don't want to find out what mine is."

The lad sneered. "Are you crazy or something?"

"It's been said. Want to find out how crazy?"

"Just ignore her, Tom." The blonde girl pulled the lad back towards the bar. "Look at her face. Ugly bitch."

That was Sarah's cue. She scooted back in her chair, ready to get up and teach these drunken idiots a lesson in manners.

James got up first and stepped away from the table. The students bristled as he approached them, but he simply reached inside his blazer and pulled out a wallet. He flicked it open and shoved it in their faces. "I suggest you go sober up someplace quiet or I'll nick the lot of you on a section five."

"You're a copper?" The lad with the average-looking muscles frowned. His Adam's apple bobbed as he swallowed. "You can arrest me?"

"An excellent deduction. Keep it up and you'll earn your degree in no time. What are you studying?"

"Um, animation."

"Huh," James raised an eyebrow. "Not what I was expecting. Anyway, get out of here before you make my companion any angrier. You think she got those scars baking muffins?"

The lad gave Sarah a glance, then looked away. After muttering something to the mouthy blonde girl, he made an announcement to the others in his group, and they all headed for the door. "Come on, guys. This place is dead. Let's go chill in the SU."

James sat back down as the students slouched out of the pub. "Sorry about that," he said. "Where were we?"

"I didn't need you to defend me."

"I was defending *them.* I know your track record, Sarah. That's why I'm here."

"No." She swigged her pint down to halfway and was

happy to abandon the rest. She stood up from her chair and pointed a finger in James's face. "Whatever you want, I'm not interested. The only reason I've humoured you this long is because I have nothing else to do today. Now, if you'll excuse—"

"Howard's dead."

She sat back down. "What?"

"Your old colleague at the MCU. Howard Hopkins is dead."

CHAPTER
TWO

SARAH SAT BACK DOWN.

Howard Hopkins was the man responsible for recruiting her into the MCU antiterrorism squad ten years ago. He'd approached her during a very bad time in her life, a time when she'd been unstable and angry, and had lashed out at everything and everyone around her. Despite his reservations, Howard had brought Sarah in and stuck by her through thick and thin. A true friend. One of the few she'd ever made.

"What do you mean he's dead? I spoke to Howard a couple of months ago."

James leant to the side and pulled a briefcase up onto the table. Sarah hadn't even realised he'd had it with him. He released the silver clasps and opened it up. From inside, he grabbed a thick pile of papers and then placed the briefcase back on the floor. He handed Sarah the top sheet. It was an incident report filed by the Major Crimes Unit.

"Agent Hopkins recruited you into the MCU, right?" James said, his voice brimming with unsolicited compassion. "I understand you two were… close."

Sarah studied the report, not wanting to believe what she was reading. "I was close to everyone at the MCU."

"But you were especially close to Howard. Even after you left."

She looked up from the paper and shot him a fiery glance. "I don't see how that's any of your business."

"Why didn't it work out with you two?" He actually sounded interested, which irritated Sarah greatly.

"Relationships." She shrugged. "They don't tend to fare well when one of you works all hours of the day and night, putting their life at risk, while the other just wants to stay home and eat toast in bed."

James nodded. "I'm divorced, I get it. You were out, but Howard felt like he still had more to give."

"And that's why he's dead." She thrust the file back at James to disguise her shaking hands. "How did he die? It doesn't go into detail."

"From what I understand, he was investigating an Albanian crime gang in Doncaster. Human trafficking, drugs, guns, murder for hire, the whole shebang. Howard was working to bring the organisation down. They got to him first."

"Did anyone go to jail?"

"There were a few arrests based on the evidence Howard had gathered, but he hadn't tied everything together yet."

"I meant for his killing. Did you collar anyone for it?" She locked her jaw and ground her teeth together. Her heart was drumming in her chest. "Did you get the bastards who did it or not?"

"No."

She shook her head and glowered at him, causing the scars on her face to stretch painfully. They were always more sensitive in sunny weather. "Like I said, there's no end to evil. Try to fight it and all you get is a bunch of dead heroes."

"Howard didn't believe that, and I don't think you do either, Sarah." He leant forward on his elbows, looking her dead in the eyes. "I get why you retired. Chasing gangsters, hunting terrorists, it's a young person's game. It's hectic, and pyrrhic, and you certainly did enough to earn your way out, but that doesn't mean you should hang up your boots entirely. How many lives did you save while at the MCU?"

"I think more about the ones I lost."

He nodded. She didn't know if he truly understood what she was saying, but at least he was earnest. "What I'm offering you, Sarah, is a place to fight the good fight without having to throw yourself out of helicopters or defuse ticking time bombs."

She huffed. "Are you writing my biography?"

"No, but I've learned enough about you to know you're the only woman capable of doing what I need done. It has to be you."

Howard's death had left Sarah reeling, but she did her best to hide it. If she tried to get up, she might collapse, so for the next few minutes she was stuck in this chair, having to listen to this man while she regained her nerves. "What the hell is this?" she demanded. "I mean, really? I've heard about the murder university – a bunch of geeks and bookworms getting off over serial killers and sex offenders. It ain't my wheelhouse, buddy. I'm more of a hands-on kind of lady."

A flash of distaste crossed James's face, which changed his entire aura. Perhaps he wasn't as benign as he appeared. "We have an undeserved reputation," he said. "I assure you that every one of my colleagues is dedicated to making the world a safer place."

"By studying sickos like Fred West and Myra Hindley? Sounds lovely."

"Sarah, do you know that ten years ago there were only two serial killers assumed to be active in the United Kingdom? We now predict there to be over thirty. Be it poverty, mass immigration, social media, or hundreds of other factors, it's clear that violent crime is on the rise. The geyser you spoke about is spewing out in full force. Are you really willing to sit back and do nothing?"

"The bad guys are winning." She sat back and folded her arms. "They always have been."

"Isn't it time to change that?"

"You can't change it."

"You proved that's not true, Sarah. Countless people are alive today because of the work you did in the MCU."

She shook her head but couldn't speak. The conversation was draining her strength. She purposefully kept her life simple; emotionless and dull. Dull was safe.

I don't want back in. I can't drown in all that misery again.

Leaning forward, Sarah rediscovered her voice, although it was shaky and full of emotion. "Do you have any idea how many friends I've watched die? I mean, literally watched the light fade from their eyes? Their last words whisper in my ears at night while I'm trying to sleep. Do you really think I want to go back to that life?"

James put another file in front of her. "This isn't about stopping suicide bombers or assassination attempts, Sarah. It isn't about trying to shut down terrorist cells only for them to pop up again bigger than before. What I'm offering is a chance to stop the monsters that prey on innocent young girls like this."

Sarah glanced at the picture attached to the file. It was a photograph of a young woman with strikingly blonde hair. She seemed sweet and full of hope, her smile genuine and unforced. "She's dead?"

James nodded solemnly. He glanced around, maybe to see if anyone was listening, then leant closer again. "Her name is Claudette Herrington, a student at Durham University. Would've turned twenty next week. Unfortunately, ten days ago, someone scalped her and left her hanging in an abandoned train station. Her killer made an anonymous phone call to let us know where to find her, and that she would be the first of many."

Sarah's stomach churned. What went on in the head of psychopaths who derived pleasure from the abduction and murder of innocent young girls? She couldn't even fathom it. Perhaps she should give James a break if stopping those kinds of maniacs was his passion. "I don't see how I can help you," she said, her voice jittery. "This isn't my area of expertise. The only psychological profile I can offer you is my own, and it makes for grim reading."

"I have a dozen people who can give me a workup of our killer's personality, Sarah. That's not why I need you. I need you because you're tough, intelligent, and female."

"What does me being female have to do with anything?"

"Let me get into it first. Will you hear me out?"

She shrugged, still too shaky to stand up. Her thighs trembled beneath the table. "I can try."

James pulled another file out of his briefcase. This one seemed like an official personnel sheet for a thirty-four-year-old man named Richard Mullins. "This is Richard," he explained. "He's quite possibly the best criminologist in the entire country. I need you to babysit him."

"What? I don't—"

He put a hand up to keep her from interrupting. "Richard Mullins changed his surname six years ago. His real name is Richard Flesch."

Sarah waited for James to continue, but when he didn't, she realised he expected some kind of reaction from her. Was she supposed to recognise the name? Strangely enough, it did seem familiar. "Wait, are… are you talking about the Chester-le-Street Cannibal? Richard Flesch? Shit, you are, aren't you? This… This is him?"

James nodded slowly. "It's him. Richard works at the Institute. He has an uncanny ability to solve murders."

"I'm not surprised. He committed enough of them himself. They sentenced him to the nuthouse for what he did, didn't they?"

"He was coerced, Sarah. His parents were Brenda and Felix Flesch, two of the sickest individuals to ever walk this earth.

They forced Richard to take part in their murders when he was just eight years old. A child."

"Not by the time they caught him."

James grumbled. "Richard was fifteen when they arrested him, but eighteen by the time he eventually took the stand. People saw an adult monster on trial instead of a damaged boy."

Sarah remembered watching a documentary on the trial a few years back. Richard Flesch had been a demented, dead-eyed young man with a strange way of talking – a monster, for sure. "So let me get this straight," she said. "You broke a serial killer out of the looney bin to help catch others like him? Do the press know?"

"There's an injunction in place preventing anyone from reporting on it. The Lord Chief Justice himself signed off on Richard's new identity."

"His new identity as a police officer, you mean? Are you insane? He tortured, killed, and ate people. You gave Hannibal Lecter a job."

James leafed through the file in front of Sarah, pointing out several sections. "He isn't a police officer. His title is only applicable as an investigator for the Institute. Richard has no powers of arrest, and he remains electronically tagged at all times."

"Comforting."

"Look, if there were any danger at all, Richard would still be at Broadmoor. His doctors released him because they believe him to be rehabilitated."

Sarah raised an eyebrow. "And is he?"

James let out a sigh and averted his eyes. "He has proclivities. Weaknesses, if you will."

"Wait, are you saying this guy still has urges to chop people up?"

He turned back to her. "What I'm saying is that Richard

Flesch endured one of the most traumatic, painful childhoods anyone has ever experienced. Yet he is eager to do good."

"He wants to atone for the twenty-odd people he murdered? How noble."

"Isn't it better than not trying at all?"

Sarah grabbed her half-finished pint and emptied it in one gulp. After this conversation, she intended to buy another one. Her hand shook as she put the glass down. "Why are you talking to me about this? How on earth do you think I am qualified to… to *babysit* your pet monster?"

"Because he can only operate with a female partner."

A brittle chuckle escaped her clenched teeth. Her body tensed up in a mixture of bitterness and disbelief. Then she outright bellowed with laughter. It caught the attention of the young barman, who seemed bemused as he polished a towering stack of glasses on the counter. "Oh, of course," she said, putting her hands together in a single clap. "I'm supposed to sit there with my tits out while he fondles himself, right? Does that help little Richie deal with his urges to kill-kill-kill?"

James tutted at her. Was it because she was mocking him, or was he offended on behalf of Richard Flesch?

"It's not like that at all, Sarah. Richard's father was brutal and cruel. It traumatised Richard to the point where most men unsettle him. The last time he worked with a male partner, he ended up wetting himself during a heated argument. He mentally shut down for two weeks afterwards."

Sarah went to say something, but decided it would only be unhelpful. James was being serious, so she should try to listen to him without the constant barbs. It took a lot of effort to stay quiet, but she managed it.

This conversation is insane.

A mass murderer who wets himself.

James seemed to appreciate the non-interruption, and he continued. "The only time Richard opens up and thinks clearly is when he has a partner to bounce ideas off, but that partner has to be female. And capable of holding her own."

Sarah eyeballed him, processing his words as she spoke her own. "You mean you need a woman who has a chance of surviving in a locked room with a psychopath?"

"Richard isn't a psychopath. He has a conscience. The problem is that he's deeply, deeply damaged. I figured you'd have a little sympathy there."

She stood up, her legs still jelly but now firm enough to hold her. "I have to stop this. It's crazy, and it's wasting both of our times. Look, thank you for the interest, Jim, but find someone else."

He stood up with her and put a hand out imploringly. "It's James, and there isn't anyone with your background, Sarah. I'm desperate. The monster who murdered Claudette Herrington knows Richard's true identity. It's caused him to become unstable, yet there is no one more capable of catching this monster than him. More young women are going to die if this killer isn't stopped. Girls with their entire lives ahead of them."

"Not my problem." She turned to walk away.

"Sarah, please!"

"I'm leaving."

There was an almighty clatter nearby, followed by the sound of shattering glass.

Incoming!

Sarah threw herself down beneath a table and pulled in her legs as the world around her clashed and rattled. A moan escaped her lips, and she tried to blink the sudden blurriness from her vision, but her eyelids had turned to stone. Her hands clenched, fingertips digging into her palms, mouth stretched in a rictus grin.

Bullets firing overhead.

Car windscreens shattering.

Men and women screaming.

Helicopters, trucks, tanks. Sand, stone, heat.

Burning. Her face burning.

Wicked grins of evil men.

Only one face was familiar. Howard Hopkins. Bleeding. Dying. Calling out to her.

"Sarah? Sarah, are you okay?"

She blinked and her vision came back. She was no longer in the desert, but sprawled on a sticky, beer-soaked floor inside a dimly lit Wolverhampton pub. James stared at her, clearly mortified. Standing behind him, the young barman appeared equally shocked. "I-is she okay?" he asked. "I dropped a stack of glasses. Butterfingers."

"It's all right," James said, waving a hand gently. "She's fine. Um…"

"I… I'm sorry," Sarah said, her entire body shivering. Sweat trickled from her hairline and inside her armpits.

James reached out a hand. "Sarah, I didn't know you were…"

She chuckled, too embarrassed to be defiant any more. "Didn't know I was a total head case?"

"Well, it wasn't in your file, I admit."

"You should've read between the lines."

James helped her up, but she pushed his hand away as soon as she was standing. Brushing herself down, she apologised to the barman, who sheepishly returned to his post to clear up the broken glass.

James opened the door for Sarah and suggested she get some fresh air.

"Stop fussing over me," she said. "I'm fine. The news about Howard upset me, that's all. Then you went and got me all worked up with your pet cannibal bullshit."

"Sarah, you don't need to explain. After all you've been through…"

"I'm not in a position to help you, James. So find someone else to be a babysitter."

He shook his head. "It needs to be you, Sarah. And I think

you need this as well. You think you're broken, but you're not. Every person you've ever worked with speaks highly of you." He waved a clump of files in her face. He had his briefcase tucked under his arm. "I've read their character references, dozens of them, all glowing."

"I'm not the same person. I'm too damaged."

He thrust the top sheet from the file at her. Claudette Herrington's picture. "It's not about how damaged we are, Sarah. It's about stopping monsters from damaging others who still have a chance of a normal, happy life. You think this is an endless war against evil, but that's only true so long as we keep fighting. If we quit, then evil wins well and truly and the war is lost. Just give me a day, okay? Come see the Institute. Come see the good we do there, and if the answer's still no, I'll never bother you again. Please, Sarah. Give me one chance. If anything, you'll get a day's pay for doing very little."

She took a deep breath.

CHAPTER
THREE

RICHARD SAT ALONE in his office, the soft *whoosh* of ocean waves drifting from his laptop's speakers. It was seven AM on a Wednesday morning, and while most of the Institute's staff started at nine, he liked to clock in early and enjoy a little silence before the hustle and bustle began. He liked his colleagues just fine, but people put him on edge. Behind their smiles, he always sensed their discomfort.

I'm an alien.

I'll never be like everyone else.

If it hadn't been for James Westerly taking him under his wing and bringing him into the Institute of Pathological Crime six years ago, Richard wasn't sure where he'd be now. Doctor Carney at Broadmoor had deemed him no longer a threat to society, but also incapable of functioning without supervision. And it was true – Richard had no clue how to lead a normal life or fit into society. He was different and always would be. That was why he was confined to the grounds and monitored through an ankle tag.

Like a wild animal.

With no friends or hobbies, Richard had little option but to seek solace in his 'otherness' wherever he could find it, and in many ways it brought him peace. While most 'ordinary' people seemed consumed by endless worry about debt, career, and relationships, Richard's life was streamlined and simple: seek out and stop monsters. It was a singular mission to which he was fully devoted. Two years ago, his involvement in capturing a mass murderer dubbed the 'Boxcutter Killer' had saved the lives of multiple future victims, and he was determined to save more. Despite two dozen forever-grieving families wishing Richard a painful death, he had one compelling argument in favour of his continued existence.

I'm saving lives now.

However, this new killer seemed to know Richard's true identity, knew that his name was Flesch and not Mullins. Were they planning to expose him? If so, then Richard's peaceful existence at the Institute was about to shatter like a falling vase. No one would tolerate the Chester-le-Street Cannibal working in law enforcement. The public would find it abhorrent. Angry mobs would clamour for his blood.

If I catch this monster, he'll expose my identity and ruin my life.

But I can't let him keep on killing. I don't have a choice but to go after him.

They demand it of me.

Every night when Richard tried to sleep, twenty-seven dead people visited him in his bedroom, with voices like nails on a chalkboard and glares like heat from a fire. They would not allow him to forget their suffering.

I wish I could take it all back.

But they don't care.

He shook his head, trying to focus. Additional evidence had been uploaded onto the crime database overnight, and he was eager to analyse it. Ritualistic killings were rare, but the killer had promised there would be more victims unless Richard stopped him.

And I will. I'm smarter than he is. I'm always smarter.

Richard glanced at the victim's background sheet for the

sixth time in the last hour. Claudette Herrington had been an economics student from Maidstone, and the granddaughter of the late Angela Montrose, a former MP in Margaret Thatcher's cabinet. It was an interesting connection because Angela Montrose had also been murdered, back in 1991, by a disgruntled ex-miner by the name of George Batchy. Batchy had bludgeoned the poor woman to death with a hammer on the doorstep of her own home. Fortunately, they caught him almost immediately, and then discovered his plans to attack several other key Tory MPs – including Thatcher herself.

Angela Montrose's only daughter, and Claudette's mother, had survived the trauma of losing a parent to go on to become a successful barrister. She'd already been in contact with several important people in the City about her daughter's death, which was heaping additional pressure on the investigation, but Richard didn't care about any of that. He would do everything he could to find Claudette's killer, regardless of who was mourning her death.

Families always get in the way of an investigation. Rich or poor.

Photographs from the crime scene cluttered Richard's desk. He skimmed through them one by one, searching for clues. The graffiti on the station platform appeared insignificant – just street tags and vulgarities – and the debris and litter had yielded no valuable information either. The station house was boarded up and sealed tight, with no signs of forced entry, so there was no evidence to collect inside the building. Traces of Claudette's blood found on the concrete platform were most likely from the piece of flesh the killer had cut away from her back. Her missing fingernails were likely taken as trophies.

None of the photographs whispered secrets to Richard, no matter how hard he scrutinised them. Nothing fed him the breadcrumbs he needed to find his killer.

Then there was the photograph of Claudette herself.

The dead girl's faraway gaze was almost peaceful. One might assume a cadaver keeps the expression made at the moment of death, but that wasn't true. When a person dies, the muscles in their face relax, and the blood drains from their cheeks. Depending on internal gases, temperature, and the position of the body, a cadaver might appear bloated, gaunt, sad, or even happy. Most often, though, they just seemed peaceful. Any tension they might have worn on their faces in life was gone in death. Fears, worries, hopes, dreams – all gone. Extinguished in an instant. You could see it in a person's eyes when they took their last breath.

Richard took a moment to ponder the impact Claudette Herrington might have had on the world had she lived. Like the fictional scientist travelling back in time and stepping on a butterfly, inadvertently changing the course of human history, Claudette's life might have influenced everyone who met her. The multiple souls destined to cross paths with her would now never get to meet her. Her future children would never be born. What might they have grown up to be? World leaders, scientists…

Monsters?

Richard's laptop awakened and he logged into the Institute's intranet. Durham's forensic lab had uploaded a victim toxicology report, a vital piece of information in any murder case. He skimmed over it once, and then twice.

Hmm, interesting.

As well as alcohol and a contraceptive pill, Claudette had had traces of benzodiazepines in her system, in an amount that would likely have been undetectable by all but the most sensitive of equipment. Benzos typically left a person's body in less than seventy-two hours. Claudette had been dead approximately ten hours when the police officers found her, which meant the killer must have taken and murdered her within a two-day period.

He drugged her, possibly by spiking her drink.

Then he held onto her for a while. Toyed with her.

According to Durham Constabulary's initial investigations,

Claudette had last been seen at a bar in Durham on a Friday night, associating with friends. Police were still interviewing witnesses and checking CCTV, but no one had yet admitted to seeing her leave. She had simply been there one minute and gone the next. All her friends had been extremely drunk, of course, which didn't help matters, but at least the group's designated driver, Oliver Morton, had offered something useful. He claimed to have seen Claudette talking to an older man that night, sharing a cigarette in the beer garden – which was unusual, he said, because Claudette didn't smoke. Morton had also witnessed Claudette drinking heavily and dancing with several young men. From his point of view, she'd been upset about something and was overcompensating, trying too hard to have a good time. It was a valid line of enquiry, because in most cases involving the murder of a young woman, there was a high likelihood of a lover being involved. Durham Constabulary was currently focused on finding out who that lover might be.

The possible use of Rohypnol, however, made it feasible that a complete stranger had taken Claudette. The killer had also made an anonymous phone call, taking credit for her painful death, which suggested a lack of remorse. A former lover, on the other hand, was likely to feel some measure of guilt or regret. Richard's gut told him this was not a crime of passion. It was something else entirely.

He went back to the photographs, and this time he studied the gruesome close-up of Claudette's skull. Not all the flesh had come away, so instead of exposed bone, a sinewy layer of flesh remained in place – a glistening red circle surrounded by crisp golden hair.

The pain must have been excruciating. With numerous nerve endings in the scalp, and with her hypodermis exposed, it would have felt like having a scorching hot frying pan pressed against her skull.

What must she have thought amidst her agony? Did she know her end was coming? Did she have any idea why this was happening to her? Why a monster was deciding her fate?

Richard had an erection.

"What? Oh, no-no." He reached down and grabbed himself, but realised that would only make things worse, so he lifted his hands and put them palms down on the desk. Next, he pulled himself on his wheeled chair further into the footwell to hide his crotch.

He glanced out of his office's internal window in a panic.

It's fine. No one's here. It's fine.

Aside from the fact I'm a freak who gets aroused by pain and torture.

The dead called out to Richard, mocking him, laughing at his misery.

He deserved their spite.

"I need to focus." He rubbed at his temples and squeezed his eyes shut. "Please, just let me work."

You're the Devil.

You're sick.

You're a freak.

Richard reached into his pocket and squeezed the auger shell so hard that he actually gasped in pain. Then he rummaged frantically through the things on his desk until he found a crossword book. He opened up to a random page and grabbed a pen from the pot beside his laptop.

Luigi's famous brother… Mario.

South Korean boy band… BTS.

Chilean dictator, died 2006… Pinochet.

Sponge cake of different sections… Battenberg.

He looked down at his crotch. His erection had gone away.

With a sigh, he went back to work.

The dead stayed with him.

———

The two-hundred-mile journey from Sarah's flat in Wolverhampton to the southern fringes of County Durham was tedious, to say the least. She had always thought of Yorkshire as the North, but this place was north of North. Scotland couldn't have been that far away. Even with a clear M1, the drive had taken over three hours, and she would have to do it all over again to get home.

James had picked Sarah up early that morning to take her up to Darlington, where the Institute of Pathological Crime was located. She'd never visited the town before, but her chirpy American companion happily informed her of its history as being the birthplace of the first steam-powered passenger railway.

Amazing.

During the long journey, they had spoken fairly little, but James had attempted to broach the subject of Richard Flesch several times. Supposedly, while incarcerated at Broadmoor, Richard, through guilt, boredom, or more likely as a ploy to be released, had started studying unsolved crimes in the UK. His correspondence with police went ignored for a long time, but Scotland Yard had eventually taken notice when his intuition, several times, proved crucial in solving some very serious crimes. Later on, Richard assisted Manchester police in catching a man responsible for kidnapping and assaulting nine women, saving countless future victims from meeting a similar fate. That was when James Westerly had started visiting the Chester-le-Street Cannibal personally with case files, and eventually negotiating for his release.

Today, Richard Flesch was Richard Mullins, a senior investigator at the Institute of Pathological Crime. Sarah hadn't yet decided what to think about that.

The murder university was on Darlington's outskirts, near a place called West Park. According to James, it had formerly been a stately home, but now it was a campus for criminology students and forensic experts. Most of the work performed there was academic in nature, but a small team of specialists assisted the police directly on certain cases. Richard Flesch was part of that team.

It must take a predator to catch a predator.

As they drove down a gravelled driveway, now approaching their final destination, Sarah nodded appreciatively. "I've stayed in worse places."

"It's a nightmare to heat," said James, dropping down into second.

"I'll bet."

The square-shaped manor was predominately made up of light-orange bricks, with grey edging stones surrounding the windows and doors. Modern PVC replaced whatever original windows might once have been in place, but the renovation had been carried out tastefully, preserving the building's stately charm. Upon the grey slate roof, four evenly spaced chimney stacks muddied the clear blue sky with puffs of smoke. Surrounding it all were meticulously maintained gardens, with vibrant splashes of floral purples and whites.

The long driveway stretched ahead, flanked on either side by a pair of angular stone gatehouses. A grand and welcoming entrance to a grim and morbid place.

"It's old," Sarah noted.

"One of Sir Christopher Wren's students helped design it," James said proudly.

"Wow."

Why did I even agree to come here?

I can't help myself. When people say they need my help, I can't just walk away. I'm covered in the scars to prove it.

Several vehicles were already parked in a row outside the house, so James manoeuvred the Mondeo into a gap between a white Range Rover and an orange Fiat. He switched off the engine. "Home sweet home."

The two of them took off their seatbelts and stepped out onto the gravel.

The sun shone overhead. The grass was emerald, the sky sapphire.

"This way," James said, leading her over to the manor's massive front door, which was sunk inside an impressive limestone archway with ornate swirls. Instead of rapping the large brass knocker, James prodded a code into a panel on the wall and the heavy wooden door swung open on its own.

"Ah," Sarah said. "Very Edwardian."

"The house is Georgian," James corrected her, "but the automatic hinges are a little more recent, admittedly."

"When were Georgian times, exactly?"

"I'm not entirely sure." He gave a bashful shrug. "But the house was built in 1722."

"About the same time I last got laid."

James blushed and looked away. Crass humour clearly wasn't his thing. The guy was uptight. At least he had dressed more casually today, wearing a short-sleeved grey polo with the collar undone and a pair of khaki chinos. Sarah, as usual, wore a T-shirt and jeans, but she had brought trousers and a blouse just in case. They were still in the Mondeo's boot.

In case of what? I hit the streets chasing down suspects? Not gonna happen.

As she stepped inside the building, a wave of anxiety crashed over Sarah. She'd swallowed half a bottle of valerian root tablets before leaving, but it had barely taken the edge off. Her carefully balanced life, of just enough danger to scrape a living, seemed painfully distant.

She was back in.

But she would be getting back out as soon as possible to return to taking money from paranoid sheikhs and nervous politicians.

"Right this way," said James, leading her into an entrance hall with high ceilings and wooden wall panelling. 'Welcome to our humble abode.'

Sarah had been expecting the grandeur of dual staircases

and crystal chandeliers, but the entrance hall was humble and unimpressive compared to the manor's extravagant facade. It was lit by a single, albeit rather large, glass sphere that was far too modern to be an original fixture. Meanwhile, a narrow mahogany staircase led up to a closed-off landing. No open gallery with curved bannisters that a lady of the house might drape herself over to welcome her husband home. Sarah had to admit that she was a little disappointed.

An IKEA desk stood in the middle of the tiled floor, sticking out like a sore thumb. An open laptop sat on top of it, but no one was around using it. Sarah supposed this was a reception area of sorts.

"We have to maintain the building's atheistic and structure," said James, blushing, "but we still gotta work here."

"Uh huh. You want to give me the full tour so I can get out of here?"

"Of course, but please try to keep an open mind, Sarah."

"I'm perfectly happy with a closed mind, thank you very much. I'm in no hurry to be convinced of anything."

"Well, at least you're here." He gave a small sigh and then beckoned her to follow him through a door at the back of the hall. As soon as he opened it, an irritating buzz filled the air that reminded Sarah of Friday evenings in town – young people talking too loudly and rushing about like the world was ending. It overwhelmed her for a second and caused her to take a deep breath.

James must have noticed her unease, because he placed a hand on her back and smiled. "You okay?"

"Just not a big fan of crowds." She stepped forward and peered through the doorway. "It's like a nursery in here."

"We have twenty-six postgrads, learning and contributing to active cases. Some of the brightest minds in the country."

Sarah watched the youngsters with grim interest. By her early twenties, she had already received her first commission as a second lieutenant in the British Army, skipping carefree youth in lieu of fifteen-mile hikes and night-time orienteering. These kids, sitting at desks and rushing back and forth, were soft. How many of them would crack after too many years studying mankind's darkest inclinations? Sarah was more than aware that poor mental health in law enforcement was a severe issue with no end in sight – unless someone could find a way to prevent human beings from being vile to one another.

There's a Nobel Prize winner if ever there was one.

The room they were in now might once have been a dining hall or a small ballroom. Old oil paintings adorned the dark panelled walls – of fox hunts and rich old dead guys – and heavy curtains hung from brass railings. If not for the floor-to-ceiling windows every six-feet, the room probably would have felt stuffy and oppressive. It was currently being used as a kind of communal office space, with a dozen desks placed face to face in pairs running through the centre of the room.

"This is some kind of hive?" she asked. "A place for everybody to put their heads together?"

James nodded. "I'm sure you've worked in similar set-ups. If you want to bounce ideas around or get some grunt work done, this is the place to be. Everyone works as a team. What we do is important."

Sarah knew it was, but she couldn't shake the feeling of being in a nightclub. She felt too old to be there, out of place and out of time. Everything seemed to have moved on without her, too busy and loud, too complicated and fast-moving. Even the laptops appeared beyond her understanding, hooked up to all manner of fancy, flashing peripherals.

I bet there's a whole lot of PowerPoint going on inside this place. PowerPointing at all hours of the day. PowerPointing themselves silly.

A skinny young woman, dressed in an olive-green jumpsuit, waved at James and grinned a white, toothy smile. Her skin was the colour of weak coffee and her frizzy black hair could only have been described as 'funky'.

James waved back. "Hello, Frances. Is everything okay?"

She threaded between the desks and came over. "I'm almost done with that rundown you wanted."

"Great. Send it to my email, and CC Charles Miner at Interpol too. I'll catch up with you in a little bit, if that's all right?"

"Okey dokey." Frances dashed back to her desk and started tapping away at her keyboard without sitting down. "I'll get right on it."

Sarah rolled her eyes. "Take me where the grown-ups are, please. There's a little too much pep in here for me."

James looked at her and furrowed his brow. "We spend our days dealing with some pretty grim scenarios here, Sarah. It's important to remain upbeat with one another. A smile is more important than you think."

"I'm not much of a smiler."

"I gathered. Okay, let me show you where the real work gets done."

"Can't wait."

They left the busy communal area and went through a door at the back. What followed was more dark wood panelling and old oil paintings, and in the rooms where the curtains were drawn, it was dark and musty, like something out of a gothic horror novel. Sarah imagined sections of the walls sliding aside and a grey phantom appearing to snatch her away. She shivered at the thought.

The Institute – or rather the manor it was operating out of – was vast, and it stretched back even further than was obvious upon arrival. The deeper James took her, the more the hairs on the back of her neck stood up. The building was a Rubik's Cube, one square room alongside another, and easy to get disorientated.

"What's the name of this place, anyway?"

"Do you mean the building?" James stopped and faced her. He seemed to lose his balance slightly. "Its name is Tithby Hall.

It belonged to a local baron named Magnus Booth, who got rich securing shipping routes to Holland, I believe."

"Sure he was a nice guy. Why did the Institute end up here? Why not some office building in town?"

He shrugged. "The house fell into public ownership and we needed a place with living accommodation for students. There are sixteen bedrooms across the first, second, and third floors. Not all students stay here, but some do."

"How about you?"

"No, I have a place nearby. Oh, let me just show you the auditorium." He pushed open a nearby door and motioned for Sarah to take a peek inside.

A grey-haired man stood at the front of the new room, pointing at a projector screen while six or seven people listened to him on plastic chairs.

"Harold Shipman is an example of a non-ego-driven killer," the man said, pointing to a fuzzy image of the notoriously murderous doctor on screen. "He did not taunt police, brag about his crimes, or try to inflate his number of victims. In fact, it's thought that he killed many more than he admitted to. No, his motives were driven by something else. Some say he was compelled to avenge his loving mother who died so young, while others say…"

James closed the door. "We have experts visit regularly to discuss various topics. There's always more we can learn. Anyway, we're about to exit the house. Our most secure work happens elsewhere. Come on, keep up."

She raised an eyebrow. "You're really into this tour guide thing, aren't you? You should go work at a museum. Or maybe at a mortuary – you have that look."

He made no comment as he led her through into an old-fashioned kitchen with a granite island and thick shaker doors. They headed straight out through a rear exit, and Sarah found herself standing in a gravel courtyard beneath a blue sky. At the other end of the courtyard was some kind of modern prefab building, made of glass panes and metal sheeting. It had a flat roof and no period features of any kind. It reminded Sarah of a Tupperware container.

"The house is unfit for certain facilities," James explained as they headed towards the boxy structure, "so we had to erect a mobile lab. We couldn't build anything permanent either, so it was pretty much delivered here by crane."

"Neat. You have a full set-up?"

"More or less. We don't always have jurisdiction over evidence, so we have to rely on outside labs quite often, but we can do a lot here ourselves too. Blood, hair, urine, spectrum analysis… we can do a lot."

"Do you have Wi-Fi?"

He frowned. "Yes, of course we have… Oh, you're messing with me. You don't like to take things seriously, do you, Sarah? Is it a power thing? You like to keep others on the back foot?"

"Don't psychoanalyse me, James."

"Sorry, force of habit. Anyway, let's put you out of your misery. This is the final part of the tour." He punched in a code on another keypad. A glass door swished open, letting out a gust of hot air.

Sarah waved a hand in front of her face. "Yikes, you got the heating jacked up in here or what?"

"Glass and metal in the sunshine isn't always a great combination, plus our equipment pumps out a fair amount of heat. It's cooler in the labs."

"I hope so, or I'm going to have to strip off."

He looked at her for a moment before blinking and carrying on.

They headed through a narrow corridor, flanked on both sides by windowed offices and open-plan labs. It was a large space, set across a single storey. Less busy than the house, the people in the various rooms all seemed very focused. Wearing goggles and lab coats, they leant over various bits of expensive-looking machinery and paid no mind to Sarah passing by.

"The smaller rooms are mostly just offices," James said, "but we have two primary labs and a couple of smaller ones for specialised usage."

"I'm not a scientist. I'm a disfigured grunt with PTSD. What am I supposed to do here, James?"

"You can keep me company," said a chirpy voice from around the corner.

Sarah exited the corridor to see a younger man with messy fair hair sitting at a glass desk with a paper-thin laptop in front of him. Thick glasses made his eyes too big and his ears jutted out from the side of his head, but despite his geeky appearance, he seemed outgoing and confident as he smiled at them both. And he didn't immediately flinch at the sight of Sarah's scars, which scored him extra points, and she quickly understood why. He had a thick red scar of his own, running from his left eyebrow to just below his ear.

"This is Donny," said James, shaking the man's hand and saying hello.

"But everyone calls me Donkey. You must be Sarah?"

"Wait, did you just say to call you Donkey?"

He pushed his glasses up his nose. "Yep, because I do all the donkey work around here. I'm the lab manager of the Box."

"The Box?"

"What we call this place," James told her. "For obvious reasons."

"I'd call it the 'hot box'." Sarah wiped a layer of sweat off her forehead. "My arse is sweating."

Donkey chuckled, but James grimaced. "Lovely."

"How many people work in the Box?" Sarah asked.

"About a dozen people on most days," Donkey said. "A team of lab techs along with the senior investigators like James and…" He glanced at James.

"It's okay, Donkey. She knows about Richard."

Donkey gave her an apologetic look, making his scar flex and tug at the surrounding flesh. Sarah knew the unpleasant tugging sensation well. "We're an odd bunch here, Captain Stone. You'll fit right in."

She raised an eyebrow. "Yeah, think I might not be weird enough, and I don't intend on sticking around."

"That's a shame," he said, sounding genuinely crestfallen. He moved out from behind his desk and pulled out a walking stick. Holding onto it, he offered to shake her hand. "It would be nice to have some fresh blood around here, so I hope you change your mind. From what I've read about you, you're a warrior."

She shook his hand and offered half a smile. "I'm a lot of things, but this isn't the place for me."

"Think about it, at least." He let go of her hand and stepped back behind his desk.

All Sarah could offer was a shrug.

"Okay," said James, clapping his hands together. "There's just one thing left for you to do. Go and meet him, Sarah."

She frowned. "Who? Wait? You mean Richard Flesch? You want me to go pop my head in and say hello to a cannibal mass murderer?"

Donkey winced. "He hasn't eaten anybody recently."

"No way," Sarah folded her arms. "I don't want to talk to him."

"It's why you're here," James said.

"There's no point. I don't want to work here."

James sighed and let his head drop. "Okay, just let me get you some lunch before I take you back, okay? It's a long drive home and I don't want you hungry. In the meantime, please give it some more thought. The work is hard and the money's average, but we find ways to make the job enjoyable."

"I'm sure it's a hoot. So where do we go to eat? I'm actually starving."

James pulled open a door and nodded inside a small room. "I'll have one of the cooks bring you something shortly. They're about to arrive for the lunch shift, so it won't be long. Take a seat in this office here. It's cool and quiet."

Sarah peered inside the room. It was a modest workspace, with a black leather sofa on one side and a long gloss-white desk on the other. The desk was covered in files and paperwork, but the rest of the room was neat and organised. There was also a wall-mounted television with a remote hanging off it by a string. Overhead, a ceiling fan rotated lazily.

"Okay," she agreed. "You have one hour before I start behaving badly."

"Understood." James grabbed the edge of the door to close it. "Donkey will be right here if you need anything. And like I said, give the job some thought."

Sarah went over to the television and switched it on, then lay down on the couch and put her feet up.

CHAPTER
FOUR

SARAH WAS SPRAWLED across the sofa with her feet up, halfway through an episode of *Countdown*, when the office door swung open. "This better be good," she said. "I could eat a horse."

"W-what are you doing in my office?"

Sarah flinched. She lowered her feet to the floor and spun around to sit up. Before her was a wiry, well-dressed man with neatly combed black hair. He stood in the doorway and stared at her as if he had stumbled upon an alien.

"*Your* office? James told me to wait in here."

The man seemed flustered. He hurriedly checked the files on the messy desk and then turned to face her again. "Y-you shouldn't be in here."

"Chill out, dude, I didn't steal anything. I'm Sarah. Pleased to meet you…" She put out a hand and raised both eyebrows, indicating he should state his name.

He tilted his head at her, clearly confused. "Um, I'm Richard."

Shit. This is him. He looks different from that dead-eyed teenager on the stand. Smartly dressed, good-looking… normal. A normal-looking cannibal killer.

Sarah stood up and moved towards the door. "You're Richard Flesch?"

He flinched, as if the sound of his own name hurt him. "Are you… Are you the new hire James told me about? If so, then this is a very poor way to begin a—"

"James told me to wait in here," she said again, unsteadily. "I had no idea it belonged to you."

"He shouldn't have done that. This is my private space. I-I don't like being surprised. I don't like it at all."

"Just cool it, Hannibal, okay? I haven't touched anything."

"Don't call me that."

"Hey, if the shoe fits."

He was breathing heavily and seemed unable to look her in the eye. "You need to leave. Please!"

"Why? What are you freaking out for?"

He put a hand on his desk to prop himself up and reached into his pocket with the other. His eyes closed, and he took a deep breath, wincing as if in pain.

This guy wasn't what she had expected. He was a total mess. Pathetic even. "Okay, okay, I'm leaving," she said. "I didn't mean to intrude."

She moved towards the door.

"I'm sorry," he said. "I don't do well with surprises. You have my apologies for being rude."

She frowned at him, confused. *This guy killed twenty-seven people?* "Apologies? Um, no need. It's fine, I'm going."

"You're watching *Countdown*?" He nodded at the television. "It's one of my favourite shows. I like puzzles."

"Uh huh."

"How did you get those scars?" He pointed at her face, asking the question without an appropriate segue.

"I walked into a door."

"In Afghanistan? James said you're ex-army, and that you were involved with the Major Crimes Unit afterwards. Why did you leave the MCU?"

"I'm not doing this," she said, shaking her head as if waking from a dream. "I have zero interest in talking to you."

He looked her in the eye, although it seemed difficult for him to do so. "Because of who I am?"

"If, by that, you mean a psycho who killed and ate people, then yeah, it's a factor in my thinking."

The way he nodded made it seem as if he agreed with her. There was no anger coming from him, just a sense of anxiety, like he was about to flee the room squealing. "Would it matter if I told you I only ate the flesh of three people?"

"No, not really. To be honest, I draw the line at one person. One and a half max."

"I can't do anything about my past." He turned the chair away from his desk and sat down on it to face her. "I'm just trying to do the best I can. Did James tell you about Claudette Herrington?"

She nodded. "Yeah. The poor chick got a rough deal."

"She won't be the last. I'm trying to stop the man responsible, but… but I struggle to focus. James thinks I need a partner."

"Yeah, you seem like a real people person."

He looked away, possibly embarrassed. "My last partner used to shout a lot. It was triggering for me."

"You have PTSD?"

Looking back at her, he shrugged. "Perhaps."

Sarah took a couple of steps away from the door, suddenly intrigued by this macabre specimen of mankind. How often did you get to have a conversation with a mass murderer? "Let me get this straight. You murdered a bunch of people, but you're the one who's traumatised? Sounds like you're full of shit."

His head lowered, and he stared at his hands. "Do you know what it's like to be terrified of your own father? To lie awake in bed, worried every time you hear footsteps on the stairs? To watch the front door, hoping he never comes home from work. Or to go your entire life without ever hearing a single kind word spoken to you?"

"Yeah, I do know actually. My dad was in the SAS. He wasn't exactly built to love."

"He was built to kill?" Richard lifted his head and looked at her. His eyes weren't as dark as they had seemed in the courtroom footage. In fact, they were a pleasant hazelnut. "My father was built to kill too. I often wonder who I would be if my parents had been ordinary and loving, instead of Britain's most reviled serial killers." He huffed and managed a thin smile. "There were never any BMXs or birthday cakes for me. No, I got to watch my father rape and butcher young women in our basement."

"You took part."

"My mother forced me to, when I grew old enough to start asking questions. I think it was her twisted way of protecting me, to keep my father from killing me too. By the time the police caught up to us, he was proud of the 'knowledge' he had passed on to me. Called it the 'family business'."

"Least he was proud of you. I was only ever a disappointment to my dad." She shook her head. *What am I doing? Chit-chatting with this guy? Sharing childhood traumas? Stop it.*

Richard cleared his throat and sat up straight. He was quite tall, slender but muscled. "From the way you're looking at me, I'm assuming you're not going to take a position here?"

"How am I looking at you?"

"Like I'm a freak."

She put a hand to her face, tracing her scars. It was a novel experience, to be the one accused of looking at someone else like a freak. However, she wasn't about to accept that they had anything in common. "What are you trying to achieve here?"

Again, he had that pathetic look about him as he shook his head slowly. "I just want to do good. Isn't that enough?"

"So that you can feel better about yourself?"

"So that innocent young girls like Claudette Herrington don't have to suffer and die because of sick monsters."

"Monsters like you?"

"Monsters like who I used to be."

Sarah didn't know what to say to that. Here was a serial killer who wanted to save people and do good, like something out of a cheesy Netflix series. It was absurd – and she had had a lifetime of absurd.

"I'm leaving," she said.

He reached out a hand to her, seeming to panic. "J-just take a look at the case I'm working on. You could offer something helpful before you go. What would be the harm?" He grabbed a file from his desk and thrust it at her. At the top was a crime scene photograph of Claudette Herrington – with her scalp missing. The sight of blood turned Sarah's stomach.

"I'm leaving," she said again, her mouth filling with saliva.

"Okay, I understand." Richard dropped the file back onto his desk. Then he stood up and reached out a hand to her again. "It was good to meet you, Sarah. Sorry about my earlier rudeness."

She recoiled, dodging his obscene offer of a handshake. "I'm not shaking your goddamn hand. You should be in a padded cell, not a sodding stately home."

He looked hurt as she turned away from him, but she didn't care. She yanked open the door and went out into the corridor. Donkey looked at her expectantly. "Did you two have a chat?"

"Tell James he's a piece of shit."

She stormed down the corridor, but she was prevented from exiting the Box because she didn't know the code for the glass doors. Fortunately, after she began yelling obscenities, a disapproving woman in a lab coat appeared and let her out.

Outside in the courtyard, the fresh air was amazing. She hadn't realised how stuffy it was inside, but it felt like she could breathe again. The gravel crunched beneath her trainers and grounded her back in reality. It helped her calm down, but she was still jittery. The photograph of that poor girl...

What kind of psycho rips people's scalps off?

She heard people chatting.

A small group of people stood about twenty metres away in

an apparent smoking area. Although Sarah wasn't a regular smoker, she felt she could do with one now, so she marched over to join them. They were all young and fresh-faced, and they all flinched at the sight of her scars. At least they tried to mask their revulsion with friendly smiles.

"Hi," said the girl from earlier, the one wearing the green jumpsuit. "You okay?"

"Frances, right? Can I nick a cigarette?"

They all looked at each other.

Sarah frowned. "Did I not speak English? You lot are smoking, yeah? You can't spare one?"

"Oh," said Frances, "it's not that. It's that we all vape. No one has any cigarettes."

Sarah eyeballed their hands. Each held either a sleek-looking gizmo or a colourful plastic stick. The air was sickly with a dozen intermingling fruity scents.

A young man in his early twenties offered Sarah a neon-green vape pen. "You can have a blast on mine if you'd like?"

Sarah peered at the plastic mouthpiece and found it less than appealing. "I really don't belong here," she muttered, and then she turned and left them to it.

Her hands shook as she walked away. Rather than try to go back inside the manor, she walked around the perimeter, hoping to find her way directly back to the car. She felt like a prisoner, two hundred miles from home.

Why the hell did I even agree to come here? I don't need the money this much.

About halfway around the building, she came up against a mesh fence. The Box was obviously only accessible by entering through the main house, with the rear gardens cordoned off from outside entry. She would have to go back inside the manor to exit the Institute.

I just need a minute first.

She doubled over, clutching her abdomen as a wave of nausea surged through her body. There had been no sense of danger coming from Richard, but the fact he had eaten human flesh and killed over two dozen people repulsed her. It was like being in a room with a surgically excised cancer – a foul, inhuman thing that represented misery and death. And then there was that grisly photograph of Claudette…

Whoever did that to her deserves the deepest pit in Hell.

She put her hands through the chain link and slumped face first against the fence. Even out in the fresh air, she struggled to breathe.

"Sarah?"

She spun around, both fists raised. Her heart thudded against her ribs.

James stood a few feet away from her. He put a hand out to her like he was trying to soothe a tiger. "Are you okay?"

"How did you know I was out here?"

He nodded upwards at a camera mounted ten feet up on the wall. "I've had eyes on you the whole time. You met with Richard?"

"You prick. You sat me down in his office."

"I'm sorry. It was a crude ploy, but I needed you both to meet. I was right next door the whole time, but you took off."

"Because you messed me around. I said I didn't want to meet him."

He took a step closer and put his hand down. "But you did meet with him. What did you make of Richard?"

"He's a fruit loop."

"Is that all?"

"Well, he's not what I expected. He was timid. Polite."

James nodded. "He lives a quiet existence. The only time he leaves the estate is to visit crime scenes."

"So he's a recluse? Probably a good thing."

"I took custody of him six years ago, Sarah, after him having spent ten years in a secure hospital. He hasn't hurt a soul in that time."

She moved away from the fence, a little unsteady on her

feet, but feeling slightly better. "Okay, so he's been defanged, but that doesn't mean I want to work with him."

"He wants you to stay, Sarah. He just told me."

"What? Why? I was pretty shitty to him."

James ran a hand through his hair and let his arm drop to his side. "He said you understand him. That the two of you are both damaged."

"We're nothing alike."

"Have you ever killed anyone, Sarah?"

"It's not the same. I killed people who were dangerous."

"Absolutely, but you have that inside you now, don't you? That darkness gives you an edge others lack. You can handle Richard, and in doing so you can save lives. You want this, Sarah, and I think you need this."

"Don't tell me what I need! This place isn't where I want to be at all."

James reached into his chinos and pulled out a small black wallet. He opened it up and there was a photograph of Sarah inside it. "I can give you the full and legal rank of Detective Inspector, with all entitlements and pay. You'll have free rein to work on cases as you see fit. It's a dream gig, believe me."

"I don't want it." She shook her head. "I'm fine as I am."

"You're not. Be honest with yourself."

She felt a little shaky again, even a little teary. "No, you're right. I'm a fucking mess."

"Then you're in the right place. This can be your salvation, Sarah. You're restless. Bored."

"Bored? Do you know what happened at my last job with the MCU? My final case?"

"Um," he squinted while he thought about it, "you neutralised a terrorist who brought down an airliner, right?"

"He wasn't a terrorist, just some dumb kid who lived his entire life on the internet. He didn't even mean to do it. Hacking into that plane was just a game to him until it went wrong."

"You weren't able to take him in alive, if I remember correctly?"

She let out a sigh. "My days of pointing guns at people are over. I've seen too many people die."

"I'm not offering you a gun, Sarah, just a badge. Maybe you and Richard really are alike in some ways. Perhaps you both need to rebalance the scales. The past clearly has its hooks in you both. But I promise, whatever baggage you're carrying, I'll help you with it."

"All right, enough with the pressure, okay? Seriously, I need to think a minute."

He let out a sigh. "I'm afraid there's not really any time for that, Sarah. I just got a call. There's been another murder." He offered her the badge again, this time insistently. "The bad guys aren't going anywhere. Don't you at least want to make it hard for them?"

Sarah stared at the badge, knowing that taking it would change her life forever.

Do I really want back in?

She looked at James and asked a question. "How well do you sleep at night?"

He frowned, clearly confused by the question. "What?"

"It's a simple question."

"Not very well, as you'd probably expect. The job weighs heavily, even in the best of times."

"So why do it, James? Why fill your nights with monsters and your days with open-mouthed corpses?"

He took a deep breath and seemed to give it some serious thought. After a shrug, he gave her an answer. "Because someone has to."

CHAPTER
FIVE

SARAH BLINKED, trying to wake from a bad dream.

"I'm sitting in a chauffeur-driven Range Rover with a serial killer," she muttered.

"Pardon me?" Richard turned to look at her from the other side of the back seat. "Did you say something?"

"Nothing. Just talking to myself."

"I do that sometimes. I find it helpful to hear my thoughts out loud."

"Uh huh." Sarah turned to look out the window at the passing countryside. County Durham's beauty surprised her. Undulating fields of green and yellow dotted with Roman ruins, snaking rivers, and picturesque lakes. It was peaceful watching it all roll by.

Too bad I'm on my way to a murder.

Before leaving the Institute, James had insisted Sarah sign a contract of employment that would also act as an NDA. Any urge she might have to expose Richard Flesch's secret identity would have to remain unsatisfied for now. James had also asked her to change into the clothes she had left in his boot, so she was now wearing straight-leg trousers and a light blue blouse.

Ready for business, she thought. *The business of death.*

A body had been found in the cathedral city of Durham. No word on the exact location of the crime scene, but their driver had been updated en route and seemed to know where he was going.

"Ever been to Durham?" Richard asked her.

"Nope."

"It's quite small, as far as cities go, but it has great historical merit due to its cathedral and university. Students make up a sizeable portion of its population."

"Uh huh."

"I'm pleased you decided to stay," he said. He looked at her for a moment, but then turned his head to stare out of the window. He seemed to enjoy the pleasant scenery as much as she did.

Probably because he spent half his life locked up in a padded cell.

"For today." She grunted. "I'm still deciding if it will be any longer than that."

"Well, give it some thought, please."

Sarah rolled her eyes. "Do we have an ID for the victim yet?"

Richard looked down and swiped a finger across his phone screen. "Not yet. Unidentified female. Blonde hair."

"Blonde hair? The same as Claudette Herrington. You think it's a pattern?"

"Could just be a coincidence, but it's a possibility."

"And..." she raised an eyebrow at him, "do you think it *is* the same killer? What are your slasher-senses telling you?"

He looked back at her with his sad hazelnut eyes. "We need to examine the scene before we can draw any conclusions..." – he paused a moment – "but the killer promised to kill again soon, so it seems likely. He's... been contacting me."

She flinched. "What? Directly?"

"Yes, through my official email address. I'm listed as DI

Mullins on the Institute's website, but the killer knows my real name and uses it when he writes."

"Does James know you two are pen pals?"

Richard nodded. "Of course. It'd be bad all around if my identity leaked to the public. James has put his career on the line for me."

"And I'm sure you don't want to give up this cushy gig. People might be a tad upset to learn the Chester-le-Street Cannibal gets chauffeured around in a blacked-out Range Rover."

"I never learned to drive." He shrugged. "And I don't choose the cars."

He sounded a little pissy, which led Sarah to wonder what would happen if he lost his temper. Would he try to bite her throat right here in the back of the car? Or snap their driver's neck and escape into the hills?

Richard let out a sigh, as if calming himself down. Then he turned to her, his expression unreadable, like a hardened clay mask. "All I want to do is catch this guy, Sarah. He's a bad one, I can feel it. He's not going to stop."

She sat up straight and rotated slightly towards him. "So, these emails he's been sending you? What have they been saying? Can you not trace them?"

"We've tried, but they're coming via a server in Brazil, which means he's probably using a VPN and IP blocking software." Richard flicked at his phone screen a few more times and then held it up to her.

To: DCI MULLINS
   Subject: Sins of a father
   Dear Mr Flesch.
   Did you like my present? How did it taste? As good as before? There's more to come. A high score to beat. All I want is to impress you.

Yours,
Student of Death

Sarah looked away, signalling that she'd read the email. Richard put the phone on his lap and locked the screen. "There's been a few messages in the last two weeks, all of them like that."

"A high score to beat? I really hope that doesn't mean what I think it does."

Richard nodded. "Because that would mean—"

"That a lot more innocent girls are in danger. And what does he mean about how it tastes?"

"The killer cut some meat from Claudette Herrington's back and left it for me."

She let out a weary groan, her stomach contracting. "I take it you didn't—"

"No, of course not!"

"Sorry, I wish it were an absurd question."

"He yanked out her fingernails too. I believe he kept them as trophies."

Sarah grimaced. "Christ, we need to catch this guy."

"I won't stop until I do."

She studied him for a moment, trying to catch a whiff of deception, but there was nothing. For all his inexcusable, horrific crimes, he seemed genuine about wanting to stop this killer from hurting anyone else.

He must get off on it, though, living vicariously through another sicko's murders…

Does it matter if he stops killers from killing?

Sarah shook her head, not wanting to get lost in her own thoughts. "What do you know about this guy, Richard? You're a whizz at figuring out psychos, right? Like *Rain Man*, if Dustin Hoffman ate Tom Cruise at the end."

"I have an ability to identify with disturbed individuals, yes."

"So what is your gut telling you?"

"Well, from what I saw at the previous crime scene, I think we're looking for an intelligent killer, probably well-educated and organised. He must also be relatively fit, as hanging Claudette Herrington from the train station roof would have taken great effort." He took a breath and closed his eyes. "Pain… It gives him something. It either satisfies an urge inside him or allows him to feel a sense of power he doesn't otherwise have. While we don't have a full victim profile yet, the targeting of young women suggests a hatred for the opposite sex – or a fascination."

"And what about the way Claudette died?" Sarah asked. "Why torture her like that?"

"Many male-on-female serial killers want to hurt women to satisfy some pathological desire for revenge, perhaps equating their victims with a woman from their past who hurt them. Other killers simply want to understand women, having not been properly socialised during their formative years. Then there are those who don't even see women as people at all, but mere objects for their own intended pleasure. The exact reasoning of our killer will make its own kind of sense when we find out what it is."

"And it's definitely a *him*? I mean, these things usually are, right?"

Richard nodded. "It's highly likely that our killer is a man. Statistically, a middle-aged white male is what we're looking for, but that doesn't mean we should eliminate other ages and ethnicities. We need more data."

"Data? You mean dead girls?"

"I mean evidence. It's true that a body is our best source of information, but let's try to make this one our last."

"Do you actually mean that?" She scrutinised him again, looking for chinks in his armour. "I get the impression you enjoy this a little bit too much. Brings back memories of the old days, huh?"

"I don't like it at all, and I resent the implication."

There it is. I just saw something in his eyes. Something that's been trying to hide.

"Resent it all you want, buddy," she said. "But most would say you should be spending the rest of your life in a cold, windowless cell for what you did, not playing detective."

Richard's eyes narrowed and a shadow crossed his face. "I'd appreciate you saying no more."

"No more about what? You killing twenty-seven young women with your mum and dad? I thought my family was a mess, but yours… Jesus!"

"Stop it."

Seeing him get upset awakened something in Sarah. It brought back memories of taking down bad guys in interview rooms. She had always found pleasure in talking down to small men who thought they were big; she couldn't help herself once they started to squirm. "I bet your internet history makes for grim reading," she said, wanting to poke him into revealing who he really was. "I can only imagine the twisted shit you're into."

"Stop it, please."

"Is there a chatroom where all you weirdos get together to share stories about how you kidnapped and butchered young w—"

"Stop it!" He lunged at her, kept back only by the clamping of his seatbelt. "Stop it, stop it, stop it!"

Sarah slunk back in her seat. "Jesus!"

Both of Richard's hands were open like claws, hovering in the air like he was about to throttle her. His face had contorted in jagged lines, as if Sarah were looking at him through a broken window.

Then the anger disappeared in an instant, replaced by an expression of utter horror. "W-why would you do that?" He hung his head, hands gripping his knees. "Why would you be so spiteful?"

"What, I hurt your feelings?"

He studied his hands; they were shaking. In fact, his entire body was shaking. He put his palms against his face and made a quiet moaning sound. All Sarah could do was watch in confusion. She had seen a glimpse of the monster, but it had vanished quickly and left behind a quivering mess.

"Is there a problem?" asked the driver as he peered at them in the rearview mirror. "Do I need to pull over?"

"No, no, Tony." Richard sounded jittery. "I apologise for the disturbance. Please, continue the journey."

"Yeah," said Sarah with a grimace. "No problems here."

Richard mumbled to himself and then looked at her. "I apologise. I shouldn't have lost my temper. James wants me to have a partner because he thinks it'll help me, but I understand now that it's impossible." He looked away and rubbed at his forehead as if he were getting a migraine. "You *should* be disgusted by the things I've done, Sarah – they were terrible and inhuman – but if you're not interested in helping me, then you should just go home. I'm here to work, and I won't let anyone keep me from doing that."

Sarah realised she was breathing heavily. Actually, she was a little freaked out.

Taunting a serial killer. Real smart, Sarah.

"You're a mess," she said, seeing the sweat forming at his temples and the rapid rise and fall of his chest. "Like, barely functioning. I thought you were going to try and strangle me."

"I've been on edge lately. With the killer knowing my real name…" He stared out the window again. "I just need to focus on what I'm good at."

"Catching killers?"

He nodded. "It's all I have, Sarah. Please don't keep me from doing it." The look on his face was now sorrowful and earnest. It left her feeling like the bad guy, which was absurd.

"Okay." She rubbed at her arms through the polyester sleeves of her blouse, stifling a shiver. "I'll give you a break, but do anything weird or cannibally and I'll kick your head in."

He winced. "Deal."

"We're almost there," said the driver.

CHAPTER
SIX

IT WAS early evening in Durham when they arrived, that odd transitional time after the workday had ended but the nightlife had not yet begun. Uniformed retail workers waited for buses, while a smattering of early birds enjoyed their first drinks of the evening while sitting at the various open-fronted bars. Sarah found it slightly perverse that none of them knew there was a dead body lying only a stone's throw away.

The world's got too big. We're stepping over corpses without even looking down.

Despite her grim reason for being there, Durham was a beautiful city. A picturesque urban sprawl that somehow seemed to be both high up and low down at the same time. Look to the left and you might see a cobblestone bridge spanning a lazy river below. Look to your right and you might see the city's majestic cathedral perched atop its hill, stained glass windows glinting in the setting sun. The city was as much vertical as it was horizontal.

As they crossed over the River Wear that ran right through the city, Richard nodded out of his window at the towering cathedral looming over them. "When the Normans built Durham Cathedral," he said, "it took decades for the cement to fully dry. The masons and craftsmen predicted this, so they built certain things askew, knowing that over time the stones would settle and come to rest in the correct position. Can you imagine the skill and dedication it would take to calculate something like that?"

Sarah looked up at the Norman cathedral, with its long straight lines and parallel ledges, and was actually impressed. "I can barely put up a shelf."

"Makes you realise what we're all capable of, don't you think? Without power tools or machinery, those men were able to build something to last a thousand years; something that today people visit for its beauty and grandeur."

"I don't know much about beauty," said Sarah, running a finger along her scars, "but I appreciate hard work when I see it."

Richard studied her for a moment, tilting his head like a curious puppy. "I understand you were struck by an IED. In Afghanistan, right? Is that what caused your injuries?"

He clearly meant no offence, and she actually considered telling him the full story. Her history wasn't a secret, but that didn't mean she enjoyed dredging through it. "My squad was travelling through the Helmand Province to visit a group of tribal chiefs in a nearby village. Just before we arrived at the meeting point, we came across a woman in the street. She was struggling with an overturned wheelbarrow full of watermelons. We got out to help her, and…" She gritted her teeth at the memory, still angry after so many years.

Richard nodded, as if he already knew what happened next. Perhaps he did.

"My entire squad died in the ambush," Sarah said flatly, "but I escaped with a badly sliced face. A piece of shrapnel must have struck me, but that's not what caused my scars. No, that happened after the Taliban captured me and a man named Wazir poured gunpowder into my wounds before igniting it with a lighter. It stopped the bleeding…" – she pointed to her scars – "and left me with this."

"That must have been traumatic."

She shrugged. "It wasn't the worst day of my life, but it certainly left the biggest mark. Anyway, I'm lucky. I made it home alive. My squad didn't."

"Sometimes surviving is harder."

"Tell that to the dead."

Their driver, Tony, turned his head. He was a bald guy with a goatee, and looked capable of doing more than just driving. "We're here," he said politely. "I'll find somewhere to park."

"Thank you, Tony," Richard said.

"Yeah," Sarah added. "Cheers."

Tony put a cherry on top of the car and switched it on. The flashing red and blue lights bounced off the plate-glass windows on either side of the street. Cars moved aside, while pedestrians stood and gawped. Sarah didn't like the attention and shrank down in her seat as they pulled into a small car park cordoned off with blue-and-white police tape. Several liveried squad cars were already there, and a small white tent had been erected in one corner.

Tony activated the parking brake and switched off the engine. Sarah and Richard got out.

James Westerly met them both with a perfunctory wave, having travelled in his car twenty minutes ahead of them. He had changed into a white short-sleeved shirt and black trousers, and along with the ID card hanging around his neck on a lanyard, it made him look like a schoolteacher. "The primary site is about a hundred metres from here," he explained. "In a small wooded area down below."

Sarah looked around. "Right in the middle of the city? Are there no witnesses?"

"We're trying to find that out. Believe it or not, the area by the river is quite secluded and difficult to navigate."

Richard turned on the spot and scanned the area like a robot.

"Our killer is bold," he muttered. "His last kill was in an unpopulated area. This is far riskier."

"What do you think that could mean?" James asked him, hands on his bony hips.

"I'm not sure. Perhaps we're not dealing with the same killer."

"Or," Sarah added, "he's looking for a bigger thrill."

Richard scratched at his chin, fingernails scraping against tiny prickles of day-old stubble. "It's a little soon for this kind of escalation. He may have picked this location for another reason, making the risk necessary."

"What reason?"

"Let's try to find out."

James reached into his pocket and pulled out some blue plastic bags. "Might want to put these on. It's muddy down by there."

Sarah took the shoe covers and wrapped them around her low-heeled boots. When the three of them were ready, they set off down a narrow path leading from the car park. It was more of a muddy rut than anything else, and they had to hop a low stone wall to get to it. A route for the adventurous, it took them down a moderate grassy slope to the river bank below. Durham Cathedral, now to their left, cast a gigantic shadow over the rushing water.

As James had mentioned, the wooded area was dark and secluded. Dense branches obscured the river bank from view and almost completely blotted out the sun. Sarah hadn't known such pockets of nature could exist right within a city, but then Durham wasn't exactly a metropolis. Even Wolverhampton was bigger.

But a whole lot uglier.

Beneath the leafy canopy, swaying shadows danced across the mud. A sour smell drifted over from the river. Underfoot, the ground grew softer and softer.

"Careful where you step," James warned. "We're about to enter the crime scene."

Up ahead was more police tape, wrapped around trees in a rough square and clearly demarcating the area of investigation. Within the cordon, a dozen little red flags had been placed down to pierce the earth.

James and Richard placed their feet carefully, stepping on a thin strip of plastic tape that had been placed along the ground as a guide. Sarah did the same, and it took the three of them right into the centre of the cordoned-off area – a clearing surrounded by willow trees, stinging nettles, and thick brambles.

Something lay on the ground.

At first, it looked like a large pile of rocks, but when Sarah saw bare feet and legs poking out from underneath, she realised it was a body.

A pair of forensics were already working the scene, crouched down and cataloguing evidence, but they moved out of Richard's way as he proceeded to walk a slow circle around the body and the rocks. "*Peine forte et dure*," he said, and when Sarah frowned at him, he elaborated. "It was a method of torture employed by French courts, usually to press a defendant into entering a guilty plea. You gradually add weight to a person's body, increasing the pain and pressure on their torso until they give in."

"And if they don't?"

He looked down at the body, a young girl with blonde hair and a wide-open mouth. "They suffocate to death. This amount of weight would have made it impossible for the victim to take a breath."

James pointed towards the body. "Her fingernails are all missing. This is our killer's work. Ritualistic, medieval, and another young girl."

"Do we know who she is?" Sarah folded her arms and stared into the girl's lifeless grey eyes.

James shook his head. "Not yet. DCI Flannigan is working that side of things. I'll liaise with her later."

"Who's that?" Sarah asked.

"Flannigan's the Chief Inspector for Durham Constabulary," Richard said.

"We'll do our part," James told her, "but this is Flannigan's jurisdiction. Our job is to help her find and prosecute the monster who did this."

Sarah knew a little bit about inter-office politics and decided she didn't need to know more. All she cared about was getting justice for this poor young girl who had been crushed to death so close to a street full of people.

"Why is her mouth open like this?" Sarah unfolded her arms and pointed. There were bloodstains around the edges of the girl's swollen lips, and her front teeth appeared damaged. "Wait! It looks like there's something inside."

James stooped to take a look, and his eyes went wide when he realised Sarah was right. "It looks like the killer forced a rock into her mouth and wedged it behind her teeth."

"Probably to stop her screaming," Richard said without emotion.

"Her wrists are tied to the ground." Sarah noted the girl's muddy hands. "Her ankles too."

"Looks like our killer used tent pegs and cable ties," said Richard, kneeling down. "She would've been powerless to fight back, and as he increased the weight on her chest, it would've got harder and harder to breathe. Depending on how long it took, she could have suffocated over the course of hours. Every inhalation painful. Every exhalation exhausting."

Sarah pulled a face, her upper lip curling. She wanted to find this guy and hurt him. Hurt him worse than both his victims combined. "How did he get her down here with no one seeing?"

Richard stayed in a crouch position, but he shimmied over to the victim's head. He snapped his fingers at one of the nearby forensics and they immediately passed him a pair of latex gloves from a small pouch on their shoulder. He put them on and touched the dead girl's face, pressing lightly against her pale cheeks before reaching behind her head and trying to lift it. "Her body is in full rigor. That would place her death at least twelve hours ago."

James nodded, seeming to agree. "The killer brought her here in the middle of the night. If it wasn't so muddy and secluded, she probably would have been discovered sooner."

"I would assume so." Richard closed his eyes, as if he were thinking. "If our killer drugged this girl like he did Claudette, then she was probably unconscious when he brought her here. There would have been no noise, and nothing to see besides a parked car."

Sarah moved over to the trees closer to the river. She looked out at the rushing water and tried to put herself in the poor girl's shoes. "She would've woken up here, all alone, with a psycho in the dark."

James glanced up at the treetops. You could just about see the cathedral on the hill though the branches. "Why do you think he picked this spot? Richard, earlier you seemed like you might know the answer."

"I think I do." He straightened up and stepped away from the body. Glancing back at the two forensics who were measuring something in the soil, he whispered so that only James and Sarah could hear. "I've visited this exact same spot before."

Sarah leant back against the gnarled trunk of a willow tree to disguise how light-headed she was feeling. The sight of the dead girl had nearly floored her, and it took everything she had not to freak out. It was only thoughts of the victim's poor family that allowed her to keep her shit together. They didn't know about this yet, but they would want answers for how such a horrible, senseless thing could happen.

"Why were you here before, Richard?" James asked. "What's the significance of this spot?"

Richard hesitated. "It's where I abducted Caroline Andrews."

Richard peeled off his gloves and tossed them into a bin inside the command tent, while James went and spoke to a uniformed woman Sarah assumed was DCI Flannigan. The sun had all but disappeared now, and after having spent almost an hour with a corpse, she wanted to go take a shower.

The cause of death was obvious. Asphyxiation due to compression of the diaphragm. A slow, desperate suffocation.

She must have been so frightened. That poor girl.

Sarah watched Richard as he went and sat on the low stone wall surrounding the floodlit car park. During the last half-hour, he'd grown increasingly glum, as if his mood had fallen with the sun.

Well, he's had his time to think. Now I want answers.

Sarah approached him but kept her distance. "Tell me about Caroline Andrews. You murdered her?"

His lips pressed tightly together, and his complexion drained of colour. "Yes."

"Who was she?"

"Just a girl."

"Just a fucking girl?"

He licked his lips. "I mean, I knew nothing about her when I… when I took her."

"How did you do it?"

"I was fourteen, not an adult yet, but I was tall and athletic. Handsome too."

"Good for you," she said. "Tell me how you abducted her."

He stared down at the water rushing down below. "I had a dog's lead. I pretended I had a beagle and that it had fallen into the river below. It didn't take me long to persuade Caroline to come and help me rescue it. She followed me down to the water, and once we were underneath the trees, I choked her unconscious with the lead."

Sarah leant over the wall, her mouth filling with saliva that she wanted to spit out. Spit right in Richard's face.

"I waited an hour or so until nightfall," he carried on, "and then I brought Caroline back to this car park where my dad was waiting for me in a van."

"How long until you killed her?"

He rubbed the back of his neck and cleared his throat. "The next day. I think I choked her for too long and caused brain damage, because she wouldn't fully wake up. It was like she was drunk or on drugs. My dad had me cut her throat and we buried her in Kielder Forest Park a couple hours north of here."

"You buried all your bodies there, right?"

He nodded. "It's big, secluded."

"How do you sleep at night?"

"I don't."

"So you're going to blame it all on Daddy, I suppose? You were scared, under his control, right?"

He looked at her, his brown eyes squinting slightly. "What do you want me to say, Sarah? I kidnapped her because he told me I needed to prove I was a man. I had to catch my own prey."

"Well, good on you, kiddo. You were obviously a natural."

"Not at all. When we had to kill Caroline early, my father blamed me for messing everything up. He beat me and locked me in the basement with her body for two days before we went and buried her."

Sarah spat into the river, wiped her mouth, and looked him in the eye. "Why didn't you just run away? Why didn't you do something? Anything?"

He turned away and stared off at the cathedral. In the night-time, Durham was a city of sinister shadows and bright, glaring lights. "I ask myself that all the time. All I can say is that my father seemed larger than the universe back then. There was no doubt in my mind he would kill me if I even thought about escaping, and…"

"And what?"

"I suppose, at the time, it just felt normal. Killing people was an ordinary part of life. I even started to… started to like it."

Sarah almost punched him then. "Did you seriously just say that?"

He didn't seem ashamed of it, merely resigned to what he was saying – as if he were speaking of a pet goldfish he had once flushed down the toilet. "It was the only time my father ever seemed to approve of me, and my mother always hugged me and sang songs to me after a kill. It was the only time I ever felt anything close to love. The doctors said I was brainwashed, that my formative years were so badly perverted that it caused me to associate pain and suffering with love and affection." He let out a long sigh and leant on his forearms across the wall. "I've spent the last sixteen years of my life trying to rewire my brain, to unlearn every sick habit my father put inside me."

"And how's that going?"

"Reasonably well until all of this." He chuckled, before quickly returning to his glumness. "This killer knows everything about me, Sarah. For some reason, these murders are about me."

Sarah nodded. It was a pretty obvious conclusion. "You obviously have a fan. Someone who's obsessed with you for some sick reason."

"You'd be surprised how many people idolise monsters. Ted Bundy had fan mail every day. So did Dahmer, Manson, and even Peter Sutcliffe in this country."

"There are too many people in this world with a screw loose."

"I'd say some people have screws that are missing altogether."

Sarah chuckled, but quickly stifled it. "Well, that's something we can agree on."

A silence settled between them, and Sarah used the time to attempt to find some sympathy for Richard, if only to tolerate his presence. If she hadn't known of his background, he would've come across merely as an awkward, yet harmless individual. Reluctantly, she accepted that she might even have liked him if he were just some random stranger.

But he's a monster hiding behind a mask, and now another monster is trying to impress him.

Wait a second…

"He's watching us," she said.

Richard's brows knitted together, his forehead creasing into a deep frown. "What?"

"If this guy is obsessed with you, then he's going to want to see your reaction, right? Killers have big egos, and they get off on watching the misery they cause."

Richard nodded, his eyes slowly widening. "The killer is grandiose. He'll be feeding off the attention."

"Especially *your* attention. He must be somewhere close by, close enough that he can watch his idol respond. You're like the Justin Bieber of murder."

"Who?"

"Seriously? Who doesn't know…" She shook her head. "Never mind, we need to see if he's watching us."

"Agreed."

The two of them turned around slowly.

Sarah scanned the area, both excited and dismayed. The police cordon had attracted plenty of attention, and portable floodlights blanched the area in blinding white light. The nosiest members of the crowd were spectating from a nearby bridge or from the upper level of an adjacent elevated street. Then there were the students who were casually drinking on the lamplit bar terraces, enjoying the commotion in the same way they might an evening of theatre.

People everywhere.

All watching.

"I'll have someone start photographing the area," Richard said quietly. "Maybe we can catch our man on camera."

"Good idea. I'm going to take a walk and see what I can see. Stay here."

"Why?"

"Because you're the centre of attention."

"I don't like that."

"Tough. If the killer is focused on you, then he won't notice me snooping around, will he?"

Richard frowned at her. "No, I mean I don't like the thought of you wandering off on your own. It could be dangerous."

"You read my file?"

"Yes."

"Then what are you worried about?"

He rubbed his hands together anxiously and looked up at the elevated street. "Be careful. We barely know anything about who we're dealing with."

"I can handle myself." Sarah took off at a brisk pace, checking her solar-powered Seiko to make it seem like she was thinking about something else rather than checking out the area for a voyeuristic killer.

What would a psycho torture-killer look like? She glanced back at Richard, who was now talking to James and the policewoman inside the tent. *Like him.*

The nearest group of spectators didn't seem to fit the bill. A wizened old man with a cocker spaniel stood with a stooped-over woman that must have been his wife. Next to them, a boyfriend and girlfriend held hands underneath an orange-glowing lamppost, looking nothing but innocent. More faces peered down from the street above, all of them disappointingly ordinary – just people gawping out of boredom or morbid curiosity.

What exactly am I searching for? Someone touching themselves with a machete covered in blood? A sack-headed, chainsaw-wielding maniac?

We need to get CCTV from the area. There must be footage of the killer carrying the girl down to the river. Nowhere is private any more.

Sarah trod cautiously along the side of the road, scrutinising the occasional vehicles whose drivers chose to ignore the police diversion. Could the killer be behind the wheel of one of them?

Further ahead, the main road ended and fed into a cobbled side street. Various signs jutted out from the buildings on iron brackets – V. Kirkpatrick Accountancy, EZkutz hairdressers, and Dave's Bakery. The businesses were closed for the evening, their interiors dark, but an aroma of fresh bread still lingered in the air.

Only a single person occupied the shadowy side street, and they were walking away with their hands in their pockets. Sarah didn't know where they had emerged from, but their quickening pace caught her attention. Perhaps they had simply stepped out from one of the businesses – or just maybe they had been skulking in the dark and watching. The entrance to the side street looked directly down at the car park.

When Sarah glanced back, she could still see Richard talking to James inside of the floodlit tent. Both men seemed to be watching her, probably discussing her theory that the killer might be lingering in the area.

She looked around, assessing the situation. A small group of students chatted at a nearby bus stop, but other than that, the stretch of road was entirely deserted because of the police diversion.

The stranger was about to disappear. Sarah needed to hurry or risk losing them.

Okay, buddy. Let's see who are you and where you think you're going.

Sarah hurried along the cobbles, the impact putting an ache in her feet. The clopping of her heels echoed in her ears as she headed further down the narrowing street. Three-storey Victorian terraces flanked her on both sides, and if not for a pair of lampposts and a blinking alarm unit, it would have been hard to see anything at all.

The stranger slunk into an alleyway to the left.

Sarah picked up her pace and considered yelling out. But would it spook the suspect?

She entered the alleyway behind them.

The stranger was gone.

How? I was right behind them.

She squinted to see ahead, her eyes adapting to the darkness. The alleyway curved to the right, disappearing around a corner.

Movement ahead.

Something was tapping against the rear side of a large wheelie bin placed up against a wooden shed door. It was the back area for a group of businesses. Was the stranger trying to hide?

Sarah realised she didn't have a radio or any way to call for backup. Of course, she had her mobile phone, but she hadn't yet added any contacts details for James or Richard. All she had was a badge.

She approached the wheelie bin cautiously, pulling her ID and holding it up. "Detective Stone. Step out where I can see you."

No reply. But the tapping stopped.

Great. We're going to have to do things the hard way, then.

It had been several years since Sarah had needed to defend herself, and while she kept herself fit, she knew there would be a certain amount of atrophy. If a fight broke out, she would need to fight dirty. *Gouge the eyes, hit the nose, attack the genitals, kneecaps, and neck.*

"Last warning," she said. "Step out now where I can see you."

When there was still no reply, she swore out loud and marched forward.

Something leapt out at her from behind the bin and let out an inhuman yowl.

Sarah yelped and sprang aside.

The ginger cat darted past her as if a pit bull were chasing it, tail low and hackles high. It raced down the alleyway, back towards the adjacent street.

Sarah put a hand to her chest. "Shit. I bloody hate cats."

Refocusing, she peered around the corner to try to relocate the suspect she'd been following. She still had no idea where they had gone.

The alleyway led to a dead end, the street terminating at a brick wall that seemed to surround the gardens of a row of townhouses up ahead. Lights were on in some of the upstairs windows, but none of the illumination reached the ground.

"Huh? Where the hell did you go?"

Something moved behind Sarah.

She spun around just in time to see something swinging at her head. She tried to duck, but the object glanced off her forehead and rattled her skull.

Her legs abandoned her.

She hit the cobbles, smacking her face and causing flashing sequins to swarm her vision. A warm, coppery tang filled her mouth.

It's him. It's the killer.
I need to do something.

Despite the disorientation of her senses, Sarah managed to yell out at the top of her lungs, fear assisting her with her volume. She was unarmed and trapped with a sadistic killer. "Somebody help! Help me!"

No one came. Her cries didn't seem to worry her attacker one bit. She would need to fight.

But I can't move my legs.

A pair of plain black trainers entered the fringes of Sarah's vision as she lay on her front, still dizzy from the blow to her head. She tried to crane her neck and see clearly, but she couldn't make it past the stranger's knees.

"What's this?" asked an unremarkable male voice as its owner stooped down beside Sarah and picked something up. She knew it was her ID card; she'd dropped it when she fell. "Detective Sarah Stone," he muttered. "Looks like they gave Richard a new friend to play with. Hope you don't mind if I keep this."

Sarah spat blood onto the cobbles. "Wh-who are you?" She tried to look up again, but her attacker kicked her in the stomach and took away her breath. Curling up in a ball, she moaned in gasping agony.

I don't want to die here.

But I can't get up. Too much pain.

Sarah felt like she was going to explode as she fought to catch a single breath, and for several terrifying moments she thought she might suffocate like the poor girl lying down by the riverbank. Then her diaphragm spasmed, and she gulped air like a baby hungry for milk.

She got a glimpse of the man standing over her.

He wore dark joggers and a plain black hoody drawn tightly around his face. Sarah got the sense her attacker was young, but her vision was so blurry that she might have been wrong. A hammer swung loosely in his hand, the object that had glanced across her forehead.

"You're not part of this," he told her calmly. "All you'll do is get in my way and keep Richard from admitting who he really is and what he's done. You're not part of the plan, but I'm going to have to kill you now."

"Help me," she screamed again, but no one was nearby. She tried to push herself up, but the killer put a foot on her back and pushed her back down. A younger version of her might have been able to put up a fight, but she suddenly felt old and afraid.

"This would be the part where you imagine yourself someplace nice," the killer soothed her. "Find your happy place and maybe you'll get to stay there forever."

He pressed down harder with his foot, pinning her against the cobbles.

Sarah tried to shout again, but her throat constricted and her voice became a strangled moan. "Please don't…"

"That's the same thing Mona Lewis said. Now stay still or this will get messy."

"M-Mona Lewis?"

He knelt down on Sarah's back and let the hammer dangle in front of her face. Then he raised it into the air. "Don't worry about it now, sweetheart. Just close your eyes."

"Please…" she said again.

"Sarah? Sarah, are you there?"

Sarah glanced past the man about to kill her and saw feet hurrying around the corner. "I-I'm here!" She gave another strangled moan. "Help me!"

Her attacker hissed and leapt to his feet. "Must be your lucky night, Sarah." His calm gave way to anger. "But we'll meet again soon enough. I won't stop until Richard accepts the truth."

With that, her attacker sprinted at the brick wall at the end of the alleyway and leapt up and over it into the gardens beyond; a six-foot obstacle scaled effortlessly.

He's athletic. Calm under pressure.

And a fucking psychopath.

"Sarah? Are you okay?" Her rescuer turned out to be Richard. He hurried over and crouched beside her, placing a hand on her shoulder as she tried to push herself up. "What happened? I heard you calling out."

"I-I'm okay," she said, shock giving way to an awful thudding in her skull. "It was him. It was… shit!" She collapsed onto her side and grabbed her head, teeth gritted. "Y-you need to get units up here now. We need to… to catch him. Ah, shit! My skull is throbbing."

"I'm not leaving you here." He pulled a mobile from inside his jacket and started dialling. "You were right about him watching, Sarah. We almost had him."

"W-what were you doing here? How did you find me?"

He looked her in the eye and appeared uncertain. "I know you told me to stay put, but I was worried. Call it a gut feeling, but I knew it was a bad idea for you to go alone. I shouldn't have let you in the first place."

Sarah felt sick at the thought of him being worried about her, but she had no doubt that she would be dead if he hadn't arrived, her brains smashed in by a hammer. Despite that realisation, she couldn't bring herself to thank him.

Her mouth was full of blood, caused from biting her tongue, and she spat it out onto the cobbles. It caused Richard to flinch and stare at the gory salvia for a moment, but then he made a call for all units to respond.

A group of people entered the alleyway, young men and women glancing around cautiously. Students most likely. They had obviously heard the commotion and finally come to see what was going on. Too little too late. The killer was gone, free to continue inflicting his wickedness upon the world.

There was no telling who the killer would target next, but Sarah decided right then, bleeding on the ground, that she was going to become his worst fucking nightmare.

I'm going to catch you, you bastard. You should have killed me when you had the chance.

CHAPTER
SEVEN

SARAH SAT on a folding canvas chair inside the command tent while a paramedic fussed over her various wounds, the worst of which was a throbbing knot on her forehead. She waved a bloody hand at the woman and grumbled. "I'm fine. It's just a bump on the head and some scratches." Her words were clumsy, her bottom lip split open and swollen from hitting the cobbles and her tongue a little sore.

"Someone whacked you with a hammer, pet. We have to make sure you're okay."

"It only glanced me. If it'd hit me properly, we probably wouldn't be having this conversation."

"You were lucky," said James, standing behind the paramedic and rubbing at his arms as if he were chilly, despite having put on a plain black jacket. There was a slight breeze coming off the river from below and the night had taken away the warmth of the day.

"Yeah, I feel real lucky," Sarah muttered, then winced as a spike of pain jabbed her in the ribs.

James rushed and put a hand on her arm. "You okay?"

"Just a bit banged up. I'll be fine."

The paramedic prodded around the lump on Sarah's forehead a few more times and then stepped back. "Well, there's no sign of concussion, but you need to stay alert over the next twenty-four hours. Any nausea or vomiting, dizziness or confusion, and you need to go straight to A&E."

"Understood." Sarah gave the woman a nod.

While the paramedic packed up, James handed Sarah a bottle of water, which she gulped down thirstily.

"Did you get a look at him?" he asked her. "Did you see his face?"

She put the lid back on the bottle and wedged it between her thighs. "Not really. He was wearing a hoodie. All I can say is that he's male and probably young. He scaled a six-foot wall like it was nothing."

"Well, that's more than we had this morning. I'm glad you're okay, Sarah."

She raised an eyebrow. "What? No lecture about me running off alone?"

He pulled a face. "You're a grown woman. Anyway, the risk of being attacked so close to the crime scene should've been non-existent. I don't see you as being at fault. In fact, it was a good call. A little more luck and we could've had him. You were doing your job. Unfortunately, our killer is surprisingly bold."

She let out a sigh, her head still pounding. "He knows the area. He led me down that alleyway on purpose. A dead end, and he managed to hide so that I walked right past him. No way that he did that by chance."

"There were several bin cupboards in that alleyway," James explained. "He must have slipped inside one while you were following him."

"He has my badge."

"Not the end of the world."

"Unless you count the fact he knows who I am now. Maybe I'll become his next obsession. The one who got away."

"Then it'll only increase our chances of catching him. He got sloppy today, Sarah. You had him cornered."

"I'd say he had *me* cornered."

"Either way, we learned something about him. He could've run, but instead he chose violence. He's confident, extraverted, and willing to take risks."

"How does that help us?"

"It means our killer is likely living his life out in the open. We're not looking for an oddball on the fringes of society or a fifty-year-old man-child still living with his mother. We're looking for someone who can blend in. Our killer wears a normal face."

"You mean like Richard? Where is he anyway?"

James glanced about furtively, clearly worried that her comment might have been overheard by the paramedic. But the woman had moved away and was packing up her stuff in the back of the ambulance. "Richard was mortified that you got hurt," he said. "I told him to give you some space while you got patched up. He went back down to the river to see if he could find any more clues."

"Do we know who the girl is? The killer mentioned a Mona Lewis. I told you that, right?"

"Yes. We're still working on an ID, but we're running that name through the system. Forensics found all they could at the river bank, so we're just waiting on a body collection now."

"Wait? Is Richard down there with that girl on his own?"

"I just told you that—"

Sarah groaned. "I need to go down there. I'm his partner for a reason, right?"

James put a hand on her shoulder and kept her in place. "It's fine. Take a minute."

"What if he's doing something creepy down there? He shouldn't be alone with her, James."

A woman walking by started laughing. When James stepped aside, it turned out to be the policewoman Sarah assumed was DCI Flannigan. "You think Macabre Mullins is a deviant as well, do you?" She took off her police cap and revealed short black hair that made her look like an evil headmistress. "He's always given me the creeps."

"Mullins?" Sarah frowned, and then remembered Richard's assumed identity. James was looking pleadingly at her. "Yeah, um, Mullins. I'm new to the team, but he gives me the creeps too."

"He's good at what he does," James said huffily.

Flannigan nodded. "Granted, but that doesn't make him any less strange." She offered out a hand to Sarah. "DCI Flannigan. James told me a little about you. Thank you for you service, Captain Stone."

Sarah huffed. "It was a real pleasure."

"One can only imagine." She nodded at Sarah's scars. "That must have smarted something bloody awful. Hope you got the buggers back."

"I did, and then some."

Flannigan grinned. "Glad to hear it. My nephew served in Afghanistan, said it was two years of the worst hell imaginable, and half of it was down to utter, mind-numbing boredom."

"Absolutely," Sarah agreed. "The other half was being shot at from a hundred different directions. And in the end, it was all for nothing."

Flannigan hissed through her teeth. "Blame the politicians for that. Doesn't make you any less of a hero though. You ever need anything, Captain, you let me know, do you hear me? James can give you my number."

James nodded and smiled.

"Thanks." Sarah stood up unsteadily but eventually found her feet. "I'm going down to the river. I want to see if Richard has found anything new."

"Just take it easy." James reached out but didn't touch her. "You've had a shock."

"Leave the girl alone," Flannigan chided. "She's probably had more bruises than you've had hot dinners."

Sarah smirked. She was quickly growing to like DCI Flannigan. "If he tries to stop me, arrest him, will you?"

"Nothing would please me more."

With a smile on her face that lasted only a few steps, Sarah headed out of the car park and over to the muddy path that led down to the river bank. Her vision blurred for a few moments, but eventually her footing grew steadier, and she became confident that she was okay. She headed down towards the river.

Since being there last, a series of hanging LEDs had been attached to a selection of trees, lighting the way and keeping things accessible in the dark. Glancing back, Sarah noticed the gawkers were finally losing interest. Drinkers in the pubs had gone back to enjoying themselves, paying very little attention to the mundane activities going on in the car park. Word must have got out that there had been a murder, but no one seemed frightened or alarmed.

Or is it just easier for people to pretend nothing's happening? James said violent crime is on the rise. How long before no one feels safe any more?

Sarah crept carefully down the muddy path, the earth squelching beneath her feet and releasing a pungent, damp odour. The little red evidence flags were still in place, as was the taped-out path. She tried her best to keep to it.

Richard was standing beneath a willow tree beside the rushing river. The trailing branches obscured his face, making him look headless. The girl was still lying on the ground nearby, buried by rocks. It didn't appear that anyone had disturbed her. Or interfered with her.

"Richard?"

He ducked under the branches to look at her, slightly startled. "Sarah? Are you okay? I'm so glad you—"

"I'm fine. Just a bit beat up."

"I can't believe you got so close to catching him. James was right to bring you in. You have great instincts."

"If my instincts were that good, I would've taken a radio for backup."

He stepped out from beneath the tree and gave her a crooked smile, as if he didn't quite know how to make one. "It's your first day on the job. I'm still very impressed."

"I don't care if you're impressed, Richard."

"Fair enough." There was a flicker of irritation on his face, a slight narrowing of his eyes. "Have you remembered anything else about our killer?"

"I already told you what I know. A young guy, athletic and confident; that's all I've got."

Richard couldn't disguise his disappointment. He blasted air out of his nostrils and tutted. "Well, that's something to go on."

She glanced down at the dead girl. "How about you? Got anything to share?"

"Yes."

"Really? What?"

He began to pace, looking down at the body. "When I came back down here, I got to thinking, specifically about another mistake I made while abducting Caroline Andrews. After I strangled her with the dog lead, I hung it from a tree while I tied her hands and feet together. I forgot to retrieve it afterwards and the police found it. It was a key piece of evidence in my trial because the leather loop had my skin cells all over it. You know, because of how tightly I gripped it when I strangled Caroline."

Sarah put a hand against her throbbing forehead and groaned in disgust. "I can't believe how casually you can talk about it."

"Beating myself up about it won't help anything, will it? I'm trying to figure out our killer."

"Okay, fine. So what does the dog lead have to do with anything?"

"I hung it from this willow tree while I worked." He pointed to the tree he had been standing under. "I checked the exact spot where I left it, and I found this…" He raised his hand and showed Sarah a small plastic card. In order to see it clearly, she had to take it from him.

"It's a student ID card." She turned it over to see a photograph on one side. A cursory glance at the body confirmed it belonged to the victim. "Caroline Boswell. Nineteen years old. Christ, he must have picked her because of her first name, just to mess with you. Hey, there's something written here in pen."

Richard nodded. "You made me."

That was what it said, written in a scrawl: **You made me.**

"What do you think it means?"

"I don't know. Maybe what I did affected our killer personally in some way, or perhaps he's referring to his obsession with me. He might feel it's out of his control, a compulsion. It would be reasonable for him to blame me."

Sarah continued to study the photograph of the girl, heartbroken to see a twinkle in her eye and the beginnings of a smile. "She had her whole life ahead of her."

"We need to take this to forensics," Richard said, reaching out to take the card back.

Sarah studied it a moment longer and then handed it back. As she did so, she left a sliver of blood down one edge. "Damn it," she said. "Sorry, I must have cut my hands on the cobbles when I fell. I should've worn gloves to come down here."

Richard didn't reply. He held the ID card in his hand and stared at it intently. Mesmerised.

He's staring at my blood.

When his breathing quickened, Sarah had seen enough. She snatched the ID card back and swore at him. "You want to lick it or something? What is wrong with you?"

"I…" His face turned white in the glow of the LED lamps. "Blood. It has an effect on me. It's… triggering."

"It arouses you? Jesus, you may say you're trying to atone – trying to help people – but you get off on this, don't you? The death and the suffering? I can see it in your eyes. It gets your blood pumping."

He looked away, as if to keep her from reading any further into his expression. "I try to stay focused, but it's like I told you – my brain is wired up all wrong. I... I can't help it."

"Oh, poor you." She put her hands on her hips and threw her head back exhaustedly. "This isn't right. This poor girl deserves better than a sicko like you perving over her remains."

"I'm not doing that!" His volume rose, but his tone lowered. "My only intention is to make sure no more young girls like her have to die, but sometimes... sometimes things get a little mixed up inside my head. I have a handle on it, okay? I'm not dangerous."

"You killed two dozen people, Richard. You're as dangerous as they come. If you can't control yourself..."

"I can control myself, Sarah, and if for some reason I can't, then that's why you're here. We can work well together, I know it, if you just help me."

"How? I can't fix your lizard brain."

He sighed and turned to face the water. In the dark, the river was like a wide black dragon's tail with silvery scales. "You know, I don't even remember if I always enjoyed doing the things I did with my family, or if it repulsed me at first. My memories of childhood... most of them are murky. The doctors say it's repression, but I keep searching my mind for something to show me whether or not I'm human; just an early glimpse of me protesting or screaming or being sick at the grotesqueness of it all. If I could see that, then maybe I could forgive myself a little more and accept that I was made into something I didn't choose to be." He turned back to Sarah, his eyes downcast. "If my parents made me into a monster, then is it possible that I made our killer into a monster? Am I responsible for Claudette Herrington and Caroline Boswell? I thought my sins were all behind me, but people are still dying because of me."

"You're not responsible for another man's murders, Richard.

Whatever this sicko's excuse, he's choosing to do what he's doing. He's not a brainwashed child."

"Do you think if he was it would make him less responsible?"

She shrugged. "I don't know. God, this has been the strangest day of my life. I just want to go to bed and sleep. Although I'm probably going to have nightmares. Nightmares about you!"

"You don't trust me, Sarah, I get that. But I promise you I'm not a killer. Not any more. The last thing I want to do is hurt anybody else ever again. Please believe that."

"I don't. I'm sorry."

Richard motioned to Caroline Boswell, her spoiled corpse crushed beneath the rocks. "Okay, then just decide whether or not you can allow monsters to get away with doing things like this. We can stop this killer, I know it."

"And then what? How many more murderers are out there?"

"Less if we work together and stop them. Please, Sarah, don't let your opinion of me keep you from doing good." He gave her the slightest of smiles, but risked nothing further. They were standing at a murder scene after all.

Sarah folded her arms and looked out over at the inky river. "If I stick around, it's only because I owe this psycho some payback. I also need to do something else."

He leant in, curious. "What?"

Sarah took a deep breath, her voice firm. "I need to make damn sure you respect Caroline and Claudette, and every other poor soul counting on you for justice. If I catch you doing anything messed up, like sniffing a victim's hair or sucking their toes, I'll make sure you pay, Richard. I'll shatter your goddamn testicles."

Richard stepped away from the willow tree and moved right against her. He looked her in the eye intensely, his breath on her face. "Do you promise?"

"What?"

"Do you promise?"

"Y-yes!"

"Good." He offered out his hand.

Pushing aside her disgust, she shook it.

Looks like we're partners.

What the hell am I doing?

"Mona!"

Richard frowned at her. "What?"

"The name the killer said in the alleyway. Mona Lewis." She turned and looked down at Caroline Boswell. "I had assumed it was the name of this girl, but it isn't. That means…"

Richard closed his eyes and seethed. "That he's already taken another girl. Damn it, we have to find him, Sarah. We have to put a stop to this."

"No shit." Sarah clenched her fists and marched back up the muddy path. "No shitting shit."

———

His heart was thudding in his chest, the adrenaline only now beginning to subside. He'd taken an enormous risk by sticking around to watch the fun and games by the river, and it had almost gone very wrong. Impulsivity was a character flaw, but he couldn't change who he was.

If that police bitch hadn't come after me by herself, she might have had me. Good thing she's an idiot.

It irked him that he had been forced to let the police officer – Sarah Stone – live. The sight of her bloody mouth had excited him, and he had desperately wanted to see her glistening brains splattered across the cobbles. He'd never killed anyone via bludgeoning before.

And they say variety is the spice of life.

"You got to keep things fresh," he told himself, which was

ironic considering he dedicated such a large portion of his time to events of the past.

He was currently sitting on the bed of his dorm room at Bailey Court, listening to fellow residents from his floor whoop and laugh as they drank alcohol in the communal kitchen. Soon he might join them, but he was too jittery right now. The expensive silver bracelet his girlfriend forced him to wear was rattling on his wrist because he was so hyped. His bloodlust was up, and if he tried to interact, he would probably come across as a hyperactive lunatic.

He could barely unclench his fists, and his legs were uncomfortably tingly, so after giving them a shake, he decided to stand up and pace the room. To occupy himself, he pulled a book from the shelf above his single bed: *Feudalism and the Middle Ages* by J. Millis.

The textbook was required reading for his Medieval History module, but he had already studied it cover to cover several times. While he had a soft spot for the ancient and classical eras, his passion was the Dark Ages. With the zeal of the Catholic Church driving it, along with multiple inbred and insane kings, mankind had truly come into its own during the medieval period. Killing, torturing, imprisoning. Wars on a massive scale. Incurable plagues. Death in the most twisted and perverse flavours. Life was a carousel of barbarity and misery. Intoxicating to think about.

He held the book by its spine and let it fall open in the middle, revealing the recess he had carved into its pages. Pretty cliched, as far as hiding places went, but there weren't many places to stash things in a four-by-four dorm room. Perhaps if he had been one of the many rich international students that occupied Durham University, he could have afforded a secret safe behind an old oil painting, but that wasn't his lot in life. He was a lowly peasant, a victim to circumstance.

But I'm here. I made it despite everything being stacked against me. A lone wolf amongst mindless sheep. No one has any idea how dangerous I am. And I'm still just a student.

From inside the book's hidden alcove, he pulled out a small plastic sandwich bag. It was filled with thirty chipped and painted fingernails, given to him by three pretty young women. Removing them had been surprisingly easy, and one of the most astounding things he had learned during his most recent studies was that some people simply accepted being murdered. They begged and cried, but they didn't try to stop you.

Some people are born to be prey.

Then there are the apex hunters like me. Top of the food chain.

There was a knock at his door, which caused him to flinch and shove the plastic bag full of fingernails back into its hidey-hole. He slammed the textbook closed and slid it back onto its shelf – just as his door opened. It always pissed him off how his dormmates felt entitled to come and go as they pleased. This was his space, not a communal hangout. Still, he forced a wide smile onto his face as he turned to see who it was.

It was his girlfriend, Prue. A rich beauty from Hong Kong, who he often thought about slicing wide open. *Are her insides the same as a white girl's? A black girl's? There's still so much to learn, so much enlightenment to gain.*

Prue smiled back at him with that sparkle in her eye she always got whenever he was around. "Oliver," she said, which annoyed him greatly, as everyone else called him Ollie. "I've been missing you all day. Where have you been? You weren't at our Connected Histories lecture."

Oliver moved over and gave her a kiss on the forehead. She'd been texting him all day, and he knew he couldn't avoid having to explain why he hadn't replied to a single message. "I've, um, been getting hassle off my dad again. It sent me into a bit of a spiral. I told Irving-Ross I wouldn't be there."

She tilted her head at him and pouted. "Oh no, did you have another panic attack?"

"Yeah, I…" He looked away, trying to appear ashamed of his mental weakness, which was nothing but a gross fabrication. It'd been more than a year since his last bout of anxiety. "I went to sit by the river. The water always calms me down."

She rubbed his arm and tutted sympathetically, her brown eyes flickering slightly as they focused on him. "Oh, honey. You should have replied to my texts, I would've come and sat with you."

"I know, I know. Sometimes, it's just better to be on my own." He put his hand against her plump white cheek, like rounded porcelain. "You deserve better."

"Don't be silly. Life's tough, I get it."

Oliver almost laughed at that, seeing as Prue was the daughter of a multimillionaire telecoms mogul and had grown up in a Hong Kong penthouse with servants. "You're so sweet, Prue. I'm lucky to have you."

She leant forward and kissed him on the mouth, but then she jolted and pulled away. "Can you believe they found a dead body today? If you were at the river, you must have seen all the commotion?"

He had to stifle a grin. He'd seen it all right, up close and personal. "Yeah, there were police up on the bridge – forensics too, I think. Must have been a murder or something."

Prue covered her mouth. "So soon after what happened to Claudette Herrington? Do you think it's another student? Is there a psychopath running around Durham?" She shuddered and threw her arms around him. "You knew Claudette, right?"

"A little bit from the gym. I had to give a statement to the police about her because I saw her the night she died."

"God, maybe you saw the killer too. It terrifies me to think about it."

He tried to comfort her with an unconcerned shrug. "You have me to protect you, don't you? And Claudette Herrington was… you know?"

"A little too friendly with guys?" Prue finished for him diplomatically.

"Exactly. The world is a dangerous place and some people aren't as careful as they should be. But you're smart, Prue. Don't worry."

She pulled away and pinched the bridge of her tiny nose as if she had sinus pain. "It's so horrible when things like this happen. Makes me depressed."

"Me too," Oliver agreed. "I suppose people are still just animals at the end of the day, huh?"

"Party animals maybe." She shook away her revulsion and went back to smiling. "You coming to hang out? We're playing Zombicide."

Oliver rolled his eyes. "Thrilling."

She gave him a playful shove in his toned chest, but the aggression sparked a mild reaction in him that made him want to strike out at her. "Maybe if you had a drink with the rest of us, you might actually have fun."

"I just don't like the taste. And I don't like losing control. My mum had a drink problem and I don't want to go down the same path."

"Oh, Oliver," she said. "I love you, but you gotta learn to enjoy yourself instead of worrying all the time."

He leant forward and gave her a smirk. "Trust me, I have plenty of fun."

"What? You mean when you're not working out or sticking your head in a book?"

He winked at her. "That's not all I do."

"Fine. So, are we going to go and—"

"Board games can wait." He grabbed her by the waist and tossed her onto the bed, quickly stripping away his clothes. His head filled with thoughts of Richard Flesch and the countless women he had tortured and mutilated. His engorged penis hardened so much it threatened to burst out of its skin.

"Oh, Oliver."

"Call me master."

Her giggling, followed by happy moaning, irritated his nerves. He much preferred screaming.

CHAPTER
EIGHT

SARAH PACED BACK and forth in the quiet room she'd set up for herself. Most of the Institute's employees did the majority of their work in the manor's former dining hall – what Sarah thought of as the Hive – but it was too busy there, too difficult to think around so much young, nervous energy. Sarah was middle-aged and set in her ways. She liked to work alone.

The reversible whiteboard was tilted slightly downwards to avoid the glare of the room's glittering chandelier. Crime scene photographs and red marker pen covered its sleek surface, spreading out from the centre. This was Sarah's mind laid bare, a map of the things bothering her.

Like where was Mona Lewis?

James had wasted no time in researching the name the killer had spoken two nights ago in the alleyway, and it had been grimly inevitable when news came back that Mona was missing. Not a student at the university, like Claudette Herrington or Caroline Boswell, Mona was a nineteen-year-old supermarket worker from the seaside town of Redcar in North East Yorkshire. She had been missing for two whole weeks.

The young girl peered at Sarah now from the very centre of

the board. She was a frizzy-haired beauty with a lopsided smile and bright green eyes. Her mother had provided the photograph and begged for her baby to be found. Sarah was going to do everything she could to find her.

The killer didn't keep Claudette or Caroline for so long. Why is he keeping Mona?

Sarah pulled the lid off her red marker and wrote on her thinking board, wincing as the tip squeaked against the sleek surface: **Killer must have space to hold a hostage/body. Has own house or business?**

It was a contradiction that bothered her, a jigsaw piece that refused to fit. Her attacker in the alleyway had seemed young, possibly even a teenager. But young people didn't typically own property in 2023. Perhaps he lived with family, but that opened up a whole new line of questioning. How could the killer hide his sadistic crimes from his family if he were living with them? Sarah's gut told her this was a monster who liked to be alone. Someone driven and focused and obsessed.

Obsessed with my partner – Richard 'the Chester-le-Street Cannibal' Flesch.

Jesus.

She and Richard hadn't crossed paths much during the past two days. Like Sarah, he preferred to work alone, burying his head in files or staring at the screen of his laptop. Occasionally, he would visit the house to share his latest theory or bounce ideas, but Sarah suspected it was more to check in with other human beings than anything else. While he was nowhere near being a people person, Richard seemed to enjoy the occasional social interaction. Sarah had noticed, however, that he would always turn glum soon after chuckling or smiling, as if he felt guilty for experiencing even a fleeting moment of happiness.

And he should feel guilty. He can never make up for the lives he took.

The door at the back of her small room opened and James

wandered in with his usual chirpiness. He had shorts on today, with a stretchy nylon T-shirt, indicating he had come back from a game of tennis. Apparently, the estate had a pair of concrete courts in the west gardens. Employees were encouraged to get plenty of exercise to maintain their physical and mental health.

"Hello, Sarah. How are you this afternoon? Are the clothes Frances brought you okay? Did you sleep well on the top floor? It gets a little stuffy."

Sarah looked down at the tight jeans and silky blouse she was wearing and shrugged. "I feel ten years younger."

"Great. How are your enquiries going?"

She turned back to her board and stared at the evidence. "No news on Mona Lewis or the sicko who took her. It's like beating my head against a brick wall with what little we have."

James moved up beside her and studied the board. "We'll get the guy. We won't stop until we do. Here, I have some things for you."

He was holding a bulky folder and a see-through plastic bag. He handed the bag to Sarah first, and when she reached inside, she pulled out two items: one heavy and one light. "A Taser and pepper spray?"

"Considering what happened in Durham, I decided it might be good for you to have some modicum of protection."

She put the self-defence weapons back inside the bag and placed them on the desk she had set up in the corner. "Would prefer my old SIG, but I suppose those days are behind me now."

"And thankfully so, I'm sure."

"What else have you got for me?" She nodded at the bulging folder still under his arm. "Some light reading, I suppose?"

"The very opposite." He moved over to her desk and placed the folder down, then flipped open the front cover and tapped the first page with his index finger. "Rundowns of active cases. The North East Torture-Killer is obviously our key focus right now, but it might be helpful for you to get up to speed with the other cases on our books."

"The papers have named him the Durham Butcher, you know?"

James shrugged. "We pay little attention to what the press says. Gone are the days when they were actually helpful to investigations."

Sarah moved to the other side of her desk and took a moment to skim through the pages. Most were typed reports of some description, but there were also dozens of crime scene photographs – of deceased girls and women mostly, but with the occasional young male. Stab wounds, ligature marks, poisonings, the brutality went on and on, an endless catalogue of depravity and wickedness. "Bloody hell, James. It's like you've just handed me a brochure for a snuff movie."

He folded his arms and gave her a pitying glance. "Nature of the job, I'm afraid. I wish I could say it gets easier, but…"

"It gets worse." Sarah knew mankind only ever raised the bar on its various exploits. Olympic records got broken, lifespans grew longer, and criminals behaved even more obscenely. The days of Hitchcock's *Psycho* had given way to *Saw* and *Hostel*. Who knew what tomorrow would bring?

Sarah closed the folder and sat down at her desk, lacing her fingers together in front of her as she looked James in the eye. "How many are in here?"

"Victims? I'm not sure."

"How many psychopaths?"

"Well, psychopaths isn't a catch-all term. Some killers are mentally ill or delusional, some have behavioural prob—"

"How many? How many monsters are in this folder?"

James sighed. His legs were quivering, probably from the exertion of his tennis match. "I would estimate the cases on your desk right now involve at least nine active killers."

"So ten, including the Durham Butcher? Ten deranged

psychopaths for us to hunt for like goddamn Pokémon. What have I signed up for?"

Rather than answer her question, he moved over to the door. "I'll leave you to work, Sarah. I have to go take a shower, but you know where to find me if you need anything."

She nodded, although she didn't actually agree. James had an office in both the Box in the rear gardens and an office on the second floor of the manor. Often, she went to find him in one place only to learn he was in the other. Instead of arguing about it, though, she just waved him off.

Once he had gone, she reopened the folder and scrutinised it more carefully, familiarising herself with the various killers currently running amok in the UK with their raging murder boners. The worst was unquestionably a monster nicknamed the Boxcutter Killer, who had already been caught once but had since escaped. The freak's favourite hobby was kidnapping people and blinding them, before taking up to a week to systematically remove their body parts. Any victim found alive usually wished they were dead.

Then there was the Orifice Killer, an unidentified serial murderer and rapist whose particular penchant was to slice a hole in a woman's—

I can't do this. I can't face this stuff. It's too much.

How am I supposed to get up in the morning knowing the world is like this?

She closed the folder and pushed it aside, wanting to get to her laptop underneath. She opened it up and checked her emails. There were several, but the only one she opened was from Donkey.

I still can't believe we all call him that.

FAO: Sarah

I got the info you wanted, but don't tell James. This kind

of thing is not in our purview, and my crooked ass is on the line if an audit flags it up.

Donk

It was short and sweet, which she had learned to expect from Donkey. She wasn't sure what had made her reach out and ask for his help, but she was still learning the ropes and needed to rely on someone if she was to get anywhere fast.

She opened up the pdf attachment and ran her eyeballs over the screen. It was a list of convictions for Albanian nationals, along with their last-known addresses and places of work (if any). The report covered the entirety of Yorkshire, England's largest county, and the place where her ex-colleague Howard Hopkins had been murdered. Despite what she had discussed with James moments before, the truth was she had eleven active cases, not ten. She intended to find the man who had killed her friend.

The next few hours flew by as Sarah delved down various avenues of thought, searching for answers about who the Durham Butcher might be and what he had done – or planned to do – with Mona Lewis. She also made multiple calls to various landlords about their Albanian tenants and their current whereabouts. Neither investigation presented anything to excite her, but catching criminals was a long and arduous process, like separating sand. For every piece of evidence that mattered, there were a thousand pieces that didn't. Sifting took time.

The sun had dulled outside, the daylight turning to burnt amber. The swaying trees cast a long shadow through Tithby Hall's lead-lined windows.

I need to take a break, Sarah told herself. She didn't even know how many hours she'd been cooped up inside this room, but her rumbling tummy told her it was too many. Furthermore, her mind had gone numb, like she had been holding a chunk of ice against her brain. Her best thinking was done for the day and she wished she was back in Wolverhampton in her flat, crashed out in front of the television. Instead, she would once again be staying overnight at a stately home-cum-university dorm.

She closed down her laptop and exited the room.

Her destination was the manor's former smoking lounge, which was now used as a small break room, with books, a television, and a fridge full of snacks. Her knowledge of the building's layout proved good enough that she was able to avoid the Hive and its peppy researchers by taking an old servant's hallway. Regrettably, the smoking room was not vacant when she arrived.

But, thankfully, it was only Donkey.

Sarah went straight to the fridge and was glad to find a cling-film-wrapped tuna sandwich inside. The kitchen crew always made extra food to stock the various break rooms, and it was a lifesaver today, as she had somehow missed both lunch and dinner.

"Hungry?" Donkey asked her, peering over the top of what looked like a computer magazine.

She held the sandwich up in front of him. "Why else do you think I just grabbed this? Because I'm horny?"

"I spend all day studying perverts and weirdos. I would never make assumptions."

"Good point." She moved over to the U-shaped seating area around the television and sat on the two-seater couch opposite the one Donkey was on. He always slumped awkwardly when he sat, one badly aligned hip jutting out to the side, but it didn't seem to cause him any discomfort. His ears jutted out too, and his eyeballs bulged behind his glasses. Donkey was not a handsome man, but Sarah felt a kinship with him due to the scar across his face, from left eyebrow to left ear. She hadn't asked where his injuries had come from, but she had heard from James that it had been a car crash during childhood. It must have sucked for Donkey, and it actually made Sarah grateful that she had at least made it through her twenties before getting disfigured for life.

"Thanks for sending me that info earlier," she said, sinking back into the couch.

"What info?"

"Right, yeah, of course."

Donkey cleared his throat and sat up a little straighter. "So how are things progressing with the North East Torture-Killer?"

Sarah unwrapped the sandwich on her lap and groaned. "I came here to get away from work. Ask me something else."

"Okay, how are you and Richard getting along?"

She groaned again. "That question is only marginally better than the last one. Tell you the truth, I've barely seen anything of him since we found Caroline Boswell's body by the river."

"You should work closer. Both of you are brilliant."

"Not sure I agree with you there, unless you mean killing and eating people. He's pretty good at that, I gather."

Donkey clearly disapproved of her attitude, but he seemed to find her sarcasm amusing enough to chuckle. He adjusted his specs and fiddled with his loose blonde hair. "I meant you both have great instincts. Look how he saved you in that alleyway. Anyone else probably would have assumed you'd be just fine, but not Richard. He knew."

Sarah bristled. Part of the reason she'd made so little effort to spend time with her partner was because she hadn't enjoyed admitting that she might owe him her life. "Yeah, well," she muttered. "It takes one to know one. Isn't that the whole reason he's here?"

Donkey nodded, then reached down the side of the sofa, groaning and struggling until he came back up with a bottle of Jack Daniels, nearly full. "Not the most refined," he said, "but easy to share. You want in?"

She grinned and felt her nose wrinkle in a gleeful expression she immediately chided herself for. "Are you planning on getting wasted?"

"I live in a place nicknamed 'the Murder University'. Sometimes you have to black out and forget about all the gory death for a while."

"You never seem to be affected by it. In fact, I'm impressed by how upbeat you are. How do you manage it?"

He wiggled the bottle of Jack Daniels next to his head. "Hello? Answer right here."

Rolling her eyes and smirking, she reached out and clicked her fingers. "Give it here, then."

Donkey handed over the booze and Sarah took a decent swig. She liked bourbon, so it went down smoothly. After gasping at the burn from her throat, she handed the bottle back. "What's your actual name, by the way? Your email address has 'dondon' in it. Is that your name?"

He smiled. "Donald Keye. Which is another reason for my nickname. I was named after my grandfather."

"Your name is Donald? Like the duck?"

Deadpan, he said, "No, like my grandfather."

"Who was a cartoon duck?"

Donkey chuckled, and then took a swig from the bottle. "Well, who were you named after?"

"I imagine my parents just picked a name out of a book. I come from a long line of military men, so it was a great disappointment when I was born a girl."

"But you served anyway, so what's the problem?"

"Tradition. I could have covered myself in medals and captured Bin Laden, but it still wouldn't have pleased my father. He used to think a woman's place was in the kitchen. Not exactly a modern man, you know? Although I did see him eat a banana once, which was quite open-minded for him. What were your parents like?"

Donkey pursed his lips and shrugged. "They were nice, normal. Crap drivers though."

For a moment, Sarah gawped, not knowing if he was being serious or not. Eventually, all she could do was laugh. And laugh they both did for another hour until James walked in and interrupted them with a blushing smile.

"Oh sorry, is this a private party?" he asked.

Sarah lifted the Jack Daniels bottle and observed that approximately one-third of it remained. It was nine o'clock, and she was feeling pretty sloppy. "No, there's a sip or two left if you want to join in."

"Well, I prefer Iron Smoke, but that's just the New Yorker in me. I'll take a hit."

Sarah handed him the bottle. Donkey got up, clutching his bladder. "Gotta pee." He pulled his walking stick from the ground and used it to hobble out of the room.

James sat down on the sofa next to Sarah, causing her to bounce a little over to the other side. He had changed now into jeans and a casual button-up shirt. His hair was damp from a shower. Although he had a place of his own in town, he seemed to prefer crashing at the manor most nights. Sarah could barely stand sleeping in the creepy old house, surrounded by peppy students who also lived and studied there. If she stuck around for the long term, she would most certainly be getting her own place.

I'm not sticking around though. Only until I catch the Durham Butcher.

But what about all the other cases inside the folder? All of those innocent victims crying out for justice.

Not my problem.

Sarah smirked as James took a short swig of bourbon. From the way he spluttered and patted his chest, he didn't appear to be a big drinker of spirits. In fact, from the shape of him, he appeared to live a clean and healthy life.

"Shall we invite Richard to come chill with us?" she asked.

"I'm sure he has some great stories he could share over a drink."

James tutted, but he gave her half a smile. "Richard doesn't drink, and I'm not sure you would be pleasant company for him."

She raised an eyebrow, her facial muscles sluggish. "And why's that?"

"Because you'll no doubt upset him with a constant stream of barbs."

"You act like I'm a bully for prodding a mass murderer." She took the bottle from him and swigged again, only a mouthful, as she didn't want to deprive him of his share.

He took the bottle back from her and swigged again. As usual, he was visibly defensive of Richard, but he didn't seem as offended as usual. Was he getting used to her personality?

"Are we going to go around in circles about this forever, Sarah? You're like Manhattan traffic, you never let up."

"I wouldn't know about that. My chief concern is how this eventually ends. How long can you keep Richard's true nature under control? How long before he starts stalking the night and reliving the good old days?"

James gave no reply. He stared at the label on the bottle and seemed to think about something. Just when Sarah was about to ask him what was wrong, he reached into his jeans pocket and pulled out his phone.

"What are you doing?" Sarah asked.

"Showing you what Richard likes to do at night." He gripped the bottle between his thighs and used both free hands to tap away at his phone. After a few moments, he showed her the screen. "I hate to invade his privacy like this, but it was one of the conditions of his release. He has to be supervised at all times."

Sarah looked at the screen. It was a camera feed from Richard's small office. She watched him sitting at his desk, leafing through papers and tapping away at a laptop keyboard.

"So he likes to work. Not surprising as it's—"

"He'll be working till about three in the morning, and he'll likely be back on it first thing tomorrow, before the rest of us are even out of bed. Since the day he arrived here, Richard hasn't taken a day off work or even taken a weekend to relax."

Sarah was silent.

"I agree his past is abhorrent, but there is zero doubt in my mind that Richard is on a mission to save his soul. I've never seen another human being more dedicated to helping people. You don't have to like him, Sarah, but I think it's time you start to respect him. He saved your life, after all."

Sarah growled and snatched the bottle back. "Yeah, yeah. For all you know it could all be an act. Maybe he's just waiting for you to let your guard down so he can eat your face."

"You may be right, but that would make me a pretty shitty psychologist, wouldn't it? Look, if you don't trust Richard, then please trust me. I believe in Richard Flesch. It's not an act. It's a genuine quest for salvation."

Sarah wanted to punch him right in his sincere face. How could he be so naïve? Serial killers didn't reform. They were born wrong; too wrong to fix. "Why did you leave New York, James?" She wanted to change the subject. "Why leave America and move to Darlington, of all places?"

He put his phone away and shrugged. "A lot of reasons."

"Such as?"

"I married an English woman, for one."

"Oh. I didn't know you were…" She nodded at his hands, which lay in his lap. "You're not wearing a ring."

"Claire died a little over three years ago now from a weak heart. She was older than me by eight years, but fifty-four is still no age for anyone to die." His eyelids flickered, and he stared off at the blank television as if he could see something reflected in its screen. "Still, better to have loved and lost and all that."

Sarah pursed her lips and tried to smile. "I'm sorry. That must have been hard."

"Is hard," he corrected her, although not unkindly. "I miss Claire every day."

"How did you meet?"

He beamed, clearly glad to think of her in happier days. "Claire was working at Hunter College as a chemistry professor while I was teaching psychology in the same building. Both of us were single, childless, and unlucky in love, and we both intended to stay that way. Since our careers left us with little time for a social life, we were only work colleagues for the first year or two, but there was always this…" He ran a palm over his chest in a circle. "There was this *magnetic* force between us – this feeling that I was only ever complete when Claire was around. Eventually, we had no choice but to give in to the attraction we both felt. We were together thirteen years after that, ten of it here in the UK."

Sarah smiled. Although she wasn't usually one for sentimentality, it was hard not to be moved by James's earnestness. "Claire missed home?"

"Yes, and I had no real affection for New York, so I was happy to move here. My home was wherever Claire wanted to be."

Feeling more than a little drunk, and uncharacteristically content, Sarah reached out and placed a hand on James's knee. "It's so obvious now."

"What is?"

"Your pain." She chuckled. "It's written all over your face. Is it bad that it makes me like you more?"

"I suppose pain is something we have in common. Something to bond over."

Her hand was still on his knee, and she found herself sinking into his brown eyes. She couldn't look away. "You must get lonely, stuck here, surrounded by death."

"When you've lost someone you love, you feel lonely everywhere."

"Amen to that."

Sarah leant forward.

What the hell am I doing?

James tilted away from her. "Sarah...?"

Sarah found herself stranded in mid-air, her face hanging out in no man's land where she'd hoped to find a kiss. She didn't even know if she liked James. It had just been so long since she'd been around a man who she didn't want to punch.

James shuffled away a few inches on the sofa. "Sarah, I really don't think that—"

She leapt up and bumped her leg against the side of the couch, almost knocking herself over and embarrassing herself further. "Yep, bad idea. Very bad idea. Shit, I'm sorry. I'm drunk. Really drunk actually. Drinking is usually a talent of mine, but I'm clearly off my game tonight. It's getting late. I'm going to call it a night and—"

"No," James said, "you're not calling it a night."

Sarah stopped dead. "What?"

"You're going to sit back down while I finish the rest of this bottle. I'm not done drinking, and I would appreciate some more of your company."

"Come on, James. You don't have to be a dick about it."

"I'm not being a dick about it. You're overreacting, so sit back down and relax a while longer. Everything is fine."

Except for the fact I can feel my cheeks burning. What the hell did I think was going to happen? Just because he doesn't wince at the sight of my scars doesn't mean he wants to jump into bed with me.

"Sit down, Sarah," James said a little more firmly, and then he pointed to the couch opposite. "Although, maybe over there."

She smirked. "Okay, now you're being a dick."

"Allow me a modicum of fun."

The door opened, making them both flinch. Donkey hobbled in, and when he saw Sarah standing in the corner with her arms folded, he tilted his head like a confused puppy. "Everything okay? You're not calling it a night, are you?"

Sarah could still feel her cheeks burning, and when she turned to look at James, she expected to see him smirking. Instead, he was sipping from the bourbon bottle as if nothing had happened.

"No, I'm not leaving," Sarah said after a moment's consideration. "I'm not going anywhere."

She sat back down on the couch. Opposite James.

CHAPTER
NINE

SARAH TEETERED BACK and forth as she headed down the wood-panelled hallway, on her way to the briefing room for a Saturday morning update. It appeared everyone at the Institute lacked any kind of life, so weekends were fair game for extra work. The briefing room was in Tithby Hall's former parlour, a moderately sized room with an ugly needlepoint rug draped across its hardwood floor that people were always tripping over. If not for the fact it was probably a hundred years old, Sarah would have taken the tatty thing away to be burned.

With a groan, Sarah asked herself how much she had drunk last night.

Only half a bottle of Jack. But on a stomach filled with nothing but a tuna sandwich.

Blergh, I can still taste both.

Last night was a chromatic blur, offering only brief, headache-inducing flashes that stoked Sarah's anxiety and told her she should have stayed in bed. She usually preferred to do her drinking alone. It was a rare lapse in judgement for her to allow herself to get sloppy in public. She was still wearing the same outfit Frances had lent to her.

I still can't believe I made a pass at James. Why can't that be part of the blurriness? Why do I have to remember that part in extreme, excruciating detail?

Sarah dreaded having to face James, but upon entering the briefing room, he just gave her his usual smile and carried on with what he was doing. No big deal, apparently. Just as well, because Sarah was prone to decking someone, the mood she was in.

The room was filled with fresh-faced students, each tasked with researching crimes and processing evidence alongside pursuing their doctorates. Their cloying perfumes and aftershaves made the air smell like something between a spring meadow and the cleaning aisle of a supermarket. The only people not attending the meeting were the lab techs from the Box, as knowing too much about a case might muddy their work by creating unintentional bias.

Richard appeared from out of her blind spot and offered an unconvincing smile. He was wearing his usual suit jacket and open-collared shirt. "Sarah? You're a little late."

"Better than a lot late."

"I suppose so. Are you prepared for the meeting?"

"We're just sharing ideas this morning, right? What is there to prepare for?"

Richard glanced about furtively, sweating from his top lip. He clearly didn't relish standing up in front of a room full of people. Sarah wasn't exactly enthusiastic about it either, but mainly because there were more productive things she could have been getting on with. Mona Lewis was still at the forefront of her mind.

"Okay folks," James said emphatically from the back of the room. "Everyone, please take a seat so Richard and Sarah can begin."

Sarah rolled her eyes. She disliked hearing her name alongside Richard's. They weren't a duo or some kind of double act.

Scarface and the cannibal.

Richard cleared his throat and ambled to the front of the room. Stopping in front of the whiteboard, he started tugging at his shirt cuffs. Sarah moved to join him, but kept three feet between them.

She decided to speak first, not wanting to seem like an assistant or a helper monkey. "I'm Sarah Stone, in case you don't already know, and the only reason I'm here is because James pestered me relentlessly until I agreed to come." A slight titter from the audience. "But now that I'm here, I intend to make myself useful. I want to find the Durham Butcher as much as you do. In fact, I have a goddamn hard-on for seeing him thrown into the darkest cell we can find."

The students gave a muttered cheer, the loudest coming from Frances, who was dressed in another of her colourful jumpsuits, this one yellow.

"You may have heard that I got close to catching this guy already," Sarah continued. "Which shows he's not as smart as he thinks he is. In fact, everyone inside this room is probably smarter, so we have no excuses for not catching him." She turned to Richard. "Right?"

"Um, y-yes, of course." He turned to face the audience, then looked across at James, who was still standing at the back. James gave him a slight nod, which prompted him to begin. "Hello, everyone. Good morning. I, um, would like to talk to you about the North East Torture-Killer. I think we can all agree that he's a very, um, disturbed individual, yes?"

Like you, thought Sarah as she watched him squirm.

"While you are all familiar with the cruel murders of Caroline Boswell and Claudette Herrington, I think it would be helpful to make some preliminary assumptions based on the evidence so far. Firstly, both crimes appear to be based on historical torture methods. This suggests we may be looking for an academic of some kind, with an expertise in the past.

Furthermore, the meticulousness of the killings, as well as the lack of evidence left at the crime scenes, supports the assumption that NETK is an intelligent individual. Methodical, not impulsive. Purposeful instead of opportunistic."

"Both victims were students at Durham," Frances said, a notepad on her lap and a pen in her hand. "Do we think the killer is targeting the university?"

"It's possible," Richard said. "Although neither girl apparently knew each other, and they weren't on similar courses. Durham has a disproportionately high student population, so it's possibly just a coincidence at this point."

Frances nodded, apparently satisfied. From the look of the attentive faces in the audience, Richard seemed to command the student's respect. None of them knew who he really was. To them, he was just an awkward, possibly brilliant, criminal profiler.

They have a right to know the truth.

Richard continued, his voice growing ever more confident. "From what Sarah can tell us about her encounter with the suspect three days ago, we are looking for a young male in his early twenties, athletic build, with no discernible accent."

"I'm not so sure about that any more," Sarah said, causing all eyes to fall on her.

Richard frowned at her, and his nervousness returned. "B-but based on what you said, along with the assailant scaling a six-foot wall—"

"I know what I said and what I thought," she snapped back. "But I've been thinking about it, and it doesn't fit. Mona Lewis."

"The possible third victim?"

Sarah looked across the audience and made eye contact with James for an awkward second. "The, erm…" She rubbed at her temples and swallowed to clear the dryness from her throat. "The pattern falls apart when you include Mona Lewis. She's not a student at the university, she's not blonde like Caroline and Claudette, and she's from the Yorkshire Coast, not

County Durham. Also, Mona Lewis has been missing for two weeks, while the other girls were murdered within a couple of days.

"Perhaps we just haven't found her body yet," someone in the audience suggested.

"Perhaps." Sarah allowed it as a possibility. "But Claudette and Caroline were discovered after anonymous tip-offs, right? The killer wanted us to find their bodies right away, so he outright told us where to find them. He wants attention as soon as possible. The only reason Mona Lewis could be missing for this long is because the Durham Butcher still has her. That means he must be keeping her somewhere."

"Okay," Richard said, sounding unconvinced but willing to hear her out. "What are you thinking?"

"Well, if our killer is around twenty years old, how on earth does he have access to his own private property? Furthermore, the nature of these killings, and all the careful planning that must have gone into them…" She shook her head. "It just strikes me as the actions of someone older."

"Almost half of all serial killers begin in their twenties," Richard informed her and the room. "Ian Brady was twenty-five, for example."

"My gut is telling me someone older did this."

"Your gut?" Richard gave no expression, but there was a hint of mocking in his voice. "Didn't your gut tell us the person who attacked you was young?"

"All I'm saying is that we should be wary of putting all our eggs in the 'young white male' basket. These killings are too complex and well researched. Would a younger killer have planned things out in so much detail? Wouldn't they be more exploratory and cautious?"

Richard narrowed his eyes. Sarah expected him to argue, but he didn't. Instead, he slowly nodded. "You're right. A killer's early crimes are usually opportunistic and impulsive. Rituals and methods typically develop over time."

"So my theory has legs?" Sarah drilled him with a stare that he failed to meet.

"Yes, it's possible that our killer is older. But it's probable that they're young, based on your encounter in the alleyway, and the fact the assailant was athletic enough to scale a wall."

"Great, so we're looking for someone whose age ranges from young to old. That narrows things down."

"Let's move on," James declared from the back of the room, perhaps feeling a need to referee. "What else can we assume, folks? Sarah's assailant seemed to know his way around the streets of Durham – and both victims lived there. Should we assume our killer is from there too?"

"It's certainly a possibility," Richard said. "The kill location of Claudette Herrington, in particular, would have taken time to scout and set up. I would say it's likely NETK is, at the very least, a native of the North East, and possibly County Durham specifically. But again, like Sarah said, Mona Lewis's abduction changes things. She was taken in Redcar about an hour's drive south of Durham. The only pattern we can comfortably establish right now is that the victims are all young women and that the killer has an interest in historical torture methods."

"And the messages," Frances called out. She looked down at her notepad, reading from it. "'Eat up, Flesch'. That was left at Claudette's crime scene, right? Along with a chunk of meat from her back?"

Sarah caught James's eye once again, and this time she saw a look of worry cross his face.

"Y-yes," Richard said. "That is correct. We, um, are still working on possible meanings. Perhaps it's a misspelling, and the killer is simply making a bad joke."

Frances frowned, her finely shaped eyebrows dropping into a V. "But that doesn't tally with what we know about the killer. He's an intelligent planner, not someone who would make a spelling mistake. Also, making jokes seems at odds with the meticulous nature of his kills."

Sarah had to turn her head to hide her smirk. *Way to go, Frances. You're not just a pretty face.*

James cleared his throat. "You're right, of course, Frances. I am working on this line of investigation myself, so leave it to me."

Frances craned her neck to look back at him and then beamed. "Of course, James. Let me know if I can be of use."

"Well, you've been working the CCTV angle, right? Have you found anything?"

"Not yet." Her face fell, crestfallen. She clearly hated to disappoint James. "I've been working on getting CCTV of both crime scenes, but there's zero footage in Pit Dean and less than you would expect in Durham. For a city, it's surprisingly low-tech."

"Too many historical buildings," James said. "People don't want to spoil the aesthetic with a blinking metal box. There are plenty of eateries and pubs overlooking the river though, right? They should all have security cameras."

Frances nodded, and then frowned. "I'm in contact with all of them, but their cameras focus on their own premises – their terraces, and beer gardens, or a small section of the street. There would be no reason for them to point their cameras at the river."

"That's unfortunate." James rubbed his fingertips together and made a steeple. "But keep plugging away. We may find something yet."

"Students," said Sarah, as a thought occurred to her. When everyone looked her way, she straightened up and said the word again. "Students."

Richard turned to her. "Yes?"

"Students have phones, right? Usually good ones. And what do students like to do with their phones when they're eating at fancy restaurants or drinking next to beautiful, historic rivers and ancient cathedrals?"

James grinned at her from the back of the room. "They like to take selfies," he said. "Lots and lots of selfies."

Sarah forced herself to hold his gaze as she nodded emphatically. "There might not be many CCTV cameras in Durham, but I can guarantee there are thousands of photographs taken in that city every single night. I suggest we contact the university and ask all students to review their camera reels. They might have captured something important without even realising it."

"I'll get right on it," Richard said enthusiastically. "We can set up a helpline for students to call. It's a good idea, Sarah."

"I know it is."

"Okay," James said. "I think we have a few leads to work with. I'll convene with each of you individually throughout the day. Let's get to it."

Sarah breathed a sigh of relief. With her head banging like a kettledrum, merely standing was exhausting, and she wanted to go sit in her quiet workspace with a giant mug of coffee warming one hand and a ketchup-slathered sausage sandwich dripping in the other.

But her attempts to slip out of the room unbadgered went awry.

Richard caught up with her in the corridor, causing her to halt beneath the oil-painting gaze of some red-coated old geezer with a spaniel in his lap. "You put forth some good theories in there, Sarah. You're a welcome addition to the team."

"Really?"

"Yes, your idea of having students check their mobile phone cameras was smart. I should have thought of it myself."

She shrugged and took a half step back to give herself more breathing room. "Pretty standard, isn't it? I mean, police put out requests to the public for information all the time."

"They do, but we're at a delicate stage of the investigation. We don't want to expose ourselves to the killer. The less he knows about what we know, the better."

"We don't know shit, Richard. In fact, you should remove yourself from this entire case, don't you think?"

He grabbed the inside edges of his suit jacket as if it were a life vest and tilted his head at her. "What? Whatever do you mean?"

She folded her arms to keep her hands from trembling by her sides. Her nerves were fried from a heady mixture of hangover and public speaking. "Those kids in there are clearly intelligent," she said, "and eager to find the Durham Butcher."

Richard nodded, following along.

"But we're making it harder than it should be for them to find answers. You and I both know why the killer left that message at Claudette Herrington's murder. We both know what it means and who it was for."

Richard licked his lips, then pressed them tightly together. After a moment's hesitation, he loosened his grimace and nodded. "James is considering whether to have everyone sign NDAs and inform them who I am."

"Good. It's the right thing to do."

"I agree. Them not knowing is…" He shrugged.

Sarah didn't let up. "Those kids should know they're working alongside a mass murderer. Hell, most of them are planning to dedicate their lives to stopping serial killers, and all the while there's one right under their noses. The Chester-le-Street Cannibal."

Richard winced and looked around. "Sarah! You need to get past this. If people knowing who I am will help our investigation, then I'm all for it, regardless of how it affects me personally. Stop blaming me for all the secrecy, because I didn't choose it. James is the one who is reluctant to reveal my identity. He thinks it could do more harm than good."

Sarah considered if James might be right, and she quickly ran some scenarios through her head. What if everyone at the university quit their placements in disgust? What if the lab techs requested transfers? Then Mona Lewis would have a lot fewer brains working towards finding her.

"Richard, how do people usually react when they find out who you are?" she asked, genuinely curious.

"Well, other than Donkey and James, no one else here knows about me. James and Donkey reacted nicer than you did."

"I can believe it. What about outside the Institute? Is there anybody else who knows your true identity?"

He shook his head, fine brown hair shimmying in front of his forehead. "No one. James handled everything alongside Dr Carney at Broadmoor and the then Justice of the Peace, Lord Norris. Norris died three years ago of old age."

"And Dr Carney?"

Richard folded his arms and tensed up. "Dr Carney had to sign off on everything in order to have me released. He declared I was no threat to the public and that he would take full responsibility for my actions alongside James. Without them, none of this would have been possible. I owe both men everything."

"But Carney knows you're working here, right? He knows who you really are?"

"Yes, but I assure you he has nothing to do with the murders."

"How do you know, Richard? How do you know that…?" Her voice trailed off as someone left the briefing room and entered the corridor. It was Frances. She gave Richard and Sarah a smile as she passed.

Sarah nodded hello. "Hi, Frances. We're in the middle of something here."

"Oh, okay. Just wanted to say that you're rocking that blouse, sister."

"Thanks. I appreciate you sparing it."

"No problem at all. Have a good day, Sarah." She trotted away without a care in the world. Richard watched her for a moment, almost leering after her.

With a growl, Sarah went back to their conversation. "How

do you know Dr Carney has nothing to do with the murders, Richard? Aren't psychiatrists all mental themselves?"

"I don't think that's accurate."

"Fine, but serial killers are good at hiding in plain sight, correct? After they kill a bunch of people, their neighbours always come out saying, 'Gee willikers, he was such a nice, quiet guy.'"

"In some cases." Richard scratched at his chin and loosened up a little. "For instance, Ted Bundy was wildly liked by both his fellow law students and his—"

"Carney could be involved, is what I'm saying."

Richard looked her in the eye, which she realised now was something he found difficult. "Dr Carney is not a killer. He's in his seventies, for one thing. No way did he scale a six-foot wall and race away into the night. Nor does he have any notable association with County Durham."

Sarah gave up, seeing he was not going to agree with her. Psychopath or not, Richard clearly had strong feelings about his old doc. "Fine," she said. "Then what if Carney simply let slip to someone who you were? What if he trusted the wrong person, or accidentally left his journal lying around? If he's an old man, he might have made a mistake." Richard went to argue again, but she cut him off. "Look, how else does the killer know who you are? Someone or something must have tipped him off. We have to explore every lead, and right now Dr Carney is the only one we have regarding this – unless you think James or Donkey is the killer?"

"No, of course not." He gritted his teeth, and the dangerous predator inside him showed himself for the tiniest slice of a second. But then he deflated like a child who had just lost his balloon. "You're right. We need to go and see Dr Carney."

"Great. How far is Broadmoor?"

"About four hours away."

"Seriously? I swear we're in the middle of nowhere here."

He chuckled, but stopped himself after a second. "Don't

worry. He retired to the countryside somewhere in North Yorkshire. The journey shouldn't be much more than an hour or two. We can leave right after lunch, if you're happy to drive?"

Sarah went to pat him on the back, but stopped herself. "If nothing else, you can slip in a quick therapy session, huh?"

"Right."

And I can ask the good doctor why he would let a lunatic back out on the streets.

But first, coffee.

CHAPTER
TEN

IT HAD BEEN a genuine challenge to remain undetected on the lamplit streets of Durham. It seemed like no matter how late at night he did his work, there would always be some antisocial weirdo prowling the streets. The cloak of darkness was no longer impenetrable in a world where twenty-four-hour supermarkets and all-night wine bars were permitted.

I need to be careful tonight, he told himself. After so much hard work and planning, he could not afford to be halted prematurely. History was being made, recorded in blood on flesh-bound pages, and he was its teacher.

Mona was a naïve young woman who should have known better than to accept a lift from a handsome stranger driving a plain black Astra. A hard day's work and aching feet had been her downfall, along with fortuitous late summer rain that had urged her to take a dryer option than walking.

Still, her worthless life was about to change. Like James Cook from Leicester in 1832, Mona would be an example to the peasants that law and order reigned supreme; something the country needed to be firmly reminded of right now. The unwashed masses needed to be cowed. Judgement. Execution. Damnation. The chaos needed to end, before it was too late.

He loaded his work onto the back seat of his car and covered it with a blanket. Then he placed a couple of boxes filled with stuffy old books on top of it all, to make it seem like he was simply moving some things from his home to his office. Not that he expected to be questioned. If the police were capable of doing their jobs, there would be no need for him to be doing this. Incompetence and indifference were the enemy he intended to slaughter. Fear and punishment were his sword and shield.

He continued packing up the car, waiting for nightfall. Mona Lewis waited with him.

———

Dr Alan Carney had resigned from Broadmoor in 2018 and moved to the Yorkshire hamlet of Haworth. Richard could understand why. The leafy, windswept area was as one might daydream if asked to picture the English countryside – a postcard in the flesh – with stone-built buildings hundreds of years old nestled together on cobbled streets. For Richard, the past was a dark and frightening place, full of screams and the copper tang of blood, but this place wore its history proudly and refused to shed its ancient charm.

They passed by cosy tearooms and old English pubs as Sarah drove them along the narrow alleyways and windy lanes, while half a mile in any direction would see them lost in the moorlands atop the Pennines. If memory served Richard correctly, Haworth was the former home of the Bronte sisters, although he couldn't claim to be a fan.

The satnav piped up, telling Sarah where to go. They entered a steep cobblestoned alley leading upwards. On either side, the houses were so close that you could peer right into people's living rooms and see what they were watching on TV. It was barely wide enough for a horse and cart, let alone a car.

Richard didn't dare try to make conversation with Sarah for fear he might disrupt her concentration.

In fact, neither of them spoke a word until they eventually crested the top of a hill and entered onto a roughshod dirt track. Wide and uneven, it was perfectly suited to the Range Rover and Sarah was visibly relieved to be back out in the open.

"Someone didn't want any neighbours, huh?" she said, bouncing up and down in the driver's seat. "This is a road to nowheresville."

Richard gripped his seatbelt with both hands as they rattled over uneven ground. "I suspect, after three decades of working with the criminally insane, Dr Carney might have wanted a break from other people."

"Guy deserves a knighthood, if you ask me. I couldn't dedicate my life to helping maniacs feel better."

He got the impression that might have been a dig at him, but he didn't acknowledge it. Sarah's feelings towards him were pretty unambiguous, and it wasn't like he could even defend himself. She hated him for being a mass murderer, which was fair enough. Still… it was starting to grate a little that she wouldn't at least try to maintain a cordial working relationship.

Oh, come on, Richard. You're lucky she's even agreed to be in the same room with you. The only reason you're not alone in a padded cell is because of Dr Carney.

"Eight times," he said.

Sarah still seemed to be enjoying the bouncy drive through the countryside, so she didn't hear him until he repeated himself. "Huh?" she said. "Eight times what?"

"That's how many times I called Dr Carney on the number the hospital gave me."

She remained focused on the dirt road ahead, clutching the steering wheel tightly, but she chuckled as she spoke. "Must have been weird for you, calling Broadmoor and asking for help. Did you get to catch up with anyone you know? Anyone from your old book club?"

"I only spoke to the hospital administrator. They were very helpful and told me to give Dr Carney their best."

"Maybe Carney's changed his number. He is retired, after all."

Richard had already dismissed that possibility. "No, the hospital's care team still consults with Dr Carney several times a year. They contact him via the same number they gave me."

"How recently did they last speak with him?"

"I never thought to ask." Richard looked out the window at the vast, uncultivated green fields and purple blankets of heather. He wondered how far the wilderness stretched. *How long could a person remain undiscovered out here?* "I called the number eight times," he said, "and he didn't answer."

Sarah didn't respond to that, but her expression turned gloomy. According to the satnav, they were three minutes away from their destination. The fact they couldn't get in contact with the doctor was a bad sign. It left both of them not knowing what to expect.

Dr Carney is a good man. He spent his entire career studying mental illness and trying to give support to those who need it. Sarah was right when she said he should have a knighthood.

He rescued me, turned me from a broken monster into... what exactly?

Something better. Something that saves instead of kills.

A minute later, the dirt road ended in a stony courtyard that might once have been paved – fifty years ago maybe. The mud had hardened and compacted, and the various rocks and boulders were buried so snugly that even a shovel might fail to get them out. The cottage, however, was beautiful, with a brand new tiled roof that had likely replaced an old thatched or stone one, and original lead-lined windows with dark wood sashes. Its pebble-dash walls had been painted a clean white, making the cottage stand out against the green-grey background of the distant moors.

It was a quarter past four. The journey had taken just shy of two hours, and they had set off very late due to Sarah feeling unwell and also wanting to pop into town to buy a new outfit. It wasn't until she had swallowed a bunch of paracetamol and put on a pair of dark jeans and a short black jacket that she had perked up enough to make the long drive. Tony, the chauffeur James employed to take Richard back and forth to crime scenes, had booked the next several days off as holiday, which left Richard dependant on the whims of his partner for the time being when it came to travel.

"Nice place," Sarah said, raising an eyebrow. "Looks well-maintained."

Richard remembered Dr Carney's office, with its walnut cabinets lined with alphabetised books and his oversized desk decorated with evenly spaced stationery. "He likes things neat and tidy. An orderly mind keeps our thoughts where we want them."

"Is that a quote?"

He nodded. "Something he used to say to me. Healthy rituals have been proven to reduce anxiety."

"Uh huh."

Sarah parked the Range Rover at the side of the cottage next to an old convertible MG. The classic vehicle was in pristine condition, and Richard remembered seeing it often through Broadmoor's library windows, which looked out over the staff car park.

This really is his home. Dr Carney's home.

"I'm not sure this is right," he muttered.

Sarah switched off the engine and turned to him, the scarred side of her face cast in shadow. "What is it?"

"Dr Carney is my doctor. This is his home. It feels wrong for me to be here. An invasion of his privacy."

"I suppose I can understand that, but we're here now, aren't we? So what are you going to do? Wait in the car and wave? I think the rules are blurry on what's appropriate when it comes to you."

"Do you think so? It's okay for me to be here?"

She scratched at her nose and stared out the windscreen at the fields surrounding the cottage. "I think whatever helps us catch the Durham Butcher is what we need to do. Screw everything else."

"NETK."

"What?"

"You keep calling our killer the Durham Butcher, but his official designation is North East Torture-Killer."

"Get out the car, Richard."

Sarah opened the door and stepped out, causing the Range Rover to bounce on its springs. Richard got out a moment later and caught up with her as she approached the front of the cottage. She walked fast, like she was eager to get this over with.

The front door was solid wood, with no glass panels or windows. There *was* a spyhole though, which made Richard uncomfortable as he stood in front of it. It was like a tiny staring eye.

Sarah rapped her knuckles against the wood – rat-a-tat-tat – then stood back and waited. After a moment, she reached out and yanked Richard backwards by the arm to join her. "Stand back, you weirdo. Why are you so close?"

The physical contact sent a spark through him, unnerving and exciting. He stuttered when he tried to speak. "I–I don't knock on many doors. Sorry."

"Don't be sorry. Just be normal."

They waited.

And waited.

"He must be here," said Sarah, stepping back further and peering through the front windows. Unfortunately, they were both obscured by net curtains. "His car is here, although I guess he could have two, right?"

Richard nodded. "The MG isn't really a practical runaround. He might have a second car with better milage and boot space.

Perhaps he's gone out on an errand."

"So do we wait? Or are we allowed to kick in front doors?"

"Not without a warrant."

"Seriously? Aren't we the murder police?"

"There are rules."

Sarah marched back up to the front door and grabbed the handle, which was a black-painted iron circlet. She twisted her wrist and the bolt released with a clunk. Grinning sheepishly, she looked back at Richard and asked, "What about letting ourselves in uninvited?"

"Also illegal."

"I hear screaming inside."

"No you don't. You're just saying that."

Sarah paused, staring into the small gap that had opened between the door and the frame. "Ah, what's the harm? If this doc is as saintly as you describe him, he won't mind a little bit of cheeky trespassing."

"Sarah!" Richard reached out to stop her, but she was already slipping inside the door, pushing it aside with her shapely hip and moving into the entrance hallway with a confident, snakelike shimmy.

There's so much I don't know about Sarah Stone. Much more than what's in her file.

While hesitant to enter without just cause, Richard forced himself to follow Sarah inside. If he wanted her to trust him and have his back, then he needed to have hers. Even when she was breaking the rules.

Please don't let me regret this.

Dr Carney's house smelled of books – that old, slightly mouldy odour that was at once both stifling and oddly comforting. It reminded Richard of the countless nights lying on his bunk in Broadmoor with whatever dog-eared read he had borrowed that day.

"Dr Carney?" Sarah called out. "Hello?"

No answer. The only sound was their feet against the cold stone tiles.

The small hallway felt crooked, with no straight lines anywhere. Warped wooden beams held up a narrow staircase to the upper floor, while the pitted walls undulated like the surface of a scab. Even the doors met their frames at awkward angles.

"Dr Carney," Sarah called out again, and this time when there was no answer, she pulled a bright yellow Taser out of her jacket's inside pocket. He hadn't even known she'd been armed.

"What do you need that for?" Richard hissed.

"Stay behind me and watch my back."

He nodded, not quite knowing what she intended, but ready to do whatever she asked.

My partner.

They sidled out of the hallway and into a rectangular lounge on the right. It had a tiny, unlit fireplace, and besides a wooden rocking chair, two-piece fabric sofa, and a walnut coffee table, the room was otherwise empty. Not even a television.

Sarah marched back into the hallway and tried a door on the left. It was made from thin vertical planks painted white and iron hinges painted black. It scraped across the stone tiles when Sarah yanked on it.

She raised her Taser and pointed it into the room.

The smell that wafted out was from more than just old books.

"Jesus!" Sarah waved her left hand in front of herself and stepped cautiously into the room with the Taser held up in her right.

Acid burned the back of Richard's throat. It felt wrong to invade his doctor's home like this, but now he began to fear what he would find.

"Sarah, I don't… I don't think I can…"

She peered back at him through the doorway and lowered the Taser. Her expression became softer than he had ever seen it.

Something in the room had clearly unsettled her. "You need to see this, Richard," she said.

"No, I… I can't…" *Stay calm. Stay focused.* He reached into his pocket and squeezed the auger shell so hard that he might have drawn blood. "Ask me something."

"What? Richard, what are you—?"

"Just ask me something. Trivia. Random facts. Quiz me. Please!"

For a second, it looked like she was considering whether or not to punch him, but thankfully she did as he asked. "What's the capital of…" – she shrugged – "Tasmania?"

"Hobart."

"Is it?"

"Yes. Another," he urged.

"All right, all right. What's the, um, fastest animal in the sea?"

"Sailfish. Seventy miles per hour."

She squinted at him. "I have no way of knowing if that's true."

"Then ask me a question you know the answer to!"

"Fine. Which six countries border Afghanistan?"

"Pakistan, Uzbekistan, Tajikistan, Turkmenistan, Iran, and… and…"

She opened her mouth to help him, but he waved at her to keep quiet. She folded her arms and grunted, but waited for him to answer.

"China."

"Impressive. But why are we doing this exactly?"

He took a deep breath and held the air in his lungs, focusing on the pressure in his chest. When he finally let the breath out, he felt a little calmer. "It keeps me from getting overexcited. The smell of blood, the sight of a body…. Is Dr Carney in there?"

"You'll need to confirm. I've never met him."

He put a hand against his face. "Oh no. Oh-no-oh-no. I don't think I want to look."

"You just said blood and guts excite you. What's the problem? Go enjoy yourself."

"Excite, not arouse." He sneered at her. "You're misunderstanding the word. I get… overwhelmed."

Her fists clenched up at her sides, and she took a half step back into the stinking room. "Overwhelmed? And then what happens?"

"And then I panic, okay? I freak out and turn into a trembling mess that's no use to anyone. You don't need to be afraid."

"Oh." She shifted her shoulders and looked away. "Maybe I can relate."

"I think I'm okay. It's not going to be a problem."

"Because we did a pop quiz?"

He nodded, wishing he could laugh at the ridiculousness of it, except that it was ridiculously serious. "I like facts and data, lists and patterns, things that are concrete. They help me concentrate when things are messy and disordered. It's a coping technique."

Sarah loosened up, and some of the tension left her shoulders. "Dr Carney really did help you, didn't he?"

"Any other doctor might have seen me as a lost cause, but he spent years proving them wrong. Yes, he helped me."

"Are you going to be okay? If this is too much…"

"No, you're right, Sarah. I was let out of the hospital for a reason, and right now, Mona Lewis is the priority. I need to take a look."

Sarah moved out of the doorway and stood aside.

Mercifully, the smell didn't get any worse as Richard stepped into what was clearly a home office. It meant Dr Carney had likely not been dead for very long, as the odour of decay usually became unbearable after forty-eight hours.

Like the office he'd kept in Broadmoor, Dr Carney's home office was stuffed with books concerning the human mind. In a single look, Richard saw a thick, hardback copy of *The*

Psychopath Test by Daniel Kahneman and several medical textbooks. But unlike Dr Carney's office at Broadmoor, this room was covered in blood.

"It's him," Richard confirmed as he stared at the lifeless face of the man who had known him better than anyone else; the one man who had known his darkest secrets and helped him anyway.

Dr Carney lay slumped in a leather high-backed chair, facing away from his desk and the crooked, lead-lined window behind it. Propped between his thighs was a bloodstained wooden mallet and a short double-edged dagger. Both had ostensibly been used to kill him. The top of his skull was dented inwards, causing both his eyes to bulge half-out of their sockets. His throat had been sliced open from ear to ear and dried blood stained his body from chin to feet. A sticky red puddle had formed in front of him on the thin, beige carpet.

Sarah waved a hand in front of her face again, wincing at the smell of excrement and decay. "Are you okay?"

Richard realised he had frozen like a statue. Slowly, he turned to face Sarah and nodded to let her know he was okay. "This was the work of our killer."

"He bashed the doctor's head in and then slit his throat? Strange combination, but a lot more conventional than the previous murders."

"*Mazzatello*," he told her. "Another method of execution used in the Middle Ages, mainly in the Catholic nations."

Sarah's upper lip curled, making the scars on the left side of her face crease like a sheet of crumpled parchment. "How does it work?"

"A state-sanctioned executioner would smash a person's skull in with a mallet and then throw them into a coffin. Oftentimes, the throat was slit as an additional measure to ensure death."

"Humane." She circled the room carefully, the Taser out in

front of her with both hands, as if she expected the killer to still be in the house. "Almost a little boring."

"It was seen as less barbaric and more efficient than prior execution methods," Richard said. "These were the times of the Pope and the Church's so-called mercy."

"You're not a fan, I take it?"

He shrugged. "Religion doesn't make a whole lot of sense to me."

"Me either, but hey, whatever helps people get through the day, right?"

"I suppose so."

"So…" She put a hand on her hips and moved back over to Dr Carney's body. "This wasn't intended to inflict pain like the murders of Caroline and Claudette? It was a quick death, almost merciful?"

Richard looked around the room, seeing if he had missed anything. All he saw were books and blood. "Either we're misinterpreting the killer's motives, or Dr Carney was killed for a different reason than the two young women."

"Misinterpreting the killer's motives? What do you mean?"

"I mean, the torture involved in Caroline and Claudette's murders might have been incidental to the killer's true goal. A goal we don't yet understand."

"Incidental? Just a little sauce on the hotdog, you mean?"

He shrugged, not having fully thought the theory through yet. "Possibly. Or maybe Dr Carney was merely an obstacle that needed to be dealt with. Painless and practical."

Sarah studied the body for a moment longer and then pulled a face. "Painless? Not sure getting your head caved in is a pleasant experience."

"The force of the blow caused his eyes to come free from their sockets, and there's blood in both his ears. I'm confident the blunt force trauma would have killed him instantly, probably before he even knew what was happening."

"Well, that's good, I guess."

Richard breathed in and then exhaled slowly, feeling something in his stomach that might have been grief. The last time he had felt something similar was when a letter had come to him in Broadmoor informing him that his mother had hanged herself in her prison cell. "The killer came up behind Dr Carney while he was facing the window," he noted.

"How can you tell he was facing the other way?"

Richard nodded at Dr Carney's feet. "He's wearing one slipper. The other is under the desk. He must have kicked it off when the killer hit him in the back of the head. The brain trauma would have caused his limbs to flail. Also, his laptop is open and there's a transparent stain on the screen. Probably saliva that flew out of his mouth or nose due to the sudden increase of pressure inside his skull."

Sarah bent slightly to see the single tartan slipper resting on its side against the wall beneath the desk. "Shit, you're good."

Richard nodded, wishing he had talents beside picturing how someone might have been murdered. "After striking Dr Carney with the mallet, the killer then turned his chair around and slit his throat. There's blood spatter here and here." He pointed at a collection of bloody dots staining the carpet to the left and right. "He then bled out on the carpet, which is why most of the blood ended up in this puddle between his legs."

"Doesn't a person stop bleeding after they're dead? The heart stops pumping, right?"

"Yes," Richard confirmed, "but brain death doesn't always stop the heart immediately and residual pressure will remain for a short while. Vital functions can continue for several minutes, and with both his jugular and carotid being severed, blood loss would have been rapid. Look, his hands are purple, which means there was probably still blood left inside him by the time his heart stopped. It settled in the extremities."

Sarah turned silent for a while. She was obviously familiar with death, and despite her mild revulsion, she seemed perfectly in control of herself. Most would have vomited and left the room by now. Richard could tell, however, that this part of the job was new to Sarah. She had little experience of reconstructing a crime scene, and she didn't see the obvious clues. But he got the impression she would learn quickly; she didn't have a choice.

"Is there anything you can add, Sarah? Have I missed anything?"

She shook her head slowly. "I have a feeling you don't miss anything when it comes to this kind of thing. What we need to know now is why our killer came here and killed the doctor. I told you Carney was involved somehow. He's linked to all this. He's the reason the killer knows who you are."

Richard wanted to argue, to jump to the doctor's defence, but all he could do was agree. "It seems likely, but I have no idea why." He rubbed at his cheeks, suddenly feeling dirty and tired and a little disorientated. "We need to call this in, but in the meantime there might be something here that can help us understand why NETK targeted Dr Carney."

"Are we allowed to search the scene ourselves?"

He shrugged. "Who's going to stop us?"

Sarah grinned, and for a moment, she didn't seem to hate him.

Sarah felt claustrophobic inside the stuffy office smelling of death. The cottage was a mile from the nearest proper road, and the only other person with her was an anxious lunatic on a quest for atonement.

Is he really reformed? He seems genuinely upset about the doctor's death.

They had been at the house for forty minutes, but Richard had only just reported the incident to James. Before that, he had remained in the office with Dr Carney, almost as if he was saying goodbye. Or trying to swallow the possibility that the man might have betrayed him.

Sarah had learned during her time in antiterrorism that coincidences were rarely natural, so as soon as Richard had told her about Dr Carney knowing his true identity, alarm bells had started to ring. But she hadn't expected to find the man dead. Had he been an accomplice who had outlived his usefulness, or was he another victim?

I guess it's my job to find out now.

Richard had warned her to be careful not to disturb the crime scene, so she stepped carefully as she explored the house, Taser in hand. The cottage was too quiet, too isolated, and she wasn't as confident in her abilities to defend herself as she had once been. What if the killer was still in the house? What if there was a repeat of what had happened to her in that Durham alleyway?

I wasn't ready for him then, but I am now. She ran her finger over the Taser's hard plastic trigger. *He won't get the jump on me twice.*

She navigated her way into the cottage's kitchen and took a look around. The shaker cabinets, painted a tranquil green, appeared thick and heavy. The worktop was a rustic oak, or some wood of a similar shade. It wasn't an old kitchen, but neither was it new. Some of the floor tiles had small chips or cracks, and the stainless steel fridge had a couple of small dents. There was a chill in the air due to an open window above the ceramic sink.

Richard had gone upstairs. Sarah heard him shuffling, floorboards creaking above her head. His reading of the crime scene had impressed her, and though she still found it obscene that he was free after so many unforgivable acts, she could at least understand why James had put him to work as an investigator.

But it still feels like a deal with the Devil. There's always a price.

The kitchen was neat and orderly, which was why the open

file on the counter stood out to her immediately. She moved towards it cautiously, fearing it might suddenly catch fire like one of those notes in an old spy show. Fortunately, it was just an ordinary loose-leaf file with several hole-punched pages held together with a string tie. A black-and-white image of a teenaged Richard adorned the first page, along with details of his arrest.

In 2006, a victim – Sadie Amberson – had escaped and made it to safety after being kidnapped by the Flesch family and held against her will at a Chester-le-Street property, Flexley Yard Farm. In response, police rapidly descended upon the old farmhouse where Richard and his parents lived, and had arrested all three after a brief physical altercation where a female police officer lost a pinkie finger when Richard's father bit her like 'a feral dog'. When later giving a statement, one officer described the farmhouse and adjacent outbuildings as a place even the Devil would fear to tread.

"Jesus." Sarah read on, learning about the squalid living conditions at the farm, where livestock had been left to starve and rot in the fields, and dozens of half-eaten victims had turned to black and brown slurry in every room of the house. It was a miracle the Flesch family had not dropped dead from sickness brought on by the pestilent gore.

Sarah placed the paper down on the counter and picked up the next sheet. This one seemed to be a handwritten letter. To see who had written it, she quickly glanced at the signature at the bottom. *A. T. Carney.*

She returned to the beginning and started to read.

After a long and drawn out trial, Richard Flesch arrived at Broadmoor at eighteen years of age with a complete indifference to pain and suffering, in both himself and others. The reality of his upbringing was so diabolical that any natural human nature he possessed was entirely occluded by his parent's vile, pervasive influence.

It took several years for the real Richard to emerge, and though damaged beyond repair, I believe he has a good soul and an unmatched mind. In different hands, Richard might have grown to be among society's highest achievers, but instead he was raised by fiends who forced him to perform irredeemable acts. Acts that will stain his spirit for the remainder of his life, and society for even longer.

While no longer compelled to commit vile acts, and no longer under his father's odious spell, Richard has slowly revealed himself to not be of an inherently violent nature. And yet I am in the unfortunate position of condemning the young man nonetheless. While not psychotic, Richard Flesch continues to present a danger to—

"What is that?" Richard walked into the kitchen, his smart black shoes tapping against the tiles.

Sarah flinched and instinctively hid the page behind her back. "Oh, I thought you'd gone upstairs."

"There's nothing up there. Two bedrooms and a bathroom. Nothing of interest at all. What have you found?"

"Um…" *Shit, what do I do? It's his file. Not like it's going to tell him anything he doesn't already know about himself.*

It says he's dangerous. He's dangerous and I'm here alone with him.

"It's your file," she admitted, not seeing a reason to lie. "It was right here on the counter. Dr Carney must have kept a copy when he left Broadmoor."

Richard nodded. "He probably kept a lot of files at home for private study. Can I have it, please?"

Reluctantly, she handed over the letter she had hidden behind her back and then stepped away from the counter and the file. Richard stood and scanned the pages, his face too impassive to read, although Sarah saw him reach into his pocket and make a fist. She took another step back, readjusting her grip on her Taser.

As he lifted the last page in the file, Sarah gasped. "Richard, look!"

He moved the page aside, out of his eyeline, and then stared at what she had seen. Someone had written a message on the inside of the folder's rear cover. Its smudgy brown hue suggested it had been scrawled in blood.

ARE YOU PROUD OF ME YET?

And then in smaller letters below: **Look inside the fridge.**

"I really don't want to look inside the fridge," Sarah said, glancing sideways across the kitchen to where the stainless steel unit stood.

Richard placed the papers back inside the file and closed it. "If someone finds this and makes a connection about my identity…"

Sarah blinked a few times, her eyes feeling a little fuzzy. Was it the stench of death drifting in from the office? "What are you saying? You can't take the file; it's evidence."

"The killer left it here for me. He's playing a game. But if a colleague gets hold of it and figures out the truth, then I'll be removed from the case."

"And probably sent back to Broadmoor," she added, knowing that was likely his bigger worry. His freedom was at stake.

But then he looked at her in a way that suggested she was wrong. She saw determination, not desperation. "I can help stop the Durham Butcher, Sarah, but not if this file gets out."

"The Durham Butcher?"

"What?"

She jerked her chin at him, enjoying his confusion as she pointed out his hypocrisy. "I thought we were supposed to refer to him as NETK."

"I'll refer to him however you want if it helps us catch the guy."

She gave it some thought, not much caring about whether or not she broke the rules, but worried about allying herself with a beast. Eventually, she made her choice. "Fine, you can sit on the folder. I won't tell anyone so long as it doesn't harm the investigation."

He nodded his thanks and shoved the folder inside his blazer, stuffing it into the waistband of his trousers at the back. "Did you read it?"

"What?"

"My file? Did you read it?"

"No. You came in just as I picked it up."

I only got to the part where it said you were dangerous.

"Okay, well, the local police will be here any moment. There's only one thing left for us to do."

Sarah groaned and turned to face the dented stainless steel fridge again. "This is going to be awful, isn't it?"

"I get that impression, yes. Would you like me to do it?"

She nodded. "I'd prefer it."

"Sure thing." Richard crept over to the fridge and grabbed the chrome handle running vertically down one side. He didn't yank the door open right away; he paused and looked back at Sarah. "After three?"

"Seriously? Don't do that. Just open it."

"Fine. Okay, here goes. Get ready. I'm opening it now. You ready?"

"Just do it!"

Richard yanked open the fridge, and the two of them yelped in unison and hopped back.

"It's worse than I thought," Sarah said, holding her nose closed with finger and thumb. "That motherfucker."

A young girl's head stared back at them from the top shelf, her eyes cloudy and her skin the colour of cigarette ash. Sarah knew from the photographs on her thinking board that this was Mona Lewis.

But where was the rest of her?

She had a feeling it wouldn't be long before they found out.

CHAPTER
ELEVEN

THEY HAD STILL BEEN at Dr Carney's cottage, surrounded by forensics, when James called Richard's phone. There had been another murder.

"No shit," Sarah said as the three of them spoke via loudspeaker. "We already told you the doctor is dead, and Mona Lewis's head is in his fridge."

But James came back, "No, there's another body been found, and it sounds like our killer's handiwork. I'll send you details. Can you both come?"

Both of them said, "Yes."

And so, at a little past nine o'clock in the evening they had left one crime scene to go to another, hopping back in the Range Rover and bouncing down the uneven dirt road towards Haworth, where they would then head east.

When they eventually hit the main roads and picked up speed, Sarah gripped the steering wheel and gnashed her teeth. Mona Lewis was dead. She had failed the girl and her family.

I should have worked faster or smarter. I should have found her in time.

This job isn't for me. I'm not super-smart like Richard or James, and my instincts aren't what they used to be either.

They reached their destination on the Yorkshire Coast ninety minutes later.

Saltburn-by-the-Sea was more beach than town, and its sandy coastline – backed by cliffs and lit by portable floodlights – seemed to stretch on forever, as did the vast North Sea in the opposite direction. By day, the beach below was probably filled with sunbathers and frolicking families, while the town was probably full of elderly residents eating sausage rolls and having cream teas. Tonight the entire area had been cordoned off. The picturesque Victorian seaside town was now a crime scene.

Sarah and Richard met up with James on the beach at the bottom of the cliffs. A chilly breeze came in off the sea. It caused Sarah to rub at her arms and give herself some warmth.

"This is turning out to be a pretty rotten day," James said, silencing his phone as it chirped relentlessly in his hand. "Yorkshire Constabulary will only allow us minimum involvement with this one, but it's plain to see our killer is to blame."

"Do we know the victim?" Richard asked.

"No, but seeing as she's missing a head, I'm assuming it's Mona Lewis. I'm sorry you guys had to find what you did up at Carney's place. How was the investigation going when you left?"

"In full swing," Richard said, "but there seemed little left to discover. The killer cleans up after himself. Maybe if we can…"

Sarah was too conflicted to have a conversation right now, so she walked away, heading towards the body that a married couple had apparently found while walking their dog just after dusk. The killer had been bold once again, risking discovery even more than he had in Durham. Once again, though, he had got away with it.

A fifty-foot area of beach had been taped off ahead, and several forensics were doing their thing, taking pictures and searching the sand for clues. Sarah wasn't interested in any of them. She was only interested in whatever poor soul had been murdered here.

She took in a breath of crisp sea air, holding it in her lungs for a moment. Breathing in the North was different from breathing in the West Midlands. It had a soothing effect, as if every oxygen-rich inhalation was curative in some way. Being by the salt-laden sea only strengthened the effect.

The blue-and-white police tape and glaring floodlights didn't just surround the beach, but also a short concrete promenade that ran ten feet above it. It was there where the body had been found.

Sarah ascended a short flight of steps and found herself approaching a modest station house that appeared to service a funicular – a small tram that ran up and down the cliff to take people from the town above to the beach below. The carriage was currently parked twenty feet up the cliff, which was why she and Richard had needed to take the long way down to the beach. A headless body dangled from its undercarriage, lit up by the glaring floodlights.

Obviously, hanging a body without a neck was impossible, so the killer had placed the naked female corpse inside some kind of cage and attached a chain to it. The russet metal strips encircled the victim's body so snugly that the apparatus must have been custom made. Three curved horizontal bars held the torso tightly in place, causing pallid flesh to bulge through the gaps. Both arms and both legs were also caged, but the stump of the corpse's neck poked through a hole at the top. The entire contraption swung from a chain attached to the bottom of the tram.

Sarah stood in silence as various crime scene professionals buzzed around her. Atop the cliff, she saw a smattering of ghostly shapes that she knew were gawkers looking down at the grizzly scene below. It was probably safe to assume nothing like this had ever happened before in sleepy little Saltburn.

The killer is making fools of us. He can't keep getting away with this.

After a while, a stranger disturbed Sarah, saying "Hello" right into her ear. She was relieved when she saw it was Donkey, propped up on his crutch and smiling grimly.

"Donkey, what are you doing here?"

"I came with James; in case you and Richard got held up at the other crime scene."

Sarah sighed. "There's been a whole lot of murder tonight. I'm glad you're here to help."

His smile widened, but the grim expression remained on his face. "I don't visit crime scenes very often, but I think this one needs all hands on deck. We've never dealt with a killer this brazen before. Everyone is taking it extra personally."

"I hear you." Sarah looked up at the body hanging underneath the carriage. "I think this is Mona Lewis. We found her head at Dr Carney's cottage."

"James told me. In the fridge." He shook his head. "You think Carney was involved in all this?"

She wrapped her arms around herself to keep the chill away and then shrugged her whole upper body. "Richard doesn't want to accept it, but it's a possibility. Someone leaked his true name to the killer, and if it wasn't you, me, or James, who was it?"

Donkey glanced back and forth as if to check they weren't being listened to. "If it gets out, the Institute is finished. I know you haven't been with us long, Sarah, but we do good work. Protecting Richard's identity is vital. The public outcry would be the end of us."

"I know." She chewed at her lip for a moment and then repeated herself. "I know you do good work. But let's do even better work and catch this sonofabitch, okay?"

"That's why I'm here."

The two of them stood there for several moments, both studying the body hanging in a cage from the bottom of the tram and trying to find answers. Neither of them said it, but they were both waiting for Richard. He was the one most likely to make sense of this.

It took Richard another ten minutes to finish up with James and join them, but as soon as he saw the hanging body, he had plenty to say. "It's a gibbet. Another barbaric remnant of the past that continued into the nineteenth century."

Sarah frowned. "A what?"

"A gibbet. Magistrates of various towns and cities would order the bodies of executed criminals to be placed in chains or locked inside cages and hung up in public to deter other would-be criminals. Sometimes, individuals were placed alive inside the cages and left to starve."

Sarah then noticed the ribs jutting out from the corpse's torso and the pelvic bones pointing out on either side. "That's why he kept Mona for two weeks," she said. "The bastard starved her."

Richard nodded. "Not long enough to starve her to death, but enough to torture her with a devastating hunger. I imagine the eventual cause of death was the decapitation."

Donkey cleared his throat and shifted his weight off and then back onto his crutch. "Why put her in a cage only to behead her?"

"I don't know. Time constraints, perhaps? Or he might have been combining the method of gibbetting with the act of displaying a disembodied head. Many times throughout history, cities placed the heads of traitors and murderers on display, shoving them onto pikes or hanging them from bridges. I think this murder was about shaming the victim. She's naked and headless, put on full display for all to see."

"Why?" Sarah demanded, shaking her head in disgust. If not for the crisp, clean air, she might have needed to sit down. Her stomach churned with dread as she imagined the poor girl's torment. "What did Mona Lewis do to anyone?"

"If this actually is Mona Lewis," Donkey said, "then I'll try to find out why she might have been targeted. Perhaps the victims are all guilty of something in the killer's eyes. Maybe they're not as random as they appear."

Sarah nodded, feeling it in her bones that there was more to this; that they were missing something. She turned to Richard and spoke quietly enough that only he and Donkey could hear. "Caroline Boswell was murdered in a spot that had meaning to you, correct?"

He nodded. "But Claudette Herrington's scene of death had no connection."

"What about this one? Is Saltburn linked to you?"

He turned away, as if to hide his face.

"Richard, what are you not telling us?"

He turned back, clearly guilty about something. "As soon as James sent us the address, I knew the killer picked this town for a reason."

"Why?" Donkey asked. "What's so special about Saltburn?"

Richard reached into his pocket and pulled out a tiny ivory-coloured shell shaped like a spiralling cone. "There's only ever been a single day in my life where I was truly happy, and it was here in Saltburn. I was fifteen years old."

Sarah folded her arms. "We're waiting."

"Let's go find a place and sit down. This is going to be hard for me."

―――

The three of them checked in with James and then went and found a pub in town that was still serving. It was an old-fashioned place, with clouded-glass lamps on the walls and paintings of sailboats hanging unevenly in brass frames. There could not have been more than a dozen people left to see out the end of the evening and the staff were collecting glasses and polishing the bar.

Sarah chose a booth near the back for privacy, and they each ordered a soft drink before sitting down. Richard took off his jacket and put both hands, trembling, on the table. He breathed slowly, as if trying to keep himself from hyperventilating. While growing increasingly impatient, waiting for him to speak, Sarah didn't prod him. She allowed him to begin in his own time.

"My dad used to have these rare lapses of sanity," he eventually said without preamble. "Randomly, and with no warning, he would shed the shadow that always hung over him and start being nice for a day or two. My mum always tried to take advantage of these brief periods, and she would convince my dad that it was important to let me be a normal kid sometimes and have fun, which is how she got him to agree to take us to the beach. Saltburn-by-the-sea. It was my mother's favourite place as a child, and she used to come here with her parents all the time."

"Lovely," said Sarah, rolling her eyes, but then she regretted it. "Sorry. Go on."

"So we went to the beach one summer's day," Richard continued, staring off into space as he spoke. "It was one of the few normal, happy days of my childhood. I ate ice cream on the pier, kicked a ball around with my dad, and built sandcastles with my mum. Then I met a girl." He paused, as if waiting to be interrupted, but neither Sarah nor Donkey said anything. "Her name was Sadie, and she was the most beautiful girl I ever saw, with wavy blonde hair like a lion's mane. When she saw me making sandcastles with my mum, she laughed at me for being babyish and laughed at my bucket and spade. She was right, of course, it was childish, but it was my first time on a beach. I didn't know – or care – that it was a childish act. My lack of embarrassment is probably what changed her opinion of me, because she wanted to hang out. My instinct was to say no immediately, but Dad was asleep on a big beach towel, and Mum was reading a book, so I did something insane and disappeared with her for several hours.

"And it was the best day of your life?" said Donkey, smiling a little. But tension hung in the air, because any story concerning Richard's past could only end badly.

"We walked along the pier and I watched Sadie play fairground games with the money her parents had given her. Then we shared candy floss and lemonade. Finally, when her parents yelled that she had an hour left before leaving, we went paddling, barefoot, in the sea together. When it was time for her to leave, we kissed." He smiled, even as he added, "Then she cried out in pain."

Sarah narrowed her eyes. "I'm not going to like this, am I?"

Richard continued to smile, clearly pleased by the memory in his head. "As we kissed," he said softly, "her foot came down on something sharp. It was this." He produced the little sea shell again, and he placed it down on the table for Sarah and Donkey to see. "It's an auger shell, from a kind of mollusc. After Sadie stepped on it, we both found it amusing that something so small could hurt so much, so she told me to keep it to remember her by. I've held onto it ever since. A keepsake from my one good day."

Sarah imagined what it must be like to live in hell and get a single day in heaven. She started to understand how Richard hadn't just gone to prison as a teenager; he'd been born in one. In fact, Broadmoor had probably felt like a full-service spa after growing up on the derelict murder farm.

But despite Richard's emotional retelling of his past, something didn't sit right with Sarah. She had no choice but to voice her concern. "Sadie Amberson is the girl that got away, right? The one who led the police to your family?"

Richard closed his eyes and squeezed the tiny shell, so hard that it must have caused him pain.

"Is it the same girl?" Donkey asked, gripping his glass with both hands. "Was the girl on the beach Sadie Amberson?"

Richard nodded, his eyes still closed. "When I returned to my parents, Dad was furious. He demanded I point Sadie out to him, but I refused, even when he threatened to beat me.

There was no way I was going to let him see her. But then Sadie passed by with her parents and waved to me. It was the biggest mistake of her life. Dad followed the family to the bed and breakfast they were staying at, and in the early evening he forced me to find Sadie and lead her out of the hotel. I found her hanging around the bar area, chatting with some other kids. She was so happy to see me. Happy, until the moment my dad shoved her into the back of our car and drove off with her."

Sarah's heart beat faster. Her knee juddered beneath the table. All she could think about was the moment that poor girl's smile had turned to a horrified scream as she realised handsome-but-weird teenage Richard had led her into a trap. Puppy love turned deadly.

"What happened to Sadie?" Sarah asked. Her voice was icy. In fact, her entire body had caught a chill.

"She was held alive for three weeks," Donkey said, no traces of his earlier smile now. "In the basement of your family's farmhouse, right?"

Richard opened his eyes and nodded. "Dad went hard on Sadie, harder than I'd seen him go on any girl before. I think he wanted to show me he was in charge, and that I could never leave and have my own life. He burned her flesh, pulled her nails, and forced me to… to…"

Donkey groaned. "Sadie Amberson claimed to have been sexually assaulted dozens of times by you."

Richard squeezed the shell harder, wincing slightly. "He made me do it. I didn't want to, but I had no choice. If I refused, he would have killed her, so I did what he told me to do. I hurt Sadie bad, did the worst things imaginable. Eventually, she begged for me to slit her throat and end her suffering. But I couldn't do it. I kept thinking about our day at the beach."

Sarah tasted blood in her mouth, teeth clamped around her tongue. Her entire body shook, a typhoon taking root inside of her. "She gave you the best day of your life," she growled, "and you gave her the worst day of hers. I bet she has no idea you're even walking around free, does she?"

Richard glanced at her hesitantly. There were no tears. No tears at all. "She committed suicide," he muttered. "One year before I was released from Broadmoor."

Sarah stood up with a start, pulled out her Taser, and pulled the trigger.

———

Donkey leapt up and almost fell, keeping his balance only by clinging onto the back of the bench. Richard bucked in his seat, jaws locked together and eyes wide. Sarah stood with her arm extended and the Taser vibrating in her fist, sending a live current down a wire and into a metal barb planted in Richard's chest. She'd never fired a Taser before, but she liked it. She liked it a lot.

"You piece of shit!" she yelled, alerting the few patrons still inhabiting the pub. They all cried out in astonishment, or swore in confusion.

Donkey begged her to stop what she was doing, but she kept her finger on the trigger. It wasn't until he chucked the contents of his glass into her face that she flinched and loosened up.

The Taser stayed attached to Richard's chest, but the current ceased and he stopped bucking. His body tensed for another few seconds, then he slumped out of the booth and collapsed onto the sticky, wooden floor.

"Sarah, what the hell are you doing?" Donkey grabbed his crutch and moved away, staring at her as if she were a lunatic. The truth was that she had just put one down.

"Did you not just hear what he was saying?" She sneered at him. "How can you listen to that?"

Donkey turned away from Sarah and reached down to help Richard, but with a crutch under one arm, it was an awkward thing for him to attempt. Richard was out of it, his eyes rolled back in his head.

Sarah almost pulled the trigger again, angered by the sight of Donkey trying to help Richard after what the man had admitted to, but a voice in the back of her head whispered for her to calm down. A second voice taunted her, telling her she'd just fucked up royally. It didn't take more than a split second to recognise that the voices belonged to the men who had died under Sarah's command in the scorching Afghani desert. Men who had fallen victim to an ambush she should have seen coming. Sarah attracted death no matter what she did. The overturned watermelon cart in the desert was just the start of it.

But I've never meant to cause suffering. That's what makes me and Richard different.

Donkey continued to turn his back to Sarah, even as she placed the Taser down on the table and stepped away from it. "I can't do this," she said. "I can't sit opposite someone who's done the things he's done."

"Keep your voice down," Donkey hissed. He looked back at her, and then past her towards the startled patrons standing by the bar. A pair of young men in black T-shirts stood shoulder to shoulder, seeming to debate about whether or not to intervene.

Richard slowly regained the use of his limbs, flexing his elbows and kicking at the floor with his feet. A line of drool leaked from the side of his mouth and down his cheek as he made a strange gargling sound. Donkey reached out his hand again, and this time Richard managed to focus enough to grab hold of it. The two of them worked together to get him to his feet.

Sarah didn't know what to do. She had just tased a guy. Should she make a hasty exit? Or should she stand her ground and demand that Richard be the one to leave?

"Are you okay?" Donkey asked, as he yanked the barb from Richard's chest and flicked it aside. "Just take some deep breaths."

"I-I think I wet myself," he muttered in reply, but when Sarah looked down at his crotch, she saw nothing. "S-she shot me."

"I tased you," she corrected. "I *would* have shot you, if I had a gun."

He took a tentative step towards her, putting a hand on Donkey for support. Sarah stood her ground, not knowing what else to do. Richard's expression was so inscrutable that there was no way to tell if—

Richard grabbed Sarah by the throat and shoved her back against the table. He lifted her off her feet so easily that she might as well have been made of straw. She tried to fight back but found herself planted on her back and struggling for air. Richard bore his weight down on her from the side, making it impossible for her to target him with her flailing knees. As he squeezed harder, her vision began to flash in time with her frantic heartbeat.

Richard brought his face up against hers, teeth bared like an enraged chimpanzee.

I knew it. I knew the monster was still inside him.

And now it's going to kill me.

Donkey cried out for help. The two barmen rushed over and grabbed Richard by his arms, trying to yank him off of Sarah, but he was too strong – too *possessed*. They couldn't even budge him. And all the while he continued throttling the life out of her and glaring into her soul with those predatory brown eyes.

Sarah's vision filled with stars, each one a pinprick of igniting gunpowder.

Her chest ached, lungs unable to draw breath.

Her bladder threatened to release itself.

Then Richard let go of her and stepped away. The two barmen immediately told him he needed to leave, but he ignored them both and went to retrieve his jacket from the booth.

Sarah lay on her back on the table, gasping for air and

rubbing at her neck. This time, Donkey went to her aid instead, speaking in a voice bordering on hysterical. "Oh my God. Oh bloody hell. This is bad. This is so messed up. Sarah, are you okay?"

"N-never been better," she moaned, deciding against trying to get up yet. Not only was she out of breath and dizzy, but her mind was awash with devils from the past. This was not the first time a man had tried to kill her.

He didn't try to kill me. He let me go.

Sarah lifted her head enough to see Richard grab his jacket and put it on. His entire body was trembling, and he had gone white as a sheet. It even seemed like he was holding back tears. Donkey didn't look so great either, leaning on his crutch and shaking his head in despair.

Then, to make things worse, James entered the pub with a smile on his face. It lasted only so long as it took him to see Sarah lying flat on her back and Richard trembling in the corner. "What on earth is going on?" he asked, glancing back and forth.

Donkey hobbled towards him, shaking his head. "We almost had another murder."

CHAPTER
TWELVE

SARAH WOULDN'T HAVE THOUGHT James even had it in him to be angry, but by the end of their conversation he was red in the face and talking like he was back in New York city. "Goddamn it, Sarah. I just can't believe you would jeopardise this whole frickin' case. If I file a report saying you tasered a colleague, then that's it for us, *capeesh*? We'll be under review for the best part of three months. You'll be suspended and fired."

"So what?" Sarah said. "I quit anyway."

They were standing in front of a stone and mortar wall that separated the town from the cliff's edge. The North Sea lapped at the floodlit beach below, forcing the investigators to work on an ever-narrowing strip of sand. The quarter moon was high in the sky, a silvery toenail.

James turned to look at Sarah, and his anger changed to something worse – something that seemed very much like disappointment. "I never pegged you as selfish, Sarah. Reckless, impertinent – hostile even – but never selfish."

"What do you want from me, James? You act like this is normal, but it's not. Would any sane person agree to work with him? It would've been better if you'd kept me in the dark about who he really is. I feel sick just looking at him." She pointed at her throat, which was sore with bruising. "Not to mention he tried to kill me."

"I thought you two were getting on? What the hell changed?"

"Nothing changed, and that's the problem. I forgot, for a moment, about the things he's done. Then he reminded me in graphic detail. If he truly had a conscience, he would come and leap off the top of this cliff."

"It's complicated, Sarah, and you know it." He shook his head and sighed. Looking at his watch, he said. "It's getting on for midnight. I'll book us all some hotel rooms across the street. Then, in the morning, I'll accept your resignation and put you on a train home."

Sarah folded her arms and stared off at the near impenetrable blackness of the night sky. "Fine by me."

James stomped away, shaking his head and muttering to himself.

Less than a minute later, Sarah heard footsteps returning.

"We're done here, James, so save your lectures, all right?"

"It's me."

Sarah spun around to see Richard standing on the pavement behind her. No one else was around, the only activity coming from the pub fifty metres away, where the last of the drinkers were going home. "What do you want?"

"To finish what I was saying earlier. You didn't hear me out."

"Because I don't want to! And if you're expecting an apology, then you've got another thing—"

"I don't want an apology." He took a step closer and put his hands up in a gesture of peace. In the soft light of the moon, he looked more like a little boy than a man in his thirties. "Apologies won't make anything better."

"Well, things can't get much worse, can they? The stuff you were saying at the table…" She placed her palms atop the rough stone wall and leant forward, looking back out to sea. "You have no remorse."

"I let her go."

She turned her head and frowned. "What?"

He took another step, only four feet away from her now. "I let Sadie Amberson go."

"What do you mean?"

He moved up beside her and peered down at the cordoned-off beach. His presence made Sarah's flesh crawl, but she tolerated him because she was too tired to fight. And because she had a stupid, nagging voice in her head telling her she was the one in the wrong.

"I did terrible things to Sadie Amberson, Sarah, just like I told you, but one night, when Dad had drunk more than usual, I snuck her out of the house and let her go. That's the reason she was the one who got away, Sarah. That's what finally stopped my family's reign of terror."

She looked him in the eye, but all she could do was shrug. It was an unexpected revelation, but it didn't change the events leading up to it.

"There were lots of times when I disliked what my family was doing," Richard said, "but meeting Sadie was the first time I actively hated it. It was the moment I realised my parents were evil and that what we were doing was obscene. It broke the spell."

Sarah huffed. "You never knew what good and evil were?"

"Not back then, but hearing Sadie's screams woke me up, and all I wanted was for it all to end. No more tricking young girls into the back of a van, no more hearing my dad grunting as he violated them in the cellar, and no more watching my mother descend deeper and deeper into madness. I wanted it all to stop. That day on the beach with Sadie changed everything."

"Romantic. She must have been so glad to have met you."

"No, you were right, Sarah. Meeting me was the worst day of her life. I can do nothing to change that." He exhaled loudly, almost howling at the moon. "I can't hide from it either, which is why I told you what happened. Perhaps I shouldn't have spoken so plainly, but it would be wrong to sugarcoat things and make them seem less wicked than they really were. Still, I could have found a better way to get it all out."

"I still would have tased you," she said. "I don't like your face."

He chuckled. "I deserve worse, so I won't hold it against you. If it means anything at all, I'm sorry I lashed out."

"You mean when you strangled me half to death?"

"It should never have happened. When you tased me, it was like nothing I'd ever felt before. I lost control."

"You lost control because you're dangerous, Richard. Dr Carney didn't trust you. You lied to me."

"What?"

"Carney thought you were dangerous."

"Sarah, what are you talking about? Dr Carney was the one who had me released."

"You're lying. I saw it in your file."

Richard shook his head, over and over again, as if he were a robot with a stuck switch. Eventually, he stopped and reached inside his jacket, pulling the file out of his waistband at the back. He'd obviously kept it with him ever since leaving Dr Carney's house. "You read something in here?"

Sarah folded her arms and gave a curt nod. "A letter written by Dr Carney."

Richard opened the file and leafed through it, eventually handing the handwritten letter to Sarah. "Read it and show me where it says I'm dangerous."

"Right here!" She scanned the page with her fingertip. "Look, it says, 'While not psychotic, Richard Flesch continues to present a danger to...' Oh."

"What does it say, Sarah?"

She sighed. "Richard Flesch presents a danger to himself."

"Carry on reading."

"'He is unable to healthily process his guilt, and this past November marks his fourth suicide attempt, the closest he's come to succeeding.'" She lowered the page and stared at the ground, realising she'd screwed up. But did it really change anything?

Richard rolled up his left shirt sleeve and showed his wrist to her. "I have scars too, Sarah. Most of them are on the inside, but not all."

She lifted her head and looked at the thick scar running along the underside of his arm. "I got it wrong, but what does it matter? The letter still says you're not fit to be out in public."

"That letter was written three years before I was released, Sarah! I put a lot of work in with Dr Carney. I found a reason to live." He pointed down at the floodlit crime scene on the beach and promenade. "This is my reason. This is the only thing I care about. If you can't see that, then just quit."

"I already did."

He took a deep breath in and studied her face, as if he was unsure whether or not to believe her. "Then I wish you the best, truly. But if there's even a tiny part of you that thinks you can do this job, then you should stay. I'll even let you tase me again if it helps."

She pulled a face, wondering if that was a rare attempt at a joke. "It's too late. James is livid about what happened."

"And so he should be; but he wants you here, Sarah. We all do."

"Really?"

He nodded, looking her in the eye more confidently than he had ever managed before. "Yes, really. But if you stay, Sarah, then you need to get over your feelings about me. My only goal is to stop the Durham Butcher and other monsters like him. You don't have to like me, but you do have to respect me. I won't tolerate any more abuse."

Sarah rolled her eyes and turned her back on him, facing the sea once again. A distant part of her imagined sprouting wings and flying off into that black nothingness. Would the sun eventually catch up to her, or could she stay ahead of it forever, becoming part of a never-ending darkness?

I already am. It lives inside me.

Richard's right. I don't have to like him, but he's not the one causing problems. He's just trying to catch a sadistic killer, and I attacked him. Because I'm a mess.

If I don't do this, I might never put myself back together. It's too lonely being alone. Too hard to find my way back into the light. I think I'm afraid to admit that I'm more comfortable around monsters than I am people.

She turned around. "Richard, I'm sorry."

But he had already left.

CHAPTER
THIRTEEN

MORNING ARRIVED.

Richard disliked being away from the Institute. He felt vulnerable outside of his comfort zone, and it made him realise how much he relied on being safe and secure. Ever since the cell door had closed on him in Broadmoor, he had found peace he'd never known growing up on his family's farm. Calm. Quiet. Orderly.

But this morning he was out of sorts, sitting at a table with James and staring at a full English breakfast, which had been served to them by a melancholy waitress who couldn't believe a murder had happened in her pleasant little hometown.

"Are you doing okay?" James asked him, holding a knife and fork in either hand and hovering them over his plate. "Last night was a debacle."

"I'm sorry. I lost control of myself, but I promise that I—"

James waved a hand in the air, seemingly unaware that he was wielding a knife. "I'm talking about Sarah tasing you. That woman is a liability. I was wrong to bring her in."

Richard ran his fingers up and down the edges of his plate, enjoying the residual warmth still remaining on the smooth surface. "She has great instincts, just like you predicted."

"Nonetheless. She's clearly unstable."

"When has that ever got in the way of a good hire? You sprung me from a secure hospital because you saw something in me."

James sawed at a pork sausage on his plate and skewered the orphaned section. "Well, she's already quit, so it's water under the bridge now."

"Give her another chance, James."

"Why? After what she did to you, why would you even defend her?"

"Because she warned you she was psychologically damaged, and you badgered her into taking the job anyway. It's not fair for you to punish her for behaving exactly how she told you she would. We should support her. Help her like you helped me."

James popped the piece of sausage into his mouth and chewed. Richard knew he had done it to give himself a moment to think.

Richard shovelled a forkful of beans into his mouth and thought about the case. Mona Lewis was the fourth victim now, if you included Dr Carney, and like the others, her execution had been based on historical methods. The killer was clearly trying to make some kind of statement, but what? Also, how did it involve Richard? Why was the killer taunting him at the various crime scenes and sending him emails from untraceable domains?

I can't figure out the link. Historical killings and me. It's almost like there are two separate motives at play.

"I think it's best if we move on without Sarah," James said after swallowing his mouthful of sausage. "You need stability in order to do your work, Richard."

"There is no stability in this line of work. What I need is a partner I can trust; someone who can accept what I'm trying to do here."

"I can accept it," said Sarah, approaching their table from

the side. "I can accept that what you were then is not who you are now. I'm sorry for attacking you, and you have my word it probably won't happen again."

Richard opened his mouth to speak, but he was taken off guard and didn't know what to say.

James cleared his throat and sat up straighter. "Sarah? I appreciate what you're saying, but what you did yesterday was—"

"Only as serious as we make it." She licked her lips and looked him in the eye. "Come on, James. If rules mattered that much to you, Richard would still be eating his eggs at Broadmoor. The only people willing to do this job are unhinged, so let's just call last night a bad ending to a bad day."

"I don't think I can do that, Sarah. You tasered Richard."

She put her hands on her hips and tilted her head to the side in order to lengthen her neck and reveal the angry, purple bruising. "And he strangled the hell out of me. Live and let live, yeah?"

"I'm sorry," Richard said, too ashamed to look at her. "It shouldn't have happened."

"But it did, so let's just move on." She shuffled sideways and forced James to move over onto the next seat over. "I can do this job, and I can put aside my feelings about Richard, okay? You were right; I need this job. If there's any chance of me putting myself back together, I need to catch the Durham Butcher and see him behind bars. If you still want me gone after that, no hard feelings."

James pulled in his new seat and sighed. "Richard, what are your thoughts?"

"I'm focused on the investigation. That's all I care about. No grudges here."

"Good," said Sarah. She reached out and nicked a rasher of bacon off of James's plate and bit a chunk off, speaking as she chewed. "Because I just got a call from one of the forensics who worked Carney's house last night. They found something."

James frowned. "They called you? Why?"

"Because I asked the guy to let me know right away if anything came up. I'm a people person."

"Right," said Richard. He leant forward, eager to hear what she had to say. "What did they tell you?"

"That they found a number tattooed on Mona Lewis's tongue."

James put an elbow on the table and turned to her with an eyebrow raised. "Tattooed? What was the number?"

"Twenty-two, oh-five, two-thousand-three." She popped the rest of the bacon in her mouth and chewed. Richard watched her mouth work for a moment, temporarily transfixed.

"What does it mean?" James asked.

Sarah continued chewing and shrugged. "Dunno."

"It's a date," said Richard, picturing the number in his mind. "Twenty-second of May, two-thousand-three."

James nodded. "Does it mean anything to you?"

"No. Not yet."

James stood up, elbowed Sarah to get out of his way, and shuffled behind her. "I need to make some phone calls to confirm. When Donkey gets out of bed, tell him to research that date. If the killer tattooed it on Mona Lewis's tongue, then it means something."

Sarah saluted with a smile. "Will do, boss."

James glared at her. "We'll revisit this conversation later, Ms Stone."

"Ooh, I like it when you call me by my last name."

He exited the lounge, clearly in a bad mood.

Richard sat in silence while Sarah ate from James's abandoned breakfast. Eventually, he asked her, "You can really put the past aside and work with me?"

Around a mouthful of sausage, she said, "You have things to atone for? Well, so do I. Good men died in the desert because of my bad decisions, and I've taken more lives in the line of duty than I'd care to admit. Death haunts us both."

"For different reasons," he said. "I know we're not the same."

"No, we're not. But we both want the same thing, right? To catch the Durham Butcher?"

"That's all I want." He reached across the table. "So… truce?"

She looked at his hand as if it was covered in cow manure, but after a brief hesitation, she shook it. "I can't promise to be perfect, and if you ever attack me again, I'll take your bloody eye out, but I'm willing to put the past behind me. Just… go easy on the reminiscing, okay? My own dad was enough of a bastard without having to hear about yours."

"Sins of the father, huh?"

"How about when this is all over we go piss on their graves?"

Richard frowned. "Huh?"

"Sorry, that was crass, even for me."

"No, it's just that my father isn't dead. He's serving fourteen life sentences in Wakefield Prison."

She jolted backwards as if he had slapped her in the face. The smudge of bean juice at the corner of her mouth only made her seem more confused. "Why did I think he was dead?"

"I don't know. Why did you?"

"Just the way you talk about him, always in the past tense. So… he's alive?"

"Yes." Richard put his knife and fork down on his plate and pushed the whole thing aside. "He's an old man now, but unfortunately in good health."

Sarah seemed to sit with that for a moment, her hands laced together on the table. "What about your mother? You speak almost fondly of her sometimes."

"She hanged herself six months after she began her sentence." He ran his fingers back and forth over the table, imaging his mother's face the last time he had seen her, sitting opposite him in court. "Fifteen years ago now. I was sad when it happened, although I feel guilty about it. Despite the monstrous things she took part in, she tried to be a mother to me as best she could. She might have even lived a normal life if she'd never met my dad. Her defence team said she was schizophrenic, but it was never proven."

Sarah seemed lost in thought, only half listening. "But your dad… Your dad is alive?"

"Like I said, he's in Wakefield. Probably less than two hours away, actually. What are you thinking?"

She rubbed at the scars on the side of her face and narrowed her eyes. "We've been assuming Dr Carney spilled the beans about your identity, but what if it was your old man?"

Richard pulled a face and tried to disguise the brief shudder that ran through him. Even thinking about his dad in the flesh made him uneasy. Already he could feel his bladder swelling, getting ready to purge itself. "I haven't seen or spoken to him since the day we were arrested. Why would it have anything to do with him?"

"He's a vindictive psychopath who never wanted you to have your own life, right? What if he found out you were released? Would that make him angry?"

Richard thought about it and then nodded. "I'm almost certain it would. How would he know about it, though?"

"Did Dr Carney ever visit him?"

"Yes."

Sarah's eyes went wide. "Really?"

Richard ran a hand through his hair and winced at the greasiness of it. He needed a shower. He usually took one every day. "Dr Carney wasn't just a doctor, he was an academic. He wrote dozens of essays about the human mind, and about mental disorders specifically. Having both me and my dad locked up and available to interview was something he obviously took advantage of. Much of his research went into a book about murderous impulses potentially being hereditary."

"The classic nature-versus-nurture debate, huh?"

Richard nodded. "A father and son serial killer pairing is, to my knowledge, unique, so Dad and I were interviewed many times over the years, by all manner of academics. Dr Carney most often of all."

Sarah slapped her hands flat on the counter, making their cutlery jump on their plates. "We need to go see him. Your dad knew Dr Carney and now the doctor is dead. He knows your true identity, and about all the crimes you committed. This must involve him somehow. It all fits."

"It doesn't fit," Richard argued, hearing a slight tremble in his voice. "He's been locked up for more than a decade, and he's never getting out. How could he be the killer?"

"I didn't say he was the killer, did I? But I bet he who knows who is."

Richard shook his head, and once he started he couldn't stop himself. "I can't see him. There's no way."

Sarah reached across the table towards him. "Hey, he can't do shit to you any more, Richard. As much as I hate to admit it, you're not like him."

"Sarah, I can't. Just thinking about him…"

"I know." She put her elbow on the table and made a fist at him. "But I've got your back. We're partners, right? If you're going to strangle anyone in the future, make it your old man, not me."

He looked her in the eye, forcing himself to fight through the awkwardness that always forced him to look away. "Can you actually honour that? Can you really work with me?"

She lowered her fist and looked away, but when she looked back, her gaze was steely and determined. "I can work with you because it's for the greater good. I see that now. Can you work with me?"

"I… I think so."

"Well, I expected more enthusiasm, but I suppose I'll take it. Partners then?" She raised her hand back up, this time flat and outstretched.

He grasped it at the top with his finger and squeezed. "Partners."

"What are you doing? Have you never shaken hands before?"

"I don't like touching hands. The germs."

Sarah stood up and wiped her mouth on the back of her arm. "Let's get to work, you weirdo."

Richard smiled and stood up with her. "I'm ready."

CHAPTER
FOURTEEN

JAMES ORDERED a mandatory day off for the remainder of Sunday, and it was clearly so he could do some thinking about what had happened in Saltburn. Even when Monday morning arrived, he was suspiciously absent from that morning's briefing. Richard saw it as a bad sign, and resigned himself to his days at the Institute likely being numbered. But, by midday, everyone was back on the case and working as hard as usual. The job came first, and no one spoke about internal dramas or spread gossip. They were now at four murders, without the slightest clue about who was responsible. And now Richard had to face his dad.

I don't think I can do it. Even after all these years, I can't bear hearing his voice inside my head. He haunts my nightmares, along with all those he made me hurt.

A voice whispered in his ear. *Stop making excuses. He didn't make you do anything. You could have refused.*

"I didn't know any better," he argued, and then looked around his office as if he might see a spectre standing there. Of course, there was no one with him, just the echo of his own madness.

You hurt us, Richard. It was your hands, your teeth, your cock.

My mother wept for days when they found my remains. You ate all of my fingers.

"I'm sorry."

Are you? Are you really?

Please kill me, Richard.

Richard flinched. That last voice belonged to Sadie.

Please, I don't want to live. I don't want it to hurt any more. Kill me.

"I can't. I can't kill you."

Then you're no better than him. You enjoy the pain. I trusted you. I liked you.

Richard shook his head and stood up with a start. With both hands to his face, he held back a sob. Since sharing his past with Sarah and Donkey, and getting tasered for it, his mind had been a disordered wasteland. Everywhere he looked was ruination, and behind every piece of debris was a monster waiting to sink its teeth into him.

No, not monsters. The people I killed.

I'm the only monster.

He needed to get some air, so he left his office inside the Box and went to see Donkey in Research Room One. It was an enclosed annexe off of Lab One, but little more than a cupboard with a high-spec computer inside. It was a quiet space where people could come to load up the crime database or various software, like e-fit and video analysers. You could usually find Donkey there whenever there was an active investigation. He was a qualified lab technician, but his day-to-day role was research, data gathering, and logistics. He did his job well, despite wearing many hats.

As expected, Richard found his colleague glued to the 4K monitor, tapping away and clicking the mouse. He didn't even notice Richard enter.

"Donkey?"

He spun around in the high-backed leather chair. "Richard? You okay?"

"I'm good. Any progress on what that date could mean?"

"Not yet. As far as dates go, it was a pretty uneventful day. Nothing big or noteworthy."

"Perhaps it's a birthday?"

Donkey made a clucking sound. "Already ahead of you, *mon frère*. I'm searching the birth register right now, but it's about sixteen hundred names long, so it'll take me a little while to search them all."

"Let me know if anything comes up, okay?"

"Will do. Hey, didn't James call a meeting for one thirty? You best get a move on."

Richard checked his watch and hissed. "Damn, I forgot."

"You never forget stuff."

"I'm distracted."

"Understandable." Donkey gave him a light-hearted shrug, probably assuming his distraction was down to having been tasered by Sarah last night. It wasn't that, though. It was the thought of having to sit opposite his dad.

"I best get going." Richard turned to leave, but then stopped. "Um, thank you, by the way. For sticking up for me last night."

Donkey spun around more in his chair to face him fully. "I can't say I don't understand where Sarah was coming from, but it was out of order what she did. You've done a lot of good here, Richard. It doesn't erase the past, but it's not nothing either. You deserve a safe place to work."

"Thanks."

Richard exited the Box and went into the manor, not stopping until he entered the briefing room. Everyone was already assembled, which caused a pang of anxiety to hit him, but he calmed down when he realised nothing had started yet. Oddly, Sarah and James were standing in opposite corners of the room and seemingly avoiding eye contact. There was clearly still tension between them. Richard wasn't great at reading body language, but James appeared to be angry from the way he refused to smile, and from how his movements were a little heavy-handed.

He was really going to get rid of Sarah. She let him down.
And she knows it.

Richard moved to the front of the room and cleared his throat. He needed to get back in control of things. He needed to take charge and put everything in order. The killer was hurting people because of him, and he needed to put a stop to it. "Twenty-two, oh-five, two-thousand-three," he said, and then paused a moment as everyone turned to face him. "Get that number in your minds. Is it a date? Or something else? We need to find out quickly, because it's a message directly from our killer, tattooed on Mona Lewis's tongue. Let's check local tattoo suppliers, okay? Our killer might own his own equipment, and he would have needed to have purchased it from somewhere. Furthermore, we now have four separate crime scenes, so let's see if we can start drawing up an area from where our killer might be operating." He noticed Sarah watching him from the corner and turned his head to meet her stare. She gave him an approving nod.

"Yesterday's crime scenes were once again set up to echo historical torture methods," Richard continued, "so I want a list of history experts in County Durham and surrounding counties. University lecturers, museum employees, we need to check them all. Start young to old, as we know our killer is fit and athletic. Frances, how is it going with the mobile phone footage you requested from the university? Frances?" He looked across the small audience.

"She's not in today," someone said. "She texted to say she wasn't feeling well."

"Oh. That's not ideal. Could someone check on her progress and report back to me or Sarah, please?"

"I'll do it," someone said.

"Thank you. Well, I think we should reconvene later at… say, seventeen hundred?"

"I agree," James said. "Thank you, Richard. Let's get to work, people."

Richard turned and walked to the side of the room, but before he reached the door, Sarah blocked him. She was still wearing the same outfit as yesterday, and it gave him flashbacks of holding her down on the table. "You're more confident than usual," she said. "Everything okay?"

"No," he said. "I'm masking to hide my true feelings. It's a coping mechanism."

"Well, it's working. Are you anxious about seeing your dad?"

He nodded. "I'm struggling to focus."

"That's understandable. It must be like meeting the Devil. Look, I'll go and see him, all right? Don't worry about it."

He let out a sigh, but not a sigh of relief. "No, it needs to be me. I know him better than anyone else, and he's more likely to speak to me than you."

"Because I'm a woman?"

"Among other things. You'll just distract him. He'll see it as a game."

"I could make myself uglier," she said, and pulled at the scars on her face so that the red of her eyelid showed. "I can do a really good ghoul."

"He'd just focus on your good side."

She frowned at him, possibly upset, but then she chuckled. "Fair enough. Send James, then."

"I'm going to go visit him myself. It's long overdue, and if what you said is true about my dad being angry that I'm free, then seeing me in the flesh will agitate him further. It's our best shot of getting the truth out of him."

"I agree, but it's not worth it if it's going to send you back to the loony bin. You should take someone with you. Me or James, or Donkey."

He nodded. It was the right approach to have someone there, an ally to step in if things got out of hand. "I'll take James.

Only because he has experience when it comes to abnormal psychology. He might be able to read my dad in ways I miss."

Sarah didn't appear displeased by his decision. In fact, she seemed relaxed and focused, as if something sharp inside her brain had had its edges blunted and no longer hurt. Yesterday, she had admitted to needing this job. Perhaps that acceptance had changed something inside her. "That's fine," she said. "I need to go out and buy some more clothes anyway, as well as clean Frances's outfit and give it back, so I'll do that while you're gone."

"I need to see Donkey first, and ask him to get me clearance to visit the prison. You want to come? The three of us could put our heads together and make a plan for the next few days."

"Good idea." She pointed towards the door. "After you."

The two of them got going.

It turned out that Donkey was eager to meet with them in Research Room One because he had found something. It was a relief, because they didn't have many leads, aside from Richard's father. The Durham Butcher was smart, but Sarah's gut told her they were starting to catch his scent. She'd even begun to fantasise about the moment they put the bastard in cuffs.

"You figured out what the numbers mean?" Richard asked, looking past Donkey at the monitor behind him.

"No, not yet, but I just got a report though from the National Crime Database. I cross-referenced all the currently employed lecturers at Durham University against the register, to see if any of them had a conviction during the last ten years."

"And did any of them?" Sarah asked, leaning back against the wall with her arms folded. It was a tiny room.

"No. None of the faculty has a criminal record. However, a

Professor Nathan Irving-Ross faced charges of stalking a student three years ago."

Sarah frowned. "Who's Nathan Irvin… Irvin—"

"Irving-Ross. He's a history professor at Durham University, with a special interest in the Dark Ages. The charges against him were eventually dismissed, but the University of East Anglia, where he worked at the time, suspended him for several months."

"East Anglia?" Richard noted. "He moves around?"

Donkey nodded. "Before East Anglia, Irving-Ross worked for a publishing company in Edinburgh, helping to produce a history magazine. Before that, he studied for his degree at Warwick."

"Where did he grow up?" Sarah asked.

"Lanchester. County Durham."

Richard started fidgeting excitedly. "It all fits perfectly."

"Maybe a little too perfectly," Sarah muttered. It couldn't be this simple, could it? Catching a killer shouldn't be as easy as printing out a report.

"You can't hide from your past," Donkey said. "You can be the most fastidious killer in the world, but unless you've lived a spotless life, you're going to show up on the radar for something."

"I'll go meet with this professor," Sarah said, already restless and eager to get back to work. She also wanted to get out of the building and away from James's ire. "Can you send me the details?"

Donkey nodded at Richard. "Are you both going?"

"No," Richard said. "I need to visit Wakefield Prison. Can you arrange a visitor's pass for me? Today, if possible."

"Sure thing. What prisoner do you need to see?"

"Felix Flesch."

Donkey's eyes went wide and he scooted back a little in his chair. "You want to go see your dad?"

Richard shook his head vehemently from side to side. "Not

in the slightest, but there's a chance he's involved with the Durham Butcher, so I have no choice."

"All right. Well, give the bastard hell, yeah?" He swallowed audibly, as if simply thinking about Felix Flesch gave him the shivers. "Sarah, do you want me to accompany you to interview the professor?"

"Yeah, that would be helpful. Thanks."

"No problem. I'm just glad you two are getting along again and that we have a plan."

Sarah blushed, her bad behaviour from last night flashing through her mind. Had she really tased Richard in the middle of a pub? She cleared her throat awkwardly and said, "We're all on the same team. I get that now."

"Good. I'm glad to hear it. You were both lucky last night." Donkey put his finger and thumb in the air. "I was this close to taking the both of you down."

Sarah and Richard looked at each other, and then started laughing.

Donkey joined in the laughter too. "Flesch and Stone, aye? Has a nice ring to it. Okay, give me twenty minutes, guys, and I'll get you both what you need. Let's catch this monster, yeah?"

"Hell yeah," Sarah added, and she left to get a sandwich before setting off to meet a potential serial killer.

CHAPTER
FIFTEEN

DONKEY WAS true to his word and got back to Sarah twenty minutes later with a letter of permission from the university. She had full access to the Department of History building in the centre of the city, and Professor Irving-Ross had been notified of their intended arrival.

"So, you can pretty much get me in anywhere?" she said on the drive from Darlington up towards Durham. Sarah was once again behind the wheel, which suited her just fine; she was a lousy passenger. Not being in control was an unnatural state for her to be in.

Donkey grinned, little dimples in his cheeks. Like Sarah, any cheerful expression caused the scar on the side of his face to flex and stretch. "Although we work directly with law enforcement," he said, "we're actually empowered by the Home Secretary herself. Very few people can say no to us. Also, they often make the mistake of thinking we're benign."

"Because we operate under the label of being a university?" she guessed.

"Exactly. We often frame our requests as academic interest, which people are usually more than happy to assist with."

"Sneaky. So what do we know about this Irving-Ross?" She

pulled onto the A1 and sped up to eighty in the fast lane. Traffic was thin, and she wanted to reach the professor before he had too much time to prepare.

"He's in his fifties," Donkey said. "Studied to PhD level, but doesn't seem to be particularly well-regarded in his field. He appears to be content just teaching and nothing else."

"Do most university lecturers have a side gig, then?"

"Yes. Many senior lecturers take part in research studies, archaeological digs, that kind of thing. Others publish papers or write books. Intellectual cachet is apparently very important amongst the academic elite."

"Maybe Irving-Ross has a hobby no one knows about. Like kidnapping young girls and torturing them, for instance."

"It's possible. Him moving around so frequently throughout his life could suggest a failure to form meaningful relationships, which would fit with an abnormal personality type. Or he could suffer from impulsive behaviour, forcing him to uproot continuously to stay ahead of the consequences of his actions."

"You mean like a stalking charge?"

"Officially, Irving-Ross is innocent of all charges, but the student he allegedly stalked claimed he was obsessed with her because she could trace her lineage all the way back to a member of Oliver Cromwell's cohort."

Sarah sniffed. "That's the Parliament guy, right?"

"From the English Civil War, yes. Seems like this Irving-Ross romanticises the past."

"Perhaps he wishes we were all still living in the Dark Ages. Is it common for psychos to fantasise and wish for alternate realities?"

Donkey adjusted his feet in the footwell, wincing slightly. "It's not uncommon. Delusions, hallucinations, breaks from reality, holy missions sent directly from God; it can run the whole gamut. As a university professor, however, Irving-Ross is clearly high-functioning and restrained. He doesn't naturally fit the profile of a pattern killer. We need to assume innocence before we assume guilt."

Sarah nodded. Just because Irving-Ross was waving red flags didn't make him guilty of anything. She had to be careful not to let assumptions cloud her judgement.

The conversation faltered for the next few miles, with Sarah having to pay attention to the roads, as she wasn't from the area. Eventually, however, Donkey cleared his throat and asked a question. "Do you regret your time in the army?"

She glanced at him. "Wow, that's a big question."

He chuckled, possibly embarrassed for asking it. "You don't have to answer. I'm just being nosey."

"You mean do I regret it because of my scars?"

"Among other things."

She gripped the steering wheel a little tighter, not really wanting to talk about the subject, but knowing it might do her some good to share. People couldn't hurt you with information you gave away freely. "Some nights," she began, "when I lie awake in bed, unable to sleep because of the dry, burning sensation in the entire left side of my face, yeah, I regret it. And every time some report comes out about the obscene amounts of money being made for Western interests because of our unwarranted incursions into the Middle East, yeah, I regret it. None of it has made the world any safer."

"I agree," Donkey said. "Wars are about money and power, not justice or freedom. The rich send the poor to fight so they can reap the rewards."

"I don't regret it though," Sarah said. "Not really. Why would I beat myself up for wanting to help make the world a better place? Why would I beat myself up for training hard and risking my life to protect civilians and fellow soldiers? I got a raw deal, for sure, and my scars are a reminder of my biggest mistakes, but they're also a reminder that I was willing to do what others weren't. I travelled to a scorching desert to be shot at by religious maniacs because I was brave enough to do what

I thought was right at the time. As much as I hate them, my scars are a part of me. Good and bad, like everything else."

Donkey smiled, but there was a haunted look in his eyes. "I didn't do anything brave to get my scars. In fact, I was asleep."

From the tone of his voice, Sarah could tell he was making a decision to share something of himself with her; something he wouldn't share with just anyone. "What happened, Donkey? It was a car accident, right?"

"Yep. Just an accident. Nothing noteworthy. A drunk driver forcing an innocent family off the road like you've probably heard a thousand times before. I was only eight at the time, but from what I learned in the years after, the idiot of a man drove down an exit road and entered the dual carriageway going in the wrong direction. He hit my family's car doing sixty and died behind the wheel. My mum and dad were killed instantly too, but I was a still-breathing broken mess on the back seat. Firemen spent four hours getting me out, and the whole time I had to lie there, calling out to my family who wouldn't answer."

"Jesus. I'm sorry, Donkey."

He shrugged, as if it were old news. "My nan raised me from then on, but it was rough. Took me over a year to walk again, and you'd be right to assume I never got a chance to be captain of the rugby team. High school was a total bitch because my scars back then were swollen and pink. I won't even tell you how old I was when I lost my virginity."

Sarah gave him a smile, but inside she thought about how lucky she was to have at least lived a normal life for so many years before being disfigured. Donkey probably couldn't even remember a time before his scars. "I'm really sorry," she said again. "I can't even imagine."

"Hey, everyone has something haunting them, right? At least our demons are easy to identify."

"I guess so." She gave him another smile, feeling her own

scars stretch tight. "Thanks for telling me, Donkey. You have no reason to trust me after all the aggravation I've caused you."

He waved a hand at her. "Eh. Let's call it a learning experience. I'm just glad you're coming around. What changed your mind about Richard, anyway?"

She shrugged and felt a tiny shiver down her spine. "I wouldn't say I've changed my mind, more my perspective. The things Richard and his family did are obscene, but I see that he really is trying to help."

"He is."

"But I also saw a look in his eyes when he was strangling me." She felt a shadow cross her face, dragging down her mood. "There's still a vicious, pain-loving monster inside him, and one day, when it finally comes out, I'm going to be right there waiting to put him down. James hired me to stop monsters, and that's exactly what I'm going to do."

Donkey turned and looked at her uneasily, but Sarah didn't care. She put her foot down and sped towards Durham, wondering if she would see that same, animalistic look in Professor Irving-Ross's eyes.

CHAPTER
SIXTEEN

THE UNIVERSITY'S history building was uninspiring, and Sarah likened it more to an old cannery or spring works than a place of learning. The blocky Victorian structure was four storeys high and sandwiched between two other buildings. Its wooden-framed windows were single-paned, and the stone archway over the doorway was blackened and dirty.

"Well," she said, as she waited for Donkey to hobble up beside her. "It's a fitting place for a history department. They should have a statue of Oliver Twist standing outside it."

"It's what goes on inside that matters, Sarah. I used to take half of my lectures down the local pub when I was studying."

"That explains a lot."

He moved over to the doorway and paused just next to it. "After you."

"How gentlemanly." Sarah yanked open the heavy glass door and went inside. She expected to find a reception area, but there was nothing except a pair of bucket seats, a rack of leaflets, and a carpeted staircase. On the wall, a blue sign noted the building's various classrooms and offices.

Donkey pointed at the sign. "There! First floor. Professor Irving-Ross, PhD."

Sarah turned to take the stairs to her right, but Donkey called her back and pointed to a small metal door on the other side of the hallway. "I'm getting the lift."

"Oh, yeah, sorry."

"No worries. You're clearly ableist, but I have no choice but to work with you, so I'll ignore it."

"Well, you do slow me down, you know? Try to keep up."

He summoned the lift and stepped inside. "I'll do my best."

Sarah stepped in after him and took a deep breath. She struggled to take a second. The lift was tiny, and it rattled and creaked as it went up. It reminded her of the wreckage of the Snatch Land Rover she had once found herself stuck inside on the burning sands of Afghanistan. The IED had taken her entire squad, but not her. She was the lucky one.

"You don't like confined spaces," Donkey noted, obviously sensing her discomfort.

"Not a big fan, no. But I can cope."

The door opened and Sarah hopped out, taking the breath she had failed to take in earlier. She felt silly, but Donkey passed by her without comment.

Several offices made up the first floor, with various names and labels printed on their doors. A couple of classrooms too.

Irving-Ross's office was at the very end of the corridor, and when they reached it, Sarah knocked on the door. Donkey caught up with her and propped himself up on his crutch. When there was no answer, Sarah knocked again.

"He knew we were coming, right?"

Donkey nodded. "He was informed, but I'm sure he has a busy schedule."

"Well, we're at the top of his schedule today." She rattled the handle, but the door was locked. "Oh, come on."

Sarah marched back down the corridor, peering into the windows at the top of the various doors as she passed by. Eventually, she found a classroom full of students tapping away on laptops and tablets. At the front of the room stood a tall, distinguished-looking gentleman in grey slacks and a shirt and tie. Was it Professor Irving-Ross? Something told her it was.

She knocked on the door. The man inside glanced irritably in her direction, then went back to lecturing his students.

"Oh, he didn't just ignore me," Sarah said, knocking a second time, this time harder and longer.

This time, the man stomped over and opened the door. His thin lips curled down at the corners. "Yes? What is it? I'm trying to teach a class here."

"And while I understand that's vital work, I need to ask you if you're Professor Irving-Ross."

"I am he, but I'm busy right now, as you can see. If you're from that crime institute in Darlington, then you'll have to wait until I'm done here. My class has only just started. Please, wait by my office."

He closed the door and went back to the front of the classroom.

Sarah opened the door back up and marched inside. "Lesson's cancelled, kids. Go play conkers for the rest of the day."

The students remained in their seats, confused.

Irving-Ross went red in the face, and his light – almost washed-out – eyes went dramatically wide. "Excuse me? How dare you barge into my classroom and—"

"You're an employee of the university, Professor, and the university has given me permission to talk with you. It might be inconvenient, but trust me when I tell you that my job is more important than yours. These kids will survive missing an hour of history."

He shook his head and grew even more livid. "Who do you think you are? If you want my help with something, this is the wrong way to go about it."

Donkey started apologising, also a little red in the face. "My colleague is right when she says our job is very important, Professor. Your help could literally be a matter of life and death, and we would really appreciate a moment of your time."

"Well, make it quick, and I'm not dismissing my students."

"Okay," Sarah said, holding up her hands. "Have it your way. What do you know about medieval torture methods and executions, Professor?"

"I…" His mouth fell open, and he side-eyed his students, who were now sitting up and appeared far more alert than they had been during his lesson. "Well, I'm a history professor, so I would say I know a great deal. Why?"

"Are you the only expert on those things at the university?"

He cleared his throat and straightened his tie. "I suppose so. I have a teaching assistant, of course, and my students are working towards their own expertise, but there isn't anyone with my qualifications regarding such matters. What is this all about?"

"Are you sure you wouldn't like to discuss this in your office, Professor?" Sarah asked.

"No, I already told you." He raised his chin, showing his clear contempt for Sarah. "I have nothing to hide and no time to waste, so ask your questions and leave."

Sarah let out a sigh. *This guy is an asshole.*

"Tell me about the stalking charges placed against you three years ago," she asked. "A former student accused you of being obsessed with her."

A mixture of gasps and chuckles erupted from the audience of twelve or so students. One of them spoke out. "Should I call for security, Professor?"

Irving-Ross appeared unable to speak for a moment, and he merely waved a hand towards the young man who had spoken. Finally, he spluttered out some words. "Th-that's quite all right, Oliver. We shall not allow this vulgar nonsense to distract us from our studies, but unfortunately this is the world you're inheriting. A world without dignity or manners. A world where the truth means nothing and privacy no longer exists."

The young man who had spoken rubbed his hands together on the table and seemed angry. He had a thick silver chain around his right wrist, and it clunked against the table as he moved.

Kid must really like his professor.

"That's a lovely assessment of the modern world," Sarah told Irving-Ross, "but I'd like you to answer my question, please? Why would a student accuse you of stalking her?"

"Because she was unhinged," he hit back, almost yelling. "That's why the charges were dropped. Just a silly girl with romantic ideas about me. It's unfortunately very common."

"Real lady's man, are you?"

"I meant it's common in teaching. We are a compassionate, authoritative presence in young people's lives, and for some students that can be confusing. Like I said, the issue was dealt with, and the charges were dropped. The girl was lying. It's all on record."

"History is written by the victors, right?"

He sighed, and it turned into a grunt. "I resent the insinuation. What is it that you're getting at? Why are you asking me about medieval torture and bringing up bogus charges from the past? This can't possibly be about that poor girl found down by the river."

"Caroline Boswell," said Donkey, standing just behind Sarah. "Did you know her, Professor?"

Irving-Ross shook his head. "No, she wasn't on any of my courses. Nonetheless, as a student at the university, we were all very upset to hear about her death."

Sarah turned to the students in the room, who still hadn't left. "Did any of you know Caroline Boswell?"

They all shook their heads. The young man named Oliver still seemed angry, staring at his clenched fists.

"I'll see if I can bring up a photograph of her," Donkey said, and he pulled out his camera, lifting it in front of his face a little awkwardly, as if he had suddenly developed poor eyesight.

Sarah frowned. *I've never seen him struggle to see before.*

She went back to questioning Irving-Ross. "Caroline Boswell was killed in a very specific way. Are you aware of the details?"

"From what I read in the news, she was crushed somehow."

"Beneath a pile of rocks. The killer slowly added them over time, increasing the weight."

Irving-Ross gasped and put a hand to his mouth. "*Peine forte et dure.*"

"That's what my partner called it. Richard Mullins. Do you know him?"

"Why would I?"

"Just asking." Sarah turned to Donkey and saw that he was still holding his phone up awkwardly. "You got a photo of Caroline yet?" she asked impatiently.

"Oh, um, yeah. Right here. Hold on." After a moment, he brought an image up and showed the professor. When he claimed not to know the dead girl by sight, Sarah asked Donkey to show the students the picture as well. While he did that, she carried on speaking. "Where were you the night before Caroline Boswell was discovered, as well as the day of?"

Irving-Ross threw his arms up and then pointed in Sarah's face. "There it is! The accusation. I have no idea why I would be a part of your investigations, but let's put this right to bed, shall we? When that poor girl was murdered, I was hundreds of miles away in Wales, guest lecturing at Cardiff University. I was gone for three whole days. Check with the history department both here and there; they'll confirm it for you."

Sarah tried to keep her face inexpressive, but inside she was yelling with frustration. Could it be possible that this pompous professor had nothing to do with the murders? Donkey, too, looked up from the back of the room with a disappointed look on his face.

"Does that put an end to this?" Irving-Ross demanded. "You might have been given permission to question me, but your rudeness is beyond the pale."

"Well, I apologise for that," Sarah said, not liking the man, but realising he was probably entitled to be angry. "I will check out that alibi, but could you please just answer one more question for me before I go?"

He folded his arms and huffed. "What?"

"Where were you last night?"

"Last night? Why, I was here in the office until late, and then I went home."

"Anyone see you?"

"Possibly. I'm not sure. Why does it matter where I was last night? Were there more murders?"

Sarah stared into his pale blue eyes. He was a man who had aged ruggedly and handsomely, but there was something ugly about him too. An anger barely hidden. "What would make you say that, Professor?"

"You're investigating one murder, so why not another?"

"That's a bit of a leap, but you're right. There were two other ritualistic murders committed last night, and you appear to have no alibi for when they happened."

He flung out an arm. "Don't be so bloody ridiculous. You can't pin one murder on me, so you move onto the next? Is that how you people work? Being a history professor does not make me guilty of a crime merely because it has a historical context to it. I want you to leave, do you hear me?"

"I hear you. You're being very loud."

"I'll be whatever I want to be in my own damned classroom."

Sarah shrugged and accepted it. "Fair enough. I'll be seeking to interview each of the students under your tutelage in the next few days. Heinous crimes are being committed by someone with a strong interest in history, as well as knowledge of County Durham and the surrounding area. I'm sure you can understand our reasoning."

"You will do so outside of lesson time. I may be an employee of the university, but my students are not. It's their choice whether or not they choose to speak with you."

Sarah looked at the students to see if they were taking note. The professor was clearly speaking loudly for their benefit, letting them know they didn't have to talk to Sarah or Donkey if they didn't want to.

What is he worried about? If he's innocent, then why not let us ask his students a few questions? Is he protecting someone?

Sarah's eyes fell once again upon the angry kid with the thick silver bracelet.

Oliver. His name is Oliver.

"Leave," Professor Irving-Ross said again, pointing at the door. He took a few steps, hobbling slightly.

She nodded to his leg. "What's with the limp?"

"None of your business, but if you must know, I was pushed down a flight of stairs during a burglary. I have a plastic hip."

"Did they catch the burglars?" Sarah asked.

"No. Unfortunately, the police are not fit for purpose. Now, if there's anything else you wish to ask me, you can go through the university's legal department."

Sarah moved towards the door and waited for Donkey to come over. "Strange attitude for an innocent man," she said.

"Like I said, we live in a world where the truth does not matter. Only a fool fails to protect himself. History is filled with injustices."

"And monsters," Sarah said as she exited the room.

Donkey struggled to keep up as she stormed towards the lift. Eventually, she had to stop and wait for him. "That guy is an asshole."

"Eh, we did kind of storm in on him. Maybe he's nicer during office hours."

"No, Donkey. There's something here. I can smell it. If not the professor, then one of his students."

"You think?"

"He asked if there had been more murders last night. Plural. He knew there was more than one. If not, he would've asked if there had been *another* murder, not *more* murders."

"That is interesting," Donkey said, "but not conclusive. You really think the professor's involved, or one of his students?"

She kicked at the carpet and swore. "Shit, I don't know. There's no way the professor scaled that wall in Durham with that limp. He's taller than the man who attacked me too. Damn it, I can't take not having the answers. We need to find this psychopath, Donkey."

"We will. It just takes time. Speaking of the students, I managed to get this." He lifted his phone and played a video – a twelve-second clip of the classroom, slowly panning across each student's face.

Sarah gasped. "When did you get this?"

"When I was pretending to bumble around trying to find Caroline's Boswell's photograph. I was really taking a video. I thought we could compare the students in that room to the CCTV footage Frances is collecting. If we can start placing people at the scene, we'll have justification for questioning them."

She put a hand on his shoulder and grinned. "I could kiss you, but I don't know where you've been."

"I've been with you," he said, blushing.

"Don't make it weird." She let go of him and summoned the lift. "Come on, Mr Donald Keye, after you."

He hobbled inside the lift and turned around, but by the time the doors began to close, Sarah was already heading for the stairs to meet him at the bottom.

CHAPTER
SEVENTEEN

RICHARD SAT in the leather passenger seat of James's Mondeo. It was strange, staring at prison walls from the outside, and a part of him gained comfort from the sight. The twenty-foot slabs of reinforced concrete reminded him of being safe; guarded from the outside world, where his parents and the families of his victims could not get to him.

But then he thought about the particular monster that was hiding behind these walls, and any fantasy of safety faded away.

"This is bad idea." James said as he switched off the engine. "After how far you've come, it would be a tragedy to let Felix Flesch set you back. Especially with what happened last week. You should be back in therapy, not here."

A feeling rose in Richard's chest, a feral beast thirsting for violence. He hadn't felt it in so long that he thought the beast had died inside him. But then, last night, it had re-awoken. "What happened with Sarah was a mistake. It shouldn't have happened."

James stared at his hands, which were stacked on top of the steering wheel. "No, it shouldn't have. Sarah provoked you, I understand that, but I need to know you're still in control of yourself. If there's even a single doubt that—"

"There's not." Richard lied. He was lying to James, the man who had risked everything for him. "It was extreme circumstances, but I held back. I let Sarah go."

"I wasn't there, but that's not the way Donkey made it sound."

He can't know how close I came to losing control completely. If he knows, he'll send me back to the hospital while the Durham Butcher continues killing.

"I promise I'm okay, James. I screwed up, but I'm going to learn from it and do better. This is too important to avoid. If my father knows anything about our killer, then I have to get answers."

James stared at him, and Richard knew he was looking for signs of deception or doubt. Fortunately, Richard knew he was difficult to read, because his face rarely showcased his emotions.

Eventually, James seemed satisfied and nodded. "Okay. I have to ask you again, though. Are you sure you want to do this? You haven't faced your father since the courtroom."

"That's not completely true. He wrote me letters the first few years I was in Broadmoor."

James raised an eyebrow. "You never told me that. What did he say to you?"

Richard squeezed at the auger shell in his pocket. He was anxious – even afraid – yet he wasn't panicking. At least not yet. "Just what you would expect. Telling me I would always be his blood and a born predator. Sometimes he would tell me to kill myself rather than rot away in prison. Then, after I failed to write back, the letters became full of hateful rambling and egotistical boasts. He said I was weak and that he should have smothered me at birth because of the disappointment I became. He promised he'd end my life one day, somehow, and that it was his right to do so as my one and only god."

"He was grasping for a sense of power," James said. "If you had killed yourself because of his words, he could have claimed you as another victim. Your father cannot function without hurting people. He needs to know he has the power to ruin another person's life. His entire self-esteem is tied to control and causing pain."

"I know what my father is," Richard said, "and I'm ready to face him. But I'm only able to do it because I know you'll be there to back me up. You might be the only person I've ever fully trusted, James, and I've never really thanked you properly for what you've done."

James patted Richard quickly on the leg, knowing he didn't enjoy physical contact. "You're paying me back every time you help catch a bad guy, so you don't have to thank me. Just keep doing what you've been doing."

Richard nodded, turned, and then got out of the car. It was a chilly day for the tail end of summer, but it felt strangely fitting. Felix Flesch had sent a chill down the spines of the nation, so cold weather was an appropriate atmosphere for meeting with him.

James got out and joined Richard in front of the car. He pressed the key fob and locked the Mondeo's doors, and they then both walked across the car park to the visitor's entrance. There, they had to show ID and wait while their appointment was confirmed on the system. Finally, they were frisked and scanned to ensure they were not bringing contraband into the prison. Once again, Richard felt odd being a visitor and not an inmate.

"We have a room set up for you," a guard captain told them, and then he led them down a long white corridor that was barred every twelve feet or so. Each one had to be unlocked with a plastic security fob attached to the guard's belt via a retractable cord.

The guard ushered them into a simple room with a single barred window. In the centre of the room was a table with a

Perspex divider in the middle, about half a foot high. Richard assumed it was to prevent visitors and prisoners from touching hands and passing things between them. Four chairs surrounded the table, each secured to a bolt in the floor by a short length of chain.

"Take a seat," the guard told them, and then pressed a buzzer on the wall to activate an intercom. He asked for the prisoner to be brought in.

My father. He's coming.

Richard sat down on one of the two chairs and immediately realised his knee was shaking. He had to grab it before it would stop. James seemed to notice, because he gave Richard a reassuring smile.

Noise sounded from somewhere close by – the sliding of metal gates and the *clomp* of heavy boots. A procession.

The room's only door was behind Richard and James, which made things a little awkward. Richard didn't know whether to turn himself around in his seat to face the door or stay facing the table. He decided on the latter.

The door eventually opened with a thin squeak of unoiled hinges. Footsteps sounded, people entering the room. James turned to look back, but Richard remained facing forward. His hand was in his pocket, wrapped around the auger shell. His knee wanted to bounce nervously again, but he focused on keeping it still.

Two guards went to opposite corners of the room, one half-hidden by the stripy shadow coming from the barred window.

"Well, well, well, it's been a long time since I had visitors," said a voice like rumbling thunder. Richard felt the vibrations in his bladder.

Felix Flesch, at six foot tall, had always been a large man, but he was substantially thinner now than when Richard had last seen him. His beer gut was gone, and his thick forearms were covered in crude tattoos. His face was gaunter, too, and his hair was wild and unkempt, but his eyes… his dark brown eyes were still full of that same malignant hate.

He sat down opposite James and Richard, then leant back arrogantly, scratching his testicles without shame.

He hasn't recognised me, Richard realised. *How long before the penny drops?*

James turned to face the guard captain who was standing by the now-closed door. "These men have signed an NDA?"

The captain nodded.

Richard was relieved. The conversation in this room was almost certainly going to reveal his true identity, and they couldn't afford to have some underpaid prison guard going to the papers for an easy payday.

"Very good," James said, and then he turned to face Felix Flesch. Richard sensed his colleague's nervousness, but it would be well-hidden from those who didn't know him. "Mr Flesch, my name is James Westerly, and this is my colleague, Richard Mullins. We would like to ask you a few questions, if you don't m—"

"I ain't answering shit, so why don't you both get down on your knees and suck my big, fat cock? At least then you'll be useful." He grabbed his waistband and began to pull it down.

The guard captain barked at him to behave and pulled a telescopic baton from his belt. "You can spend the week in solitary, Flesch."

Felix smirked. "I'm sure you can get some action too, boss. More than your wife gives you, anyway."

"Last warning."

"Must be hard," Richard said, surprised by the coolness of his own voice. "A devil in human flesh, reduced to hurling pathetic insults. Nobody fears you any more. You've been neutered."

The smirk fell away from Felix's face. He sat upright and leant forward. "Oh, they fear me, all right. I see the goosebumps on their arms, the dryness of their mouths. My face haunts their dreams."

Richard chuckled and looked his father in the eye. "I expected them to bring you to this room wrapped in chains, but you're not even handcuffed. All I see is a seventy-year-old man in need of a good meal and a haircut."

Felix's soulless brown eyes narrowed, and he leant forward another inch. "Worm? Is that you? Are you really sitting opposite me right now?"

"I don't know who you're talking about. My name is Richard Mullins. I'm a special investigator working for the Home Office. As my colleague said, we're here to ask you some questions."

Felix appeared genuinely caught off guard. He didn't seem to know if what he was seeing was real, or if he was imagining it. After a moment, his confusion wore off and a grin took its place. "Oh, it's you all right, Worm. You think I can't recognise my own spunk? What the hell are you doing here? They using you to get to me, are they?"

"Why would anyone need to get to you? You're impotent."

"You know better than anyone that your old man is anything but impotent. It's you who don't know what being a man is. Look at you, being led around like a puppy dog. Did this Yankee prick promise to let you out the funny farm if you helped him?" He turned his head and spat on the floor. The guard captain went to make a move, but James put a hand up to keep him at bay.

Richard took a slow, measured breath and continued to look his father in the eye. "As I've already said, you have me confused. My name is DI Richard Mullins. Now, can you please tell us what we need to know? We would be most grateful."

Felix sat back and put his hands behind his head, threading strands of wild grey hair through his fingers. "All right, I'll play along for now, Worm. So, what do you faggots want?"

James winced at that, and Richard was glad that his father

missed the brief wound he had scored. His focus remained on his son, which suited Richard just fine. "What do you know about the killer the papers have dubbed 'The Durham Butcher'?"

"Nowt. Why would I know anything?"

"Just asking out of interest. There hasn't been a serial killer like this in County Durham since you were active. I suppose I thought you might take a professional interest."

"Guy seems like a nutter to me," Felix said, without any hint of irony. "Staging those girl's deaths like something out of a history book. Didn't even shag 'em. What a waste."

James rolled his eyes. "It seemed the killer has different motives from yours. We believe he's trying to make some kind of statement. He also murdered Dr Allen Carney, who I believe you met with many times."

"That headshrinker? Always knew he'd end up dead. Messing with people's minds is a dangerous thing, pal. Messing with their bodies is way more fun, eh, son?" He winked grotesquely.

Richard folded his arms, but when he felt his own rapid heartbeat, he loosened them again. "Do you know anyone who would want to harm the doctor?"

"Aye, me. Would've loved to have been the one to do him in. Cannit think of a man more deserving."

"Why?"

"Because he spent his life under the illusion that there's something wrong with men like me." He nodded at Richard. "Like us. Human beings forget that they're just animals, and animals kill. There's nothing wrong with me. I just understand what it means to be human, to be a predator at the top of the food chain."

"You don't seem to be top of the food chain," Richard said.

"You can cage a lion, but it's still a lion. You can let one out too, and it will always return to killing. No point in fighting nature. What game are you playing, Worm? How did you get out of Broadmoor?"

Richard forced himself to grin, knowing it would incense his father. "Again, I have no idea what you're talking about."

"Is this why you never replied to my letters? The fuckers let you out? Do the victims of the families know? What would they do if they knew you got out scot-free? What about Sadie? Does she know? Oh, right, that bitch offed herself a few years back, right? Probably couldn't take the memory of your tiny cock inside her. You really tried your best with her, too. Took her every which way, remember? Remember how she begged? How she bled?"

Richard's vision faltered. His heart drummed in his chest.

James leant forward and banged a fist on the table. "I suggest you stick to answering our questions, Mr Flesch, or we'll end this conversation right now."

Felix shrugged. "End it, I don't care. I'm just trying to reconnect with my son. She really liked you, you know, Worm? Sadie was such a sweetheart, wasn't she? I was almost sad to take my turn. Maybe I should have let you keep her."

"She got away from you," Richard said. "She's the reason you're in here."

"She's not the reason, Worm. You are. Do you think I don't know you let her go. Your weakness is the reason I'm here, and yet you get to go free." He sneered, yellowing teeth like broken matchsticks, black eyes like chunks of volcanic glass. "Well, enjoy it while you can, because you'll never be free while I'm still breathing. I am your universe. Your heart beats only because I allow it to. Your dear old mam understood that. That's why she did as she was told and cut her own throat. She hated you at the end, you know? Hated that you betrayed your own family."

"Shut up," Richard said. "You made her what she was, twisted her until she had no free will of her own. She loved me, in her own way. She did."

"Really?" He leant back in his chair once more and grabbed his cock again. "Then you think she might have done more to keep you safe at night. Don't you remember how she used to watch while I taught you how to be a man? She used to get off on it."

"Shut up. I'm warning you."

"Oh, you finally got the balls to fight back, 'ave ya? Too late to help Sadie though, ain't it? Or any of the other girls you fucked, killed, and ate."

James smashed a fist on the table again. "This conversation is over. Guard, can you—"

"I'm going to kill you!" Richard leapt up out of his seat and launched himself at his father.

"Richard!" James wailed. "Richard, stop!"

"I'll kill you," he screamed again, leaping on top of his father and squeezing his skinny throat with both hands. "You're a monster. You made me do those things."

His father grinned, even as he spluttered and turned red.

Richard's entire body coursed with violence, his muscles flexing, his jaws locking. But even now, as he attempted to snuff out his father's evil black flame, he still felt like a frightened child, beaten and abused and forced to do things beyond his comprehension. He had come here to stop the Durham Butcher, but instead he had found a chance to stop the Chester-le-Street Cannibal. A name they both shared.

"That's my Worm," Felix managed to splutter. "Let me 'ave it, killer."

Richard roared and bit down on his father's cheek, sinking his teeth in and feeling that familiar yielding of soft human flesh accompanied by the sharp tang of coppery blood. Richard heard his father scream for the first time ever, and it sent his body into ecstatic convulsions.

Hands grabbed Richard from behind and pulled him back. He tried to keep his hands wrapped around Felix's neck, but he lost his grip. Snarling in frustration he thrashed against the interference and spat his father's blood.

"Get 'im away from me!" Felix roared. "I'll snap his rotten neck."

"I'll kill you," Richard bellowed, fighting against the guards as hands continued to pull at him. His fury took an even greater hold, and he spun around, swinging his fists.

James went sprawling backwards, caught by the guard captain behind him. He was dazed, his pupils rolling about in his head like loose marbles.

"You're fucked!" Felix yelled, half his face awash with blood. "You were supposed to learn from me, but you were a fucking failure. My new student is much better, and by the time he's done with you, you'll be back in the loony bin where you belong. You may be my blood, but you're not my son."

Richard lunged at his father again, but the three guards in the room rushed to restrain him. "You're done," the captain said. "Bloody lunatic."

"What do you know?" Richard yelled, his arms shoved up behind his back. "Tell me what you know about the murders."

"I know that they won't stop. Kid has a taste for it now, and we both know what that feels like. They should never have let you out. Not while I'm stuck wasting away in here."

"Who is he?" Richard roared. "Tell me. Tell me who you've been talking to."

Felix grinned, blood staining his teeth. But he said nothing.

"Restrain him," James yelled, rubbing at his jaw and snarling like Richard had never seen him before. "Get him the fuck out of here."

For a moment, Richard thought he was talking about his father, but then he realised he was wrong. The guards dragged Richard backwards through the doorway. He continued to yell out at his father. "Tell me who the killer is. Tell me!"

CHAPTER
EIGHTEEN

SARAH ANSWERED HER PHONE. It was a call from James. She placed it on loudspeaker so that Donkey could hear. The two of them were sitting in the car outside the history department.

"James, everything okay?"

Or are you calling to give me a hard time because you're still mad?

"S-Sarah." He sounded dazed, slurring her name. "Where are you?"

"In Durham. We just interviewed a suspect."

"Irving-Ross, right? Donkey updated me before you set off."

Donkey waved at the phone, which was a pointless thing to do, and then said, "I'm here, boss."

"Good. It's good I've got you both. I'm afraid there's been an incident on my end."

Sarah and Donkey exchanged glances. "Um, James," she said, "you sound weird. You're slurring your words. What's happened?"

He breathed heavily down the phone. "Richard will no longer be working with us. The meeting with his father turned violent."

Sarah swore, more out of shock than anything else. "No way."

"Did anyone get hurt?" Donkey asked, a hand over his mouth.

"Felix Flesch is in the infirmary having his face stitched up," James replied, "because Richard bit him. Then he lashed out at the guards."

"And you?" Sarah said. "Is that why you're slurring? Are you hurt?"

"I'm fine. We just need to focus on the investigation. Did anything come up with the professor?"

Sarah propped the phone against the car's automatic gearstick and placed her hands in her lap. "It's unlikely he's the killer, but there's something off about him. I got the sense he knew more than he was letting on."

"We're thinking it might be one of his students," Donkey added. "I took video footage of those attending his class today. We can cross-reference it with anything Frances has managed to dig up."

"That's interesting," James said, sounding a little more upbeat. "Felix Flesch claimed to know our killer. He referred to him as a 'kid'."

Sarah and Donkey glanced at each other again. Sarah said, "So it is someone young then, like I originally thought?"

"It appears that way. It's possible our killer is getting guidance from Felix. That would explain why the killings have been targeting Richard. I think, somehow, his father learned about him being released and is determined to get revenge."

"Why did Richard go off?" Sarah asked. "What made him lash out?"

James hissed, the sound high-pitched and distorted through the tiny loudspeaker. "It was a bad idea from the start. He assured me he would be fine, but he was screwed the moment he stepped into the room. His father just kept prodding at him until he lost control. It was always going to happen."

"But we got confirmation that Felix Flesch is involved in this, so it was worthwhile, James. Can we turn the screws on him?"

"Of course, but I need to get authorisation from a judge first or else he can just refuse to meet with me. It's going to take a little time. In the meantime, I need you working every angle. I'm heading back to Tithby Hall to regroup and maybe have a stiff drink."

"Don't be so hard on yourself," Sarah said, hearing the pain in his voice. "Like you said, it was a disaster waiting to happen. At least Richard went in there for the right reasons."

"He's dangerous, Sarah."

"No shit. I've been telling you that since the start. You hired me to be a babysitter because you knew Richard was a bomb waiting to explode. You might not be able to admit it, but you've always known."

"Perhaps you're right. Either way, I've learned my lesson now."

Sarah sat for a moment, contemplating the events of the last few days. Slowly, something terrible dawned on her. "We need him, James. Richard is our best chance of catching the Durham Butcher. The murders are all linked to him for a reason. Get rid of him later, but we need him on this case."

James took a moment to answer. Sarah thought, for a moment, that the call had dropped. Then he grunted and said, "I think we're past the point of that being an option, but you need to put it out of your mind for now. What's your next move?"

Sarah's phone vibrated, prompting her to pick it up. She had a message, but she would check it out after the call. "We need to see the CCTV footage Frances has collected. We know the killer was watching Richard in Durham, and we now also know that he's young enough for Felix to consider him a kid. Along with the footage Donkey took of Irving-Ross's classroom, we can start looking for familiar faces. It must be a student."

"And you're sure it's not the professor?"

"He claims to have an alibi," Donkey said. "I'll check it out, but apparently he was in Wales at the time of Caroline Boswell's murder."

"Okay, well, don't figure him out of the picture yet, and keep me updated, okay?"

"Will do," Sarah said.

James ended the call.

Donkey looked up at the history department building. "We should get going. Unless you want to wait for the professor to leave and follow him?"

"Nah, who knows how long we might be waiting?"

"Head back, then? Work with what we have?"

She nodded. "Just let me check my messages. Something came through while we were talking with James."

Donkey yanked his seatbelt and fastened it before sitting patiently while Sarah swiped at her phone. The notification alert had been for an email. She didn't recognise the sender – just a bunch of numbers and a domain she'd never heard of.

She opened it up, expecting spam.

She got something else.

Hello Sarah,

I've been thinking about you a lot since our dance in the alley. A shame Richard had to interrupt us. Do you know who he really is? If you do, then may I ask you how you sleep at night, knowing the crimes he has committed? Didn't you used to be one of the good guys? A war veteran and crusader for justice? Now you're nothing more than an enabler of evil.

Everyone who works willingly with a monster is a monster themselves. All of you need to be punished. And it starts now. History shall be made. My next masterpiece will be dedicated to you, Sarah.

The Student of Death

Sarah just stared at her phone, unable to speak. Eventually, Donkey noticed something was off and asked her if she was okay.

"It's an email from the killer," she said.

Donkey gasped. "You're kidding me."

"Nope. It's right here. He signed off as the 'Student of Death'."

"Guess he didn't like the nickname the press gave him."

"Guess not." She looked at him. "He's been emailing Richard too. You know that, right?"

"Yeah. I tried tracing the messages for a location, but it was impossible. How did the killer get your email address?"

"It's listed on the website of my security agency. He saw my ID. It wouldn't take a genius to search for me online." She looked at him and tried to swallow, but her throat was too dry. "There's a video attached to the message."

"A video?"

"Yeah. Should I open it? It can't… you know?"

"What?"

"Make my phone explode or something?"

Donkey chuckled, but when he realised she was serious, he grew serious too. "It's just a video, Sarah. It can't do anything, provided it doesn't contain an executable. I say open it. What choice do we have?"

"We could just quit, run away to the Bahamas. I can work in security for a hotel. You can be a cabana boy."

"Sarah."

"Okay, okay, I'm opening it. I just hope it's better than what we found in Dr Carney's fridge."

It was worse.

———

Two hours later, everyone was back at Tithby Hall, watching the video that the Student of Death had sent to Sarah on a pull-down projector screen in the briefing room. Richard was sitting in the corner of the room, barely present. James had admitted to not knowing what to do with him right now, but he wanted him where he could see him.

He looks like he did on the stand as a kid. Dead-eyed. Inhuman. Broken.

It was obvious how damaging Felix Flesch was to his son – from the moment of his birth all the way until now. It had been a mistake putting them both together. Cruel, even.

Frances was in the killer's video.

The Student of Death – formerly known as the Durham Butcher and NETK – had Frances.

She couldn't talk because she was bound and gagged, straddling some sort of a triangular bench in a gloomy, cement-floored room. She was clearly uncomfortable and moaned miserably around the rubber ball in her mouth. Both her legs were tied together beneath the bench so she couldn't get off.

"It's a Spanish donkey," James announced at the front of the room. His speech was less slurred now, but a nasty black bruise had taken over one side of his jaw. "The killer is going to attach weights to Frances's ankles, slowly forcing her down onto the wedge. Eventually, she'll be torn in two from the groin up."

Everyone in the room whimpered, some even crying.

"How did we let this happen?" Sarah said, hands against her face. "How did the killer take her without us realising?"

"She called in sick," Donkey said. "Sent a text."

"A text the killer probably forced her to send," Sarah said. "Do we think he got to her at her place? Where does she live?"

"I think she has a flat in Merrybent," Donkey answered. "It's about twenty minutes from here. Maybe he followed her from work. It would be easy enough."

"We need to find her!" Sarah barely knew Frances, but she

couldn't bear the thought of the peppy young woman being tortured.

"We will," James said, almost matching her anger. "This killer has been yanking our chain for weeks, but now he's made things personal. His boldness is the thing that is going to get him caught, though, you mark my words. I want everyone here working non-stop until we have what we need to put a stop to this maniac. No breaks, no downtime; I want everyone working every angle until I say stop. Frances is one of us. She needs us to come through."

"We will," Sarah said, baring her teeth. "We are going to find the bastard and make him wish he'd never been born." She looked over at the corner of the room. "And Richard is going to help us."

He didn't even look up at the sound of his name. He remained dazed, staring at the floor.

Sarah marched around the edge of the room until she was standing in front of him. "I know your head is fried right now, Richard, but we need you at your best. You say you want to atone for the things you've done, then this is your chance. Help us find Frances before it's too late. Put that messed up, tortured mind to good use. Tell us what we need to know. Don't let your old man destroy you all over again."

Sarah glanced back at James, who licked his lips nervously. The students in the room had no idea what was wrong with Richard, who had suddenly returned to base in a traumatised state, but they clearly knew something was going on. Perhaps now was the time to tell them all who Richard really was, but that wasn't her call.

Richard glanced up at Sarah, his eyes red and bleary. "I can't do this. I need to go back."

Assuming he meant the hospital, Sarah was inclined to agree, but not until the Durham Butcher was behind bars.

"You can do this," she said. "No one is better capable of

catching this guy than you are, Richard. So get your head back in the game. Put your thoughts back in order."

Richard shook his head, a tear falling from his eye. It was the same look Sarah had seen on the faces of men lying in field hospitals after getting hit by an IED or struck by a bullet. He was shellshocked.

Sarah was about to turn away and give up, but decided to make one last attempt to snap him out of his daze. "What's the chemical symbol for… mercury?"

He looked her in the eye. "Hg."

"I'll take your word for it. What's the largest planet?"

"Jupiter."

"Tallest tree?"

"Redwood. I forget the exact species."

"It still counts. Third American president?"

Richard frowned, apparently stumped. Then there was a twinkle in his eye as he answered, "Thomas Jefferson."

Sarah turned to look back at the students. "Anyone know if that's true?"

Someone tapped away at their phone and nodded a few seconds later. "It is."

Sarah turned back to Richard. "You can do this. We're so close."

He began to nod, slowly at first, but then more enthusiastically. "You're right. We almost have him, and I think that's exactly what he wants. The killer wants my attention, so his end goal must be to reveal himself to me. That's his payoff."

"Let's not give him the satisfaction, then. We're going to catch him before he does anything to Frances. You're going to beat him, because you're smarter than he is. Tell us why this is happening, Richard? What is this all about?"

He stood up unsteadily but quickly got a hold of himself. "Sadie Amberson. She's the key to all of this somehow."

"How do you know?"

He shrugged. "A gut feeling."

"I'll take it," she said.

Behind her, the students began whispering to each other. James turned pale.

———

"There, there." Oliver stroked his guest's frizzy brown hair. She wasn't his usual type of victim, but it was time to take things up a notch. He was done taunting Richard Flesch. Now it was time for torment.

Does he even have the capacity to feel? Or is he dead inside like me?

All I feel is rage. Rage that I was ever brought into this world.

He turned to the young woman strapped to the Spanish donkey and smiled pleasantly, in a way he knew was usually attractive to the opposite sex. She didn't seem enamoured by him, though. Her moist eyes bulged, and she quivered and shook as the hardwood wedge bit into her groin and no doubt caused her immense agony. Soon, he would start adding weights to her ankles, dragging her down, inch by inch, until she eventually split open like an over-ripe tomato. The coppery scent would replace the acidic odour of piss and sweat that currently wafted from his victim, and there was no doubt her dying screams would arouse him to orgasm. Something he shared in common with Richard.

His phone was on silent, but when he glanced at the screen, he saw several text notifications. They were undoubtedly from Prue, who had been trying to reach him all day. He'd decided he was going to kill her at some point, but he had a plan to stick to first. This was bigger than his own selfish desires. This was about putting fear back into the meek-hearted peasants. Once all was revealed, people would fear the word 'justice' again. Things would be better, and monsters like Richard Flesch would be stoned to death in the street, not put in secure hospitals and then let go.

Oliver picked up the pliers from the table beside the Spanish donkey, then grabbed one of the young woman's slender brown hands. "You have beautiful nails," he said. "Do you mind if I take them?"

Her screams gave him a hard-on.

CHAPTER
NINETEEN

LUCKILY FOR THEM, Frances had collected all the camera footage from Durham on her workstation in the Hive. She had set up several folders denoting various sources of footage, such as CCTV, traffic cams, and mobile phones/cameras. The majority of the footage existed inside the mobile phone folder, some two hundred students of the university having provided photos and videos taken with their phones on the night of Caroline Boswell's abduction and murder, as well as footage taken on the day her body was found. Surreally, Sarah found several images of herself, taken by nosey photographers snapping candid shots of the police investigation – probably for social media clout.

Richard was presently in his office inside the Box, working on a theory with James, but Donkey had chosen to sit with Sarah in the Hive. Both of them now sipped coffee as they swiped through the gallery of images that Frances had put together. She'd even catalogued them by time and date.

"She did good work here," Sarah said. "There's a tonne of stuff."

"Which is going to take time to sort through." Donkey rubbed at his jaw and sighed, likely worried about how long

Frances could wait for them to find her. Sarah worried about it too.

Just hold on, girl. We're coming.

They searched through the images carefully but quickly, most featuring glammed-up teenagers posing for selfies and group photographs. Some of the pictures were slightly less vain, including several lovely snaps of the cathedral or the river, but these tended to be less useful, as the photographers had clearly sought to avoid the faces of strangers ruining their pictures. Durham truly was a beautiful city, that much was clear. Too bad monsters had to ruin it.

And the Flesch family of course. This all started with them.

"Are these photos making you feel old?" Donkey asked as they looked at a group of teenage girls in barely existing dresses.

"I am old," she said. "Or at least I feel like it. The killer was wearing dark clothing when he attacked me in the alleyway. He wasn't dressed for a night out like most of the students in these pictures."

"But he attacked you on the day we found Caroline's body. These are from the night before."

"You're right. Let's focus on the time after Richard and I arrived on the scene. People were being nosey at the start. Some of them must have taken pictures."

Donkey agreed.

Sarah separated the pictures featuring a police presence into a separate folder until they eventually had just over forty images to comb over. The first few showed nothing of interest, just faraway shots of the police tent in the car park and the various personnel around it. Each one they opened that showed nothing lowered their odds of success. It was like losing at scratchcards.

Sarah brought up a new picture, this one taken from high up. The quality was striking.

"Professional," Donkey said with a whistle. "Looks like it's up on the hill. Maybe on the grounds of the cathedral."

Sarah grunted, about to move on, but then she noticed that the sweeping image of the river and city captured more detail than any of the more intimate pics. "Can we… zoom in on this? That's just in the movies, right?"

"Depends on the resolution. This is a very high-quality shot, so give it a try."

Sarah spun the mouse wheel, but too hard because the image zoomed in so much that it became a collection of large, multicoloured blocks. More slowly, she rolled the wheel backwards until the image became clearer, and the blocks merged back together to show the river, the car park, and the elevated street above.

The quality held at a decent level, allowing Sarah to make out the people standing on the street. She couldn't recognise faces, but she could see the colours of their clothing and their general age and sex. From the fact the sky was still bright, it must have been soon after Caroline Boswell's body was found, but shortly before Sarah had arrived herself.

"It's too hard to make anybody out," Donkey said, shaking his head and sighing. "We could be looking right at our killer."

Sarah squinted, examining the image almost pixel by pixel. Then she saw something that caused a jolt of electricity to strike her. "There. You see? That person standing on the elevated street, all in black. They're watching the car park below."

"You think it's the person who attacked you?"

"I think the killer would have been there the whole time, watching it all like his own private television show. This is right after Caroline Boswell was found. I know this is him. He's enjoying the commotion he's caused. Is there any way to zoom in closer?"

"Now that is just in the movies," he said. "This is probably about as good as it gets. But at least it tells us we're on the right track. Our killer was there the whole time. Someone must have taken a decent picture of him."

Sarah was still squinting. She had zoomed in slightly more, causing the black figure to blur slightly. "What's that?"

Donkey frowned. "What? I don't see anything?"

"Those few pixels there. They're lighter, white and grey. Something's on his arm."

"It's probably just daylight shining through or a shirt sleeve coming out from his hoodie."

Sarah shook her head. "No. No, it's not. It's a bracelet. One of those thick silver ones that look bloody awful."

Donkey said nothing. He just looked at her.

Sarah raised her lip into a satisfied sneer, realising what they were both thinking. "Remind you of anyone?"

"Oliver. The student in Irving-Ross's classroom."

"Kid was pretty pissed off we were there, huh?"

Donkey started fumbling with himself. "Let's look at the footage I took on my phone."

Sarah waited impatiently, her knee bouncing underneath the desk. She looked up from the desk and peered around the Hive, watching the young professionals and realising how dedicated they were. The concentration on their faces, as they tried desperately to find clues to help Frances, was absolute.

"Here it is." Donkey played the video on his phone and held it out so both of them could see. The footage was a little wobbly at first, and the image blurred, but gradually, Donkey's hand steadied and things came into crisp focus.

Oliver was sitting in the second row, both elbows on the table, his mouth curled downwards in the beginnings of a snarl. He seemed to glare at Sarah, which she hadn't noticed at the time. But she had noticed his bracelet, and she saw it again now, plain as day. A bright silver link bracelet on his right wrist.

"Got you," she said.

Richard struggled to concentrate with James being in the room. The guilt he felt for having struck his mentor threatened to tear him apart, and he was realising something about grief. It faded over time, no matter how awful it felt to start with. For years, he feared himself to be a psychopath for being able to function after committing so many vile acts, but the pain he felt now, for hurting James, demonstrated that he could still feel the emotions he was supposed to. He wasn't remorseless or apathetic.

But he was dangerous.

He kept glancing at James, trying to catch his eye, perhaps to apologise, but James stared only at the screen in front of them. They were researching Sadie Amberson, trying to learn more about the events leading up to her suicide. Many times during the last few years, Richard had considered looking into her life, but it had always felt perverse. He also didn't want to know the ongoing misery he had inflicted upon her life. Sadie Amberson had escaped Flexley Yard Farm, but she had never been free.

"The autopsy mentions missing fingernails," James said, staring at the screen through a pair of specs he sometimes wore. "That can't be a coincidence."

"They were found at the scene," Richard said. "It's likely they tore off when she struggled with the noose. Even when it's a suicide, the victim can't fight their instincts to try to save themselves. That's why most successful suicides are via irreversible acts such as hanging or jumping off of buildings."

James nodded, probably knowing all that. "You're probably right. Nothing else suggests foul play. Unmarried, no kids, no criminal record other than a few incidents of drunk and disorderly. Looks like she had a problem with alcohol. Her risk of depression and suicide would have been higher than the average population because of that. Not to mention the lingering effects of severe trauma."

Richard straightened up in his chair and sighed. "I'm not

seeing anything here. Maybe I'm wrong and this has nothing to do with Sadie."

"We need to dig deeper. The answers are somewhere. They always are."

"You're right. Look, James, about what happened this morning at the prison."

"I really don't want to talk about it, Richard. Let's just focus on—"

"I'm sorry. You have no idea how much I thought I could face my father, but—"

James put his hand up. "We'll discuss it another time. Let's just—"

The door to Richard's office burst open and Sarah leapt inside. She was bright red and panting, waving a sheet of paper in her hand like a madwoman. "Oliver Morton. Oliver frickin' Morton."

James ran a hand through his hair and turned in his chair. "What?"

"We've got the bastard," Sarah said, thrusting out the sheet of paper. "Oliver Morton is one of Irving-Ross's students and he was at the scene of Caroline Boswell's murder. See the bracelet?"

Richard glanced at the page. Two images were printed side by side. One looked like a still taken from a video of a classroom in session. The other was a zoomed in, slightly blurry image of what looked like the elevated street in Durham that overlooked the car park. Circled in red on both images was a silver bracelet. It was harder to make out in the zoomed-in picture, but there was definitely something light-coloured against the black arm of a man's clothing.

"Wait," Richard said, putting a finger to the tip of his nose. "Oliver Morton? I recognise that name."

Sarah nodded. "Donkey checked it out. He was the designated driver who gave us a statement about Claudette's

Herrington's movements the night she was abducted. This places him in proximity to both crime scenes."

"It's not conclusive," James said. "Durham is a small place."

Sarah focused on Richard. "My gut is telling me this is him. I saw the kid in the flesh. He has an anger inside him, barely contained. Smart, of course, but clearly unstable."

"Then I guess it's worth bringing him in," Richard said, wondering if she'd jumped the gun, but also knowing that she had good instincts.

James cleared his throat and thought for a moment. "The police found no evidence to back up his claims about Claudette. No one else saw her smoking or talking with an older man. It's possible he was trying to throw off our investigation."

Sarah nodded. "If he's an arrogant killer, he probably thought he was smart enough to send us on a wild goose chase."

"Many killers enjoy being part of the police investigations. If I recall, Oliver Morton came forward voluntarily to give a statement. I just don't understand what his connection could be to me?"

"It's time to find out," she said. "Get your jacket. We're going to the university right now."

Richard checked his watch. "It's past eight. Probably better to check the dorms and the student union."

"Whatever, let's just go. Sooner we leave, the sooner we can catch this guy."

"You're not going anywhere." James put a hand on Richard's arm. "After what happened today, you can't be trusted."

Richard shuddered, unnerved by the sustained human contact. He didn't pull away, though.

"Hey," Sarah said, eyeballing James. "You hired me to babysit him, so give me back my Taser and we're all good. I want to see Oliver Morton's reaction when he sees Richard. It's time we backed him into a corner."

James stared at her for several seconds, saying nothing, but then he let out a protracted sigh. "I'll catch up with Donkey and try to find out as much as I can about Oliver Morton. I'm not done digging into Sadie Amberson either, so they'll be plenty for me to do, but I want hourly updates from the both of you." He glared at Sarah. "And if Richard shows even the slightest sign of losing control…"

"I'll kick him right in the balls."

Richard grimaced. "Really?"

"Really," James said, with no hint of irony. "You're not even on your last chance, Richard. It's beyond that. Let's just catch this killer. We can figure out the rest later."

Sarah left the room. Richard grabbed his jacket and quickly followed.

CHAPTER
TWENTY

THE UNIVERSITY WAS A MAZE, and it took them twenty minutes of asking around to find the main offices. Upon flashing their badges, a senior administrator called the dean, who was less than happy to be disturbed. Nonetheless, the stuffy old man with a horseshoe haircut was cooperative, and he eventually confirmed Oliver Morton was a history student domiciled in Bailey Court.

That's where Sarah and Richard were now, heading up the stairs to the first floor – specifically to 'Room Three' where Oliver purportedly lived. They passed by students on their way, but no one stopped them or asked them why they were there, too wrapped up in their own plans to care. It wasn't until they reached Oliver Morton's room that anyone approached them.

Sarah was just about to knock on the door when a young girl called out. She was Asian and pretty, and spoke with a refined English accent. "Are you looking for Oliver Morton?"

Sarah turned and nodded. "Yes, do you know him?"

Her scars clearly took the girl aback, as she flinched and then stuttered. "I-I'm his girlfriend. I've been trying to get hold of him since yesterday. Is he okay?"

"We're looking for him too."

The girl folded her arms and turned defensive. "May I ask who you are? You look like a pair of bailiffs."

Sarah showed her badge. "Inspectors. We need to ask Oliver a few questions."

"About what, precisely? Claudette Herrington?"

Richard chimed in, raising his chin with interest. "What would make you say that?"

"You interviewed Oliver once already about it, but he doesn't know anything, so I don't know why you're bothering him. He barely even knew Claudette. She wasn't…" She shrugged her slender shoulders. "She wasn't particularly nice, I'm afraid to say."

Sarah thought it a little harsh to denigrate a dead girl, but there may well have been good reasons. Best to find out. "Why do you say Claudette wasn't nice?"

The girl shrugged and averted her eyes, as if ashamed of what she had just said. "Her mother is a fancy lawyer in London. Claudette used to threaten people all the time if they got on her bad side. She even sued the university last year because she claimed they were giving better marks to foreign students like me. I don't know if there's any substance to the accusations, but the uni quickly gave in and upped Claudette's grade. She always got whatever she wanted, no matter what. And when it came to boys…" The girl shook her head and pulled a face. "She got whatever she wanted then, too."

"Fine," Sarah said. "She was an entitled brat at a top university. Not a reason for her to be murdered, though, is it?"

"No, no, you're right, of course. I didn't mean that at all. I was simply informing you that Oliver didn't associate with Claudette Herrington, and that there are plenty of other people you should be bothering about her death."

"Her murder," Richard corrected.

"Semantics," she said, a little standoffishly.

"We just need to ask Oliver a few questions," Sarah said again, as friendly as she could make herself sound with so much adrenaline in her system. She wanted to get her hands on the young student so badly it was making her dizzy. "It's important that we speak with him. Do you know where he might be?"

"I told you. I haven't seen him for over twenty-four hours, and he's not answering my calls. I'm worried actually."

Richard stepped forward. "Worried? Do you think something might have happened to Oliver?"

She leaned back, away from him. "Well, I have no way of knowing, do I? But I don't see a reason for him not to answer my calls, and no one else has seen him since yesterday, either."

"Are you genuinely worried?"

"Yes, a little bit. He's my boyfriend."

Richard looked her right in the eye. "Is it possible Oliver may have hurt himself?"

"What? No. Oliver wasn't depressed or anything like that."

"Are you sure? Because, if you're worried, we can check out his room right now and see if he's okay. If you're saying there's zero possibility that he's hurt himself, then fine, but if not…"

The girl's face slowly drained of colour. "Well, he has been having problems with his dad lately, and he's been very distracted. Oh God, what if I missed it? What if he did something stupid because I was too selfish to see that he needed help?"

"Would you like us to check, ma'am?"

The girl nodded.

Sarah banged on the door. "Oliver Morton, this is Detective Inspector Sarah Stone. We've been asked to perform a wellness check. Can you open the door, please?"

No answer.

Sarah went through the routine again.

Still no answer.

"Kick it in," Richard said.

She looked at him. "Do I have grounds?"

"Oliver Morton might be in need of medical attention. His

girlfriend has communicated to us that she has a legitimate concern for his welfare." He moved closer and whispered to Sarah. "Frances."

Sarah nodded, stepped back, and unleashed a kick right below the door's handle. It broke open in one hit, the doorframe cheap and thin. The door banged against the inside wall, but it didn't bounce back due to the raised fibres of the navy-blue carpet biting hold of it.

Oliver's room was like an army barrack – bedsheets pulled tightly around a single mattress and not a single thing out of place. His desk chair was pushed all the way in and his bookshelf was neatly stacked. This was an orderly place.

Of an organised killer?

"Oh thank God," said the girl. "He's not here."

"He might still be in trouble though," Richard told her. "Is there anything here out of place?"

She looked around and shook her head. "All Oliver cares about are his history books. He studies harder than anyone I know. I think he's a genius."

Sarah nodded at Richard. "I have one of those. Insufferable, aren't they?"

The girl smiled. "At times. Tell me honestly, why do you want to speak to Oliver? Is it just to help with your investigations, or is it something else?"

"We believe he might know something that can help us," Sarah said soothingly. She didn't have enough evidence to risk impugning Oliver's reputation with his girlfriend. "You say he likes to study a lot, but what are his interests?"

She rolled her eyes. "His studies are his interest. If I had a pound for every time I caught him with his head in a book, I'd have no space left in my flat. Especially that one right there. He's always reading it." She shuffled over to the bookshelf and grabbed a thick tome with a muted brown spine. Sarah tilted her head to read the title as the girl lifted it: *Feudalism and the Middle Ages* by J. Millis.

As Oliver's girlfriend turned the book around to show the cover, the pages fluttered unnaturally, as if the insides of the book were falling apart. Something fell to the ground. "Huh?" She seemed confused, and she slowly turned the book around to show Richard and Sarah the interior. "There's a hole in it."

Sarah stepped forward and gasped. A square compartment had been hollowed out of the book's pages. A poor man's safe.

Richard knelt down to pick up the object that had fallen out of the hidden recess. It appeared to be a plastic bag with something inside. He shook it slightly and held it up to the light. Then he glanced over at the young girl. "What's your name?"

"Prue Li-Kashing."

"Well, Prue, I need you to exit this room, please. It's now a crime scene." He straightened up and held the bag out in front of Sarah's face. It took her a moment to realise that it was full of women's fingernails.

Oliver Morton was the Durham Butcher.

AKA the Student of Death.

―――

The police were on scene twenty minutes later, and during that time, Sarah had found a bundle of letters in Oliver Morton's desk. Felix Flesch had written them, and it appeared the two of them had been in contact for a while, although it was unclear how they had first got in touch. The content of the letters was sickening, and Felix had clearly been getting off by discussing his many vile acts, going into so much detail that it was more like fetishistic porn than a factual account. He referred to Oliver throughout as his 'student', but the letters also mentioned Richard several times, always referring to him as 'Worm'. That was how Oliver knew so much about Richard.

Sarah had read the letters aloud at first, but when Richard became upset, she switched to reading silently, reciting only the most pertinent information.

"What do you think this means?" she asked, standing out in the hallway while the police searched inside Oliver's room. Richard was standing beside her, deep in thought. He looked at her now as she spoke. "Your dad says, here and here, that he want's Oliver to 'restore my place to its former glory'. He says it twice. What do you think it means?"

He shrugged, sullen and distracted. "Continuing his crimes I suppose."

"Really? Oliver's crimes are different from your father's. He's not a cannibal or a rapist. There's no continuation of legacy. Do you think…"

"What?"

"Restore my place to its former glory?" She chewed at her bottom lip for a moment. "Do you think he actually means a place? We've been trying to figure out where Oliver is taking his victims after he abducts them. Maybe your dad provided the location."

Richard frowned as if he didn't buy what she was saying, but then something seemed to dawn on him. "Wait! Do you have the video of Frances on your phone?"

She grimaced. "I've watched it a dozen times, trying to figure out where it could be."

"Show it to me."

Nodding, Sarah pulled out her phone and unlocked it. She located the video attached to her email and hit play. Richard leant in while she held the screen up to him. His eyes were like two swirling brown pools of poison.

Sarah knew the video frame by frame by now. A dusty room with a featureless concrete slab for a floor. A bare lightbulb hanging from a long brown wire. Oily stains on the floor.

Richard shook his head, over and over. "Why didn't I see it before? It's so obvious."

"What?" Sarah felt her heart skip a beat. "It's another location from your past? You know where this is?"

"Yes." He looked at her. "It's where I grew up."

CHAPTER
TWENTY-ONE

RICHARD CALLED and updated James while Sarah gunned the Range Rover down the A167, overtaking dangerously but unable to think about anything besides Frances. They knew where she was, but were they too late?

The satnav said six minutes remaining.

The muted lights and historical ambience of Durham faded away behind them as they headed away from civilisation and into the countryside bordering Chester-le-Street. It seemed you never had to travel far in County Durham to lose yourself amongst fields, farmland, and towering wind turbines.

And somewhere amongst those fields and wind turbines was a house of horror.

Richard finished his call with James. He was sweating, and visibly agitated by the thought of going home after all these years. Would he lose it again? Despite her earlier conversation with James, Sarah had not taken a Taser along with her, so she was unarmed. The bruised fingermarks on her neck began to throb.

"James is sending the police," Richard informed her, "but we're probably going to arrive first."

"We can't wait on them. We can't delay." She turned to him

for a second, her hands gripping the steering wheel hard enough to make the plastic creak. "How is your family's farm still standing after what happened there?"

"Because my father still owns it. I'm assuming the local authorities just sealed the place up and left it to rot."

"It was rotting when you lived there."

"You're right, but it must be falling down by now. It's been abandoned for nearly twenty years."

They entered a windy country road with cobbled walls on either side. It forced Sarah to slow down a little, which caused her to curse under her breath.

She shook her head, trying to make sense of everything. "How did Oliver and your dad end up in contact? How would they ever even meet?"

"All I can think is that Oliver is a fan of my father's. Serial killers often find kinship with others like them. My dad thinks he's a superior species to the rest of us. Perhaps Oliver Morton thinks the same."

"Maybe." She turned on her high beams, struggling to see the bends coming. The last thing they needed was to crash. "So… your dad referred to you in his letters as 'Worm'. That what he used to call you as a kid?"

Richard stared out of his window at the night sky. It was half past ten. "It started as a joke about my penis being too small." He shrugged. "Maybe it is. What do I care?"

"Do you ever…" She cleared her throat. "Do you ever get the urge to use it?"

"To have sex? I think that part of me is buried forever. I'll never have a normal, consensual relationship, so I don't waste time worrying about it. Eventually, I think my body came to terms with it too."

She looked at him and saw that he was serious. He truly believed there was no chance of ever being with a woman in a healthy way. No hope for love or companionship. A deep loneliness existed within him. She should have spotted it earlier.

"You never know what life has in store for you," she said, feeling pity on him for the first time. "Take a look at me. A couple of weeks ago, my life was boring. Now I'm chasing serial killers in a place so far north that I can almost hear the Scottish yelling obscenities."

He turned to her, expressionless. "I guess you're right."

"Take it from someone older and wiser. Life exists in chapters. You just have to keep turning the page."

Then they were silent for the rest of the journey, eating up the final few miles that would take them to their final destination: Flexley Yard Farm.

———

It had to be night, thought Richard, as he returned home under the cover of darkness, like a skulking beast retiring to its lair. The sun's purity, and the honesty of its light were many hours away, and the moon was afraid to come out, barely visible against the ink-black sky.

This was a land of the dead, echoing with the screams of the tortured and mutilated.

"I'll turn on the high beams," Sarah said quietly. "There's no way to do this stealthily."

Richard nodded in agreement. Better to be able to see than to go in blind. The farmhouse was likely a deathtrap after all these years.

The high beams flicked on, and Flexley Yard Farm appeared before them. Its white stone walls were now grey and crumbled, scarred by time and neglect. The branches of overgrown trees scraped against the roof and had already knocked down dozens of tiles. Weeds and long grass had overtaken the gravel courtyard.

"You okay?" Sarah asked him, moving up to join him in front of the car. Blocking the high beams, their shadows were giants upon the landscape.

"It's changed," he said. "It's like nature's trying to pull this place down into the earth, to erase it from existence."

"Nature's good like that. I asked if you're okay?"

He shook his head. "I'm a monster, and this is where I was born. But the only thing I prey on now is other monsters. Let's go get Frances."

She looked him in the eye and nodded.

He was being honest about not being okay. Okay was something he could never hope to be, because he was twisted and broken, like barbed wire wrapped around splintered bone. But he was no longer a killer. Echoes of horror, misery, and death surrounded him, but not desire. He had zero desire to kill.

"Come on," he said, tapping Sarah on the back of her arm. "Frances is in the cellar. I recognise the floor."

Sarah shuddered and clutched at herself. "Just when I thought this place couldn't get any creepier, there's a cellar."

Richard said nothing. The time for words was over. Frances needed them now.

He crept through the long grass, his work shoes slipping on the moist roots. Every dip in the ground felt familiar, mapped out by his childhood steps. The fenced-off paddock to the east conjured the ghosts of mewing lambs, as well as their screams whenever his father slit their throats.

The front door to the farmhouse was missing, probably lying somewhere amongst the long grass. The space where it had used to be was now a featureless black rectangle, an entrance to a hellish abyss. His father's voice sounded inside, yelling and cursing. Anger. Rage. Hunger. Richard had never truly left this place. A part of him would always reside here.

Sarah stopped beside the open doorway and peered inside. Richard stood on the other side and did the same. The hallway inside was empty. The bare stone floor had cracked into pieces, and someone had taken away his mother's old wooden bureau.

Richard stepped inside and quivered, like he was plunging into icy water. For a moment, his senses froze up completely, leaving him unable to breathe. But then he snapped back to life, refreshed and alert. "This way," he whispered.

Sarah crept along behind him, bent at the knees. Neither of them were armed, but they only needed to take on one young man between them. A young man who might have been unprepared for them to find him here.

But he would have heard us arrive. He would have seen the headlights.

Where are you, Oliver Morton?

They reached the end of the dusty hallway, where they could continue into the kitchen or turn right into the parlour. The door to the cellar, however, was on the left. Richard tried the door, but it refused to open. Almost without thinking, he put his foot underneath the door and lifted. It pulled the warped wood away from the frame and unstuck it.

"Old hinges," he said when he saw Sarah's eyes glinting in the darkness beside him.

"Place hasn't changed much, huh?"

"Unfortunately."

Richard didn't need to see the stairs to use them. His feet found every step by instinct, having gone down them a hundred times before. But there the familiarity ended. The stench of death was gone, replaced by a mouldy stink, and the animalistic grunts of his father were no longer to be heard.

This is where you tortured us, Richard's victims whispered in his ear. *You took us from our families. You extinguished everything good inside us.*

I'm sorry.

Your apologies are worthless.

I know.

I trusted you, Richard.

And you saved me, Sadie. You showed me what humanity looked like.

I showed you what you will never have.

Sarah put a hand on Richard's back, which caused him to

flinch, but he realised she was only doing it to keep from falling on the pitch-black stairs. He descended slowly, guiding her step by step.

The darkness lifted several feet below. The cellar light was on.

Richard reached the bottom of the stairs and stepped out into the open.

Frances's eyes were closed. Her body was slumped forward on the Spanish donkey. The air smelled stale.

We're too late. Damn it, we're too late.

Sarah reached the bottom of the stairs behind Richard and then immediately pushed her way past. She raced over to Frances and lifted the girl's head. Her frizzy hair was damp with sweat. "Frances? Frances, please wake up. Please don't be dead."

"Sarah. I think we're too late."

"No! We're not losing anyone else to this sick bastard." She shook Frances by the shoulders, and her body flopped lifelessly like a rag doll. The hanging light bulb in the centre of the low ceiling highlighted Frances's injuries in graphic detail. Dark, sticky blood stained the crotch of her pale-yellow jumpsuit where it met the wooden wedge. Several dumbbell weights hung from her ankles.

Sarah shook Frances a little less frantically, slowly coming to terms with the situation. The girl was gone. They were too late.

Frances's eyes sprang open. A pained gasp escaped her lips.

Sarah leapt back, taken by surprise, but then she was right back on Frances, hugging her tightly. "You're alive? Shit. Oh. F-Frances, you're okay. It's okay. We've got you, sweetheart. It's gonna be all right."

"S-Sarah? Help me." She came to consciousness quickly. "Please. Help me. Get me out of here. Help me." Hysteria took over, and she let out a scream.

Sarah tried to shush the girl, tried to keep her calm.

Richard peered around the cellar, aware that Oliver Morton

could still be on the scene. Shadows drenched the cellar's corners, but nothing seemed to move within them. He looked back at the stairwell, but saw nothing beyond a few feet. At the far end of the room was a rickety metal door that he knew led to a small cupboard space with a sink and some shelving. He didn't think there was room enough for someone to hide there, although he had fitted as a child.

"Help me get her off of here," Sarah yelled. "Richard!"

He rushed over and grabbed Frances by the other arm, but her hands were bound behind her back and her legs beneath the bench. Every time they moved her, she wailed in agony.

"Get the weights," Sarah yelled at Richard, and he immediately dropped to his knees, feeling the familiar cold cement through the fabric of his trousers. The dumbbell weights had been attached with cable ties. He had nothing to cut them with and didn't know what to do. Searching the ground desperately, he wished he could find a tool from his father's old torture kit, left behind by incompetent police investigators.

But the cold, cracked floor was empty.

Empty of everything except broken chunks of cement that time had pulled loose.

Richard grabbed a shard of rubble shaped like a V and scraped it against the floor repeatedly, sharpening one edge. When he was confident it could cut, he got to work on the cable ties.

"We should have come better armed," Sarah said, looking around as she cradled Frances. "Fuck, where are the local police?"

"They're coming," Richard said, trying to concentrate through Frances's agonised begging and the dizzying scent of her blood. The floor was damp with what must have been urine.

He sawed and sawed and sawed at the cable ties attached to the weights. The plastic had dug into the flesh of Frances's ankles, exposing raw flesh.

The dumbbell weight clunked against the ground, cracking the old cement further.

Frances moaned, but there was a twang of relief to her pain.

"Good," Sarah said. "Now do the other one. Quickly!"

Richard sawed at the cable tie around her other leg, and the weight came free a lot quicker than the other one had, so he got to work on the cable ties securing her bare feet beneath the bench. When they snapped away, Frances moaned almost orgasmically, her entire body quivering as her legs spread apart.

But her relief didn't last long. As Sarah and Richard slid her off the wooden wedge, she bellowed in agony. Blood stained the thighs of her jumpsuit and she was grotesquely bowlegged. She needed medical attention ASAP. Sarah lay her down on the ground and started stroking her head as she faded from consciousness.

"I'm glad you're here," Richard told Sarah, realising how much he needed her; how much he needed her compassion.

"Just call an ambulance."

He nodded and reached into his pocket to retrieve his phone.

Shuffling footsteps sounded on the cold, hard steps.

"I wouldn't do that." Oliver Morton stood half in shadow at the bottom of the staircase. He was pointing a small, antique-looking crossbow at Richard. "We don't want it to get overcrowded in here. Do we, Dad?"

CHAPTER
TWENTY-TWO

RICHARD BLINKED, the glare of the naked lightbulb suddenly too bright. He wasn't sure he had heard correctly, so he asked Oliver Morton to repeat himself.

Oliver's grin seemed to glow in the shadows, his canines on full display, giving him a wolf-like appearance. Dressed in a black hoodie and joggers, there was little doubt he was the one who had attacked Sarah in the alleyway. "I think you heard me well enough." He pointed a wooden crossbow pistol at Frances, who was trembling, half-conscious on the floor. "The family business is thriving. Aren't you proud?"

"You called me 'Dad'."

He continued to grin. "The rotten apple that fell from your tree."

"You're not my son. How could you be?"

"The usual way. You stuck your dick in a woman and she had your baby. Wow, you really are detached from reality, huh? I'm surprised they even let you out of Broadmoor."

Sarah remained on the ground with Frances, but she was watching the conversation play out with interest. Richard didn't know if she was planning to act, but he was pretty sure he couldn't move his feet right now. "W-who?" he asked in a pitiful voice. "I don't understand."

"Who? The one that got away, of course. Who else could it have been? You killed all the others. How many bodies did they find in this place? Twenty?"

"Twenty-seven."

"Wow. I'm not even close to meeting that number, but I think I get extra points for creativity. We're a dynasty, Dad. Three generations of apex predators."

"Why are you doing this, Oliver? I don't understand."

"Dad, Dad, Dad, I thought you were smarter than this." He shook his head and chuckled. "This all started with the one you couldn't bring yourself to kill. Poor Sadie, remember her? It was cruel that you let her live. You broke her and abandoned her."

Richard felt woozy, drunk on the stench of blood and the toxic kiss of bad memories. "S-Sadie Amberson? You're her son? B-but she never had a family."

Oliver's cheeriness went away, replaced with something ugly – something Richard knew was a family resemblance. He saw his father, and he saw himself. "She could have had a family, she could have been a mother, but she gave me away as soon as I was born. Because I was your son. Because she saw you whenever she looked at me."

"You were adopted?" Richard took a step forward, but stopped when Oliver pointed the crossbow at him.

"Adopted by a young couple who were divorced by the time I was three. Apparently, having me didn't help their marriage. Dad left, Mum became an alky, and I haven't spoken to either in years. Families… am I right?"

Sarah finally spoke out, with Frances passed out in her arms. "How did you find out Sadie Amberson was your real mother? It would have been confidential."

Oliver shrugged, as if they were having a casual conversation at a cafe. Richard knew this was all a part of his egotistical need for attention. This was his moment, his audience. "I sent a request via the adoption agency," he explained. "You see, there was this great big hole inside me that nothing would fill; some sense of the unknown that I needed to explore. The agency contacted Sadie and asked if she wanted to see me. When she said yes, I was actually thrilled. I suppose she thought she at least owed me a meeting after tossing me away as a baby, but I hoped maybe it was more than that. Maybe she wanted me in her life."

"And did she?" Richard asked.

"I'm still not entirely sure." He took a step away from the staircase, leaving the shadows behind him. "Things were good at first – we met up a few times and we spoke on the phone – but she would never tell me who my dad was. Well, not until one night when she got pissed on two bottles of wine and totally lost it. She said I was the spawn of the Devil and that I was just like you – just like Richard Flesch, the Chester-le-Street Cannibal. It was quite the shock, but that was the night I learned who I really was, the son of a legend. The emptiness inside me was gone in an instant and as I wrapped a cable around Sadie's neck and strung her up from the living room light, I discovered who I was meant to be. Watching her dangle gave me the stiffest boner of my life, I swear."

"She was your mother, you sick fuck." Sarah sounded like she wanted to throw up, and she was clearly in two minds about whether to let go of Frances and launch at him, but the crossbow kept her at bay. Oliver only had one arrow, but it would be hard for him to miss up close like this.

Oliver tilted his head slightly to look at his watch. "Police should be here by now, don't you think? I swear, this country's going to the dogs. People don't fear the repercussions of their actions any more."

Sarah placed Frances carefully down on the ground and stood up. "And what about you? Do you think you're going to get away with this?"

He looked at her with dripping contempt. "Are you stupid?

Of course I don't expect to get away with it. You've clearly identified me, and I've had about fifty texts from my girlfriend telling me the police raided my room and found my little bag of treats. No, you brainless bitch, I do not expect to get away with this. In fact, getting caught is kind of the whole point. My only regret is that it's so soon. I had some really great plans."

Richard put a hand out, worried that Sarah might act rashly and get a steel bolt in the guts. The crossbow was old and rusty. "Why do you want to be caught? Is it notoriety you're after?"

"Everybody these days wants a platform, but how do you cut through the noise, with all the vapid Instagram whores and TikTok clowns? To be seen and heard these days, you have to go big. Shock and awe, that's what the people want. This is my opportunity to speak to the world and tell the peasants to be afraid. Monsters like me are lurking around every corner, waiting to feast on their misery. You, me, Grandpa... we're only one family, yet we've preyed upon dozens of the vain and mindless. Don't you see? We punish the world for its sins. It's in our blood."

"Is that what this is?" Richard asked, unable to fully disguise his scorn. "Is that why you killed those innocent women? Claudette Herrington was entitled, and she trampled over people to get what she wanted? How about Caroline and Mona? What did they do?"

Oliver scowled and raised the crossbow a little higher. "What did they do? What did they do? Mona Lewis let her three-year-old daughter drown in a pool in Benidorm because she was passed out on a sunbed from too many sangrias. She should've been sentenced to life in prison, but she faked enough tears that a jury took pity on her. As for Caroline Boswell, well she—"

"Blah, blah, blah," Sarah said, pulling a face. "They were all bad. They needed to be judged. I am the one who decides their fate. I am powerful. I am God. I am an impotent, woman-hating loser. Jesus, dude, do you think you're original? You're a one-off

Netflix special at best. The world is full of angry, violent sociopaths like you. Nobody's interested any more. We're all just getting on with it."

Oliver was clearly stunned. His eyes were like flat brown discs, catching only the slightest of light. His mouth hung open and his tongue poked in and out of his lips. "W-what the fuck did you just say?"

"You heard me well enough," she said, echoing his earlier words. "You're just a nutcase. Don't you see that? Don't you realise that every serial killer in history thought themselves righteous in some way? They all had some twisted version of the truth in their head, but they all ended up the same way – locked up and forgotten about. The world moves too fast to care. Once you're behind bars, you're last week's news."

"My actions have shocked the nation. My work is on the front page of every newspaper."

She shrugged. "I remember when the papers went wild about Tesco selling horse meat. Nothing sticks for very long."

What is she doing? Richard thought. *She's trying to make him angry.*

Oliver closed his eyes for a second and took a breath inwards. The crossbow wavered in his hand, and he might have been trembling in anger. "You don't know anything. You're just a stupid, ugly bitch. I'm gonna scar the other side of your face."

"Easy," Richard said, raising a hand. His mind was reeling, and he couldn't process that this might be his son, but he knew things were spiralling out of hand. Sarah was prodding an egotistical killer.

What game is she playing?

"I should have smashed your brains in that night," Oliver said, still glaring at Sarah. "I should have killed you."

"Yeah," Sarah said, upper lip curling. "You should have."

Without warning, she threw herself forward, deceptively quick as she started her movement down low, where Oliver's eyeline failed to reach. By the time he reacted, she had both hands out, reaching for the crossbow.

Richard tried to move, but his feet were rooted to the floor. He was standing in the cellar where he had helped butcher two dozen people with his father. And now he was a father of a killer too.

Oliver's my son.

Sadie and I had a son.

No, said Sadie. *You violated me, and this is the vile result.*

Sarah grunted and doubled over. For a moment, Richard feared she'd been shot, but the loaded crossbow was now pointed at the ceiling. Both she and Oliver fought over it, and while Oliver was the bigger and stronger of the two, Sarah had planted her feet better and was twisting his wrists to keep him on the defensive.

She wouldn't be able to keep it up for long though.

I need to move.

I need to help her.

I… I need to stop my son from hurting anyone else. Every one of his murders is because of me. I created him.

"Richard, help me," Sarah called out breathlessly. "Get over here and he—"

Oliver headbutted her in the nose, causing her to lose her grip on the crossbow. Snarling like a wolf, he levelled the weapon at her and readjusted his grip on the handle. Before he could pull the trigger, though, Sarah lashed out with a kick and struck him in the stomach. It knocked the wind out of him and sent him reeling backwards across the room.

"Richard!" she yelled again. "Grab him."

"I… I can't."

"Goddamn it." Sarah raced forward, trying to keep the pressure on and keep Oliver from taking a shot. She launched another kick, but this time she missed as Oliver leapt backwards to give himself some space. Unable to see behind him, he collided against the metal door that led to the cupboard.

Oliver lifted the crossbow. Aimed right at Sarah's chest.

Sarah was too far away to avoid being shot, several feet between her and the crossbow.

She skidded to a halt and threw up her hands. "Wait!"

Oliver snarled. "Time to die, bitch."

Richard watched in horror. *I have to move. I have to help Sarah.*

Sadie spoke in his ear. *Save a life. Do something right.*

Richard unplanted his feet and leapt forward. Sarah was several steps ahead of him, but he moved every muscle at once and propelled himself through the cellar. Rather than try to get to Oliver, or distract him from shooting, he shoved Sarah as hard as he could, sending her flying.

Richard let out a massive *oof* as all the air got punched out of his lungs.

Sarah hit the ground hard, landing on her side. She looked up at Richard through dazed and confused eyes. "Richard? What the hell?"

Oliver, still standing by the cupboard door, let out a whistle. He lowered the crossbow and nodded approvingly. "Wow! You launched that bitch. Nice one."

Richard chuckled, but he wasn't sure why. He felt lightheaded, his head full of buzzing.

"Richard," Sarah moaned, still lying on the ground. "Richard…"

He turned to her, sorry he had hurt her, and no longer even sure why he had pushed her in the first place. His confusion only grew when his legs folded involuntary and he fell to his knees. As his chin hit his chest, a dark stain began to bloom on his white shirt. Something was sticking out of him. He placed a hand around the thin metal object and gave it a tug, but it was stuck. Stuck inside him.

Everything started to get dark.

―――

Police sirens blared in the distance, muffled by the farmhouse floors and walls above them. Help was here, but time had run out.

Sarah's pelvis was numb from impacting against the cement floor, and when she tried to get up, her legs wouldn't work. In front of her, Richard had slunk back on his heels with a rusty metal bolt sticking out of his ribs.

He pushed me out of the way. That shot was meant for me.

Oliver Morton was unarmed, but he wasn't beaten. Tossing down the now-useless crossbow, he produced a nasty-looking stiletto blade from a sheath inside his hoodie's front pocket. He pointed the sharpened tip at Sarah, a dark fury on his face. "You just made me shoot my own father! Do you have any idea the trauma that can cause?"

Sarah dragged herself across the ground, fighting to get feeling back in her lower extremities. She crawled towards Frances, wanting to try to protect the girl, if nothing else.

Oliver didn't pursue her, probably realising she wasn't going anywhere for now. Instead, his focus turned to Richard. He grabbed his father by the jaw and forced him to look at him. "Why do you fight it? Why not give in to nature and be what you are?"

Richard was still alive, but breathless and weak. When he spoke, he wheezed out the words. "I-I never got a chance to be who I am. Never had a... choice."

"There is no choice in what we are. We're born killers. There's no shame in it. In the Dark Ages we would've been headsmen, or great warriors and knights. We could have been battlefield heroes striking fear into our enemies. When did killing become wrong? When did it stop being a part of human nature?"

"It's not the Dark Ages, Oliver. You need to stop. You don't have to be a monster like me."

Oliver shoved the steel spike against Richard's Adam's apple. "I'm a Flesch. It's in my blood. And there are others like us. I will inspire them. It's my destiny to speak on their behalf."

"You could have been normal. You could have…"

Sarah shuffled her legs back and forth across the cement, slowly regaining control of them. Frances murmured on the ground beside her. She stank of blood and urine and sweat. If she didn't get help soon, she would die from blood loss or infection. "Hold on, sweetheart. Help is coming."

She opened her eyes, her eyelids drooping. "W-where is he?"

"Who?"

"The killer."

Sarah frowned. Frances was looking right at Oliver Morton, who was still snarling in Richard's face. "He's over there, but don't worry. The police are right upstairs. I'll keep you safe until they arrive."

Frances shook her head weakly. "No, the other one. The… the professor."

Sarah's eyes went wide.

Oliver raised the stiletto to the side of Richard's neck. Baring his teeth, he was red with rage. "We could have worked together. Father and son. You, me, Grandpa, and Professor Irving. We could have changed the world."

Richard teetered back and forth, his voice barely above a whisper. "The professor? Irving-Ross?"

Sarah yelled out a warning just as a high-pitched squeal filled the cellar. The metal door at the back of the room burst open and a figure leapt out. Irving-Ross took Oliver by surprise, grabbing him from behind and yanking him backwards so hard that he was flailing on his tiptoes. "You fool. You told them my name."

Oliver started to apologise, but it was too late. Professor Irving-Ross drew a nasty-looking chef's knife across the lad's windpipe and shoved him to the ground like a sack of rubbish. Oliver thrashed wildly on the cement, kicking his legs out and clutching at his throat, but within ten seconds it was all over. Dark red blood pooled around his neck.

Richard slumped to the ground right beside Oliver, bleeding from wounds of his own.

Sarah was alone in the cellar with Irving-Ross. Frances was in and out of consciousness and unable to get up. Trying to escape would mean leaving her behind.

I won't do that.

Sarah climbed to her feet. Irving-Ross watched her with a venomous smile on his lips. He clearly intended to play. In fact, he was dressed for it in a pair of blue overalls.

"You really shouldn't have barged into my classroom, Ms Stone. I can't abide rudeness."

"It's Captain Stone. I can't abide it either, Professor."

His grin stretched wider. "Touché."

Sarah looked past him, at Oliver Morton's body. "Why kill him? Weren't you partners?"

"Far from it. He was a student and I was master. Oliver was supposed to take credit for the murders and rally the bloodthirsty from his cell. But then he had to go and implicate me. That boy, he was all impulse. I could have comfortably waited things out in that dreadful little cupboard, but he made it impossible, so now my only chance is to kill you and try to escape without being seen. With any luck the police will find Oliver and assume he and his father killed each other, with you ladies simply caught in the middle."

"They'll catch you. You've made too many mistakes."

"I have made no mistakes. Everything I have done has been with the utmost precision." He stepped towards her, brandishing the knife. "Now, hold still."

Here we go. Time to live or die.

Sarah launched herself on her half-numb legs and grabbed for the knife. A flash of pain tore through the back of her right forearm, but she managed to get her hands around the professor's wrist before he could stab her. Catching him by surprise, she shoved him backwards into the brick wall and drove her knee into his stomach. He bellowed in pain, but he didn't drop the knife. He had almost a full foot of height over her, but he was not a well-built man.

And he has a dodgy leg.

Sarah kicked at his shins, causing him to cry out shrilly.

Above her, she heard shouting, police officers trying to secure the scene.

Hurry your arses up.

Irving-Ross tried to shove Sarah away, but she buried her shoulder in his chest and used all her strength to keep him pinned. All she needed to do was keep him contained for a few more minutes.

"I'll kill you," he snarled. "Just like I killed all those other useless women."

"Why?" she asked, grunting with exertion. "Why kill them?"

"Because they were vapid harlots who needed punishing, like the drunken wretch who ran me over after too many beers at the student union, or the bitch who closed down the mines and ruined my grandfather's life. Women need to know their place. Things need to go back to how they were, when Britain was great."

Sarah ground her head against his ribs, trying to keep him from taking a proper breath. "Women got out of the kitchen a long time ago," she grunted, "and you'll never get us back in. We see through the weak, jealous little men like you."

He roared at the top of her head and redoubled his efforts to get away. She did everything she could to keep him off balance.

"You disfigured detritus. I'll strip you of your insides."

"I bet you say that to all the girls. Give it up, Professor, it's over. The police are upstairs right now. Don't you hear them?"

He grunted and struggled. "Then killing you will have to be the last good thing I do."

Sarah's foot slipped as Irving-Ross brought up his knee and

caught her in the flesh of her thigh. She tried to right herself, but it caused her to lose concentration on keeping her hands on the knife. Irving-Ross yanked his hand across his chest and managed to strike her in the jaw with his elbow. By the time the stars cleared, Sarah was falling onto her back as Irving-Ross kicked her legs out from under her. She tried to get back up, but he dropped on top of her, his face a mask of hatred in the glare of the naked lightbulb.

The first punch felt like a hammer hitting her cheek. The second one she barely felt. She imagined the third and fourth would send her into a sleep she would never wake from. Unable to do anything else, she spat blood at him. "I-is that the best you got?"

He sneered right in her face, her blood dripping off his chin. "You really shouldn't have come here unarmed, you foolish woman."

"She didn't come unarmed," said a voice behind him. "She brought me."

Sarah blinked as blood spattered across her face. Richard was standing behind Irving-Ross, Oliver's stiletto in his hand. He stab-stab-stabbed it into Irving-Ross's jugular, over and over again, a dozen times in a matter of seconds. He was possessed, glassy-eyed and open-mouthed, and still stabbing long after the professor was dead. Blood poured out of the man's ruined neck, soaking Sarah underneath. Eventually, she had to shove the slumped body off of her and shove Richard back.

"It's over," she yelled at him. "Over!"

Richard stared at her, but his mind was someplace else, someplace dark. Sarah didn't know if it was safe to approach him, so she kept her distance.

"It's over, Richard," she said again, clutching her forearm, which was sliced wide open. "You're at the beach, enjoying the sun and sand. You're making sandcastles for the first time in your life, feeling like a little kid. It's the best day of your life, because it was the day you learned you could be normal, and that you didn't want to hurt anybody."

His eyes flickered, a little life returning to the tiny pinpricks of his pupils.

"And you rode on a little train that goes up and down the hill. What are those called again?"

"Funicular," he muttered vacantly.

Sarah nodded and smiled. "That's right. Not quite like a train. Hey, what was the first train to ever take passengers from A to B?"

"Locomotion No.1."

"It ran to Darlington, right? Huh, James told me all about that when we first met. You know, James? We all work together at the Institute. You and me are partners. Like Mulder and, um…"

"Scully."

"Who played her again?"

He blinked and then stared at her. "Gillian Anderson. She's British, but she played an American, Dana Scully."

"That's right. Richard, are you here with me?"

He looked down at the professor, and then at his bloody hands. "S-Sarah? Sarah, what have I done?"

"You took down the professor and saved me. Everything's okay."

"No, it's not. It's not." He started shaking his head, bloody hands trembling in front of him. "I killed again. I'm the Chester-le-Street Cannibal. It's in my blood. I can't stop. I can't stop killing."

Damn it. He's losing it.

Sarah hopped forward and threw her arms around him in a hug. He was tense at first, but then she heard the stiletto clatter to the floor, and he collapsed into her arms, sobbing and trembling like a frightened little boy. "I'm Richard Flesch," he said in a high-pitched squeal. "Not Richard Mullins. I'm a monster. A murderer. A monster. A murderer."

She stroked his back and spoke softly. "You're not a monster. Richard Flesch is your past. Now you're my partner, DI Mullins. Monsters fear you, because you know them better than they know themselves. You did it. You caught the killers and put a stop to their evil. People are going to live because of you."

He continued to tremble and sob in her arms, and he didn't manage to say anything else.

Someone cleared their throat behind Sarah, causing her to rotate with Richard in her arms – a strange kind of waltz. Once she was facing the staircase, she saw DCI Flannigan standing there with her police cap in her hands. The woman was shaking her head and surveying the carnage in the room. Frances was out cold beneath the naked lightbulb. Oliver and Professor Irving-Ross were dead on opposite sides of the room.

"Seems like we got here a little late," Flannigan said.

Sarah nodded, squeezing Richard protectively and praying he didn't say anything that would put him in hot water. "I'd say a lot late. How much of that did you hear?"

Flannigan stared at her for what seemed like forever. Eventually, she asked, "How much did I hear of what?"

"Nothing," Sarah said with a sigh. "I'm just glad it's over."

"And yet the paperwork has only just begun. I suggest you take DI *Mullins* upstairs. It looks like the both of you need medical attention. Is it worth getting any down here?"

Sarah pointed to Frances. "She needs urgent help. Make her the priority."

"Will do. Now get out of here while I do my job."

Sarah looked Flannigan in the eye, trying to read her expression. Eventually, the woman gave Sarah a small nod and stepped aside for her to pass. Sarah helped Richard upstairs, muttering that they needed to "burn this place down."

CHAPTER
TWENTY-THREE

SARAH SAT in the sun-drenched gardens of Tithby Hall, allowing her various wounds to warm and heal. James was sitting in the deckchair beside her. "I can manage a twenty per cent increase in pay if you stay," he said.

Sarah groaned. "I said I'll think about it. Stop pestering me. I'm injured."

He scoffed. "It's been over a week. I think you're out of the woods."

"I'm recuperating then. Leave me alone. Or pass another beer."

He did as requested, even popping the tab for her. The crisp, icy lager was like heaven on her tongue. Who'd have thought she'd be seeing out the summer drinking on the grounds of a stately home?

In the North East of all places. Am I a Geordie now? Or is that just Newcastle? Guess I'll have to learn the lingo if I stick around.

If *I stick around.*

She still didn't know if she wanted to stay on with the Institute, but she had to admit it felt good having put a stop to the Durham Butcher and the Student of Death. Her only regret was not figuring out that there were two killers all along. It should have been so obvious.

From what the postgrads in the Hive had figured out, it appeared Irving-Ross had become obsessed with Oliver Morton upon learning who his father was. That the son of a serial-killing family was sitting in his classroom had felt like a green light for his latent fantasies of murdering young women. Oliver Morton, looking to please a substitute father-figure, was willing to take all the blame for the murders, purposely killing Caroline Boswell while Irving-Ross was away in Wales in order to provide him an alibi. The professor had convinced the tormented young man that he was destined to become famous, like Charlie Manson and Fred West, and that in jail he would be royalty. For someone still searching for their place in the world, the temptation had been too hard to resist.

"How is Frances doing?" Sarah asked. She asked it every day.

"She's upbeat, despite everything. Back on her feet, but she needs to take things slowly. Hopefully, her wounds heal… well."

"Yeah. She's a strong one. Let's hope for the best."

She might never get over this. We failed her.

Someone called out to them both from the other side of the grounds. It was Donkey, hobbling towards them at full speed – at least full speed for him. He was waving a piece of paper. "I found it," he cried. "The connection."

James raised an eyebrow. "What?"

He came over to them, grinning. "Irving-Ross's grandfather was George Batchy, the miner who killed Angela Montrose back in the nineties and planned on taking out Thatcher."

Sarah sat up. "Angela Montrose? Claudette Herrington's grandmother?"

"Yes. That's why Claudette was the first murder. Irving-Ross wanted revenge. His grandfather died in prison, an old man, but apparently they were close before he lost his mind. A young

Irving-Ross had to watch his dear old grandpa descend into madness and ruin. It must have deeply affected him."

"His parents must have changed their surname," James said. "To avoid being linked to George Batchy. It caused quite the stir at the time."

Donkey nodded. "Anyway, it looks like both of our killers were third generation killers. It's remarkable. It must be in the blood."

Sarah shook her head. "No, it's not. It was in their history. Oliver Morton thought that coming from killers meant he was supposed to be a killer too, but he didn't hurt anyone before he found out. Learning his history changed him. Sometimes it's better not to know where we come from."

Everyone gave that some thought.

Sarah passed Donkey a beer. There were several spare seats in the area next to the flowerbeds and after the exhaustion of the last week, Sarah was able to tolerate company quite well.

Donkey took the beer and sat down with a relieved groan. "So, are you staying, Sarah?"

She rolled her eyes and stood up. "Seriously, you two are as bad as each other."

"We just want you to stay," James said, lazing back to catch the sun on his face. "Don't hate us for it."

"I'm heading to the Box," she told them. "I'll be back in a bit, so keep the beers cold."

James patted the plastic cooler between the chairs. "Will do."

Sarah headed inside the large glass prefab and immediately felt hot. She spent as little time in the stuffy lab building as possible, but it was important to pop in from time to time.

Richard was sitting in his office, which was not surprising, as he hardly ever left. James hadn't yet decided what to do with him, so perhaps he was trying to delay his sentence by staying out of sight. "You okay?" she asked him, startling him and causing him to lift his head away from his notes with a yelp.

"Oh, Sarah? Yes, I'm... coping. I'm just writing a letter to the prison authority, letting them know Felix Flesch was assisting an active serial killer. I'm guessing he'll get a few months in segregation."

"Petty," she said with a smile. "I like it." She sat down on his little sofa, causing him to swivel on his chair to face her. "So has Flannigan finished her report yet? Are we in the clear for our cellar showdown and the carnage that ensued?"

"No, she hasn't closed the case yet, but the public seem happy with the end result. Two killers off the streets, and no costly court case for taxpayers to fund. I think everything will blow over."

Except I'm pretty sure Flannigan knows you're the Chester-le-Street Cannibal and could expose you at any time.

"Good. I'd say as far as cases go, this was as bad as things could ever get."

He nodded. "I can't believe Oliver Morton was my son. Prison records showed that he got in contact with Dr Carney several times, probably assuming I was still under his care. He must have eventually learned I'd been released and tracked me down."

"What a twist, huh? Wonder what we can do to top that in the future?"

"Sounds like you intend on sticking around?"

"Haven't decided yet."

He gave a half-hearted chuckle. "Yes you have. You belong here, and this place needs you."

She nodded slowly, staring down at the spotlessly clean floor tiles. "You're going to be okay, you know? I understand you think you lost control during this case, but it involved a lot from your past, and the past can be deadly. But it's over now, right? No future case is ever going to be able to mess with you like this one has. You got through it, and the only people you hurt were the ones who deserved it."

"I hurt you too, and James."

"Eh, colleagues fight. I tasered you. You throttled me half to death. It's water under the bridge."

He put his hands in his lap and stared at his twiddling thumbs. "I think James is going to send me back to Broadmoor."

"Maybe. Or perhaps I'll have a word and make it a condition of me staying that you stick around."

He looked her in the eye, seemingly confused. "You would do that for me? Why?"

She shrugged and threw out her arms, as if it should have been obvious. "You took a crossbow bolt in the chest for me. Guess I owe you one."

He lifted up his shirt and showed the clean white dressing. "It still really hurts, but the doctor says I'm lucky it only nicked a lung."

"Yeah, real lucky." She rolled up her sleeve and showed her stitched-up wound. "I'm running out of places for scars."

"Maybe you should try to avoid them then."

"I try my best, but they always seem to find me. Anyway, you should take a break from your work. I know you're on this great quest for atonement, but it's okay to be happy now and then. At least allow yourself a few minutes a day to smell the roses."

He let his head sag. "I don't deserve it. The amount of blood on my hands."

"We're all dirty, Richard, and we all have ghosts wailing inside our heads. That's what alcohol is for. We're all out in the garden, enjoying the sun. You should join us. It's one thing being a ghoul on the inside, but you don't have to look like one too. Get some fresh air."

"I don't think I can—"

"Ten minutes," she said, standing up. "If you're not outside by then, I'll come drag you out. You want to be normal, then spend more time around people. That's the only way you'll learn that there's no such thing."

He nodded. "Okay, Sarah. Thanks."

"No problem."

"No, really, I mean it."

"I know you do."

"Don't leave yet. I want to give you something."

She frowned and stayed put. "What is it?"

He reached out and dropped something into her hand. It was the tiny little auger shell.

"I used to think this was a reminder of my best day, but it's really a reminder of my worst. I've been keeping it to punish myself, but I realise that's not helpful. It's the only thing I own, so I want you to have it."

"I can't take this," she said, not even sure she wanted it.

"You can. Let it be a reminder of the danger innocent people in this world are facing. We stopped the killers, Sarah, but there are always more. Little, sharp shells hiding in the vast ocean ready to draw blood. Are you really ready to dive in?"

She closed her hand around the shell. "I'm already wet."

He smiled.

But she groaned. "That sounded wrong. I'm leaving. Ten minutes, okay? Or I'll come drag you out."

"I promise."

She stepped out of his office, placing the tiny shell into her pocket, but she didn't exit the Box yet. Instead, she went into the research room off of Lab One. Richard was right about her intending to stay at the Institute. It was fun to keep James dangling, but she knew this was where she was meant to be. She needed its resources to right a wrong, and if sticking around to chase serial killers was the price she had to pay, then so be it.

"Watch out, monsters, because Sarah Stone is going to get you."

CHAPTER
TWENTY-FOUR

FIVE WEEKS LATER...

Sarah knew it was somewhat of a conflict of interest to keep a prisoner in the back of the Institute's Range Rover, but it had the boot space she needed. Also, no one would miss it at this time of night.

She opened the boot and dragged the bound and gagged man out by his hair, dropping him over the ledge and dumping him on the gravel. She'd checked out the abandoned quarry several times over the last week, making sure nobody ever went there. Overgrown, and surrounded by barbed wire fences, it was a quiet place to play.

The bulky man struggled up to his knees and tried to get away, waddling like a penguin with his hands behind his back, but Sarah booted him in the back and threatened to use the Taser again. The yellow plastic gun was quickly becoming her favourite toy.

"Stop struggling," she said. "You're not going anywhere and you know it. It's just your instincts kicking in. You're panicking."

He got back on his knees and turned to face her. His eyes were wide and terrified.

"Just take some deep breaths," she said. "In… and out."

Nodding hysterically, he did as she asked, taking deep breaths and slowly calming down.

She pointed at his head. "Look at you. Big scary gangster with a shaved head covered in scars. Now you're pissing yourself in front of a little woman. Are all of you drug-dealing scumbags pathetic, or is it just you?"

He didn't even get angry. She'd broken him, and the fact he had no clue who she was probably scared him even more. The fact she had cut off both his thumbs after tasering him unconscious and tying him up probably didn't settle his nerves much either.

"I'm going to murder you and dump you in this quarry," she said evenly. "It's happening, so just deal with it. But you probably would like to know why first, right?"

He nodded, snot dripping from his nose and tears in his eyes.

"Someone in your filthy little gang killed my friend, Howard Hopkins. He made the mistake of having a problem with Albanian criminals dealing drugs and forcing people into prostitution. I mean, what an idiot, right? You probably had no choice but to kill him."

The man shook his head, trying to spit out his cloth gag. She stood and let him. There was no one around to hear him scream.

"I do not know what you speak about. I am innocent."

"No, you're not innocent. Don't be silly, Bujar. I've been researching you and your buddies for weeks now. I know every little seedy thing about you. The bad news for you is that I'm not like my dead friend, Howard. I'm not collecting evidence and hoping to see you all in jail. I'm just going to kill the lot of you. You see, I realised recently that I'm a bit of a monster. In fact, it took working with one for me to realise it. Death follows me, and no matter what I do, people keep dying while I go on. I figured I would make sure it only happens to those who deserve it. Do you know my partner used to eat people? Can you believe that? I've strangely come to terms with it. He's working on himself, you know?" She shrugged. "Maybe change really is possible."

"Please, let me go. I will help you. I tell you who killed your friend. I find out."

"All I know is that it was one of your gang, so just to be sure, I'm going to kill all of you. That's a foolproof plan, right?"

He snapped his teeth at her and tried to get up. She kicked him back down with ease. "Easy there. I thought we were past all that."

"I'll kill you, bitch."

She rolled her eyes. "If I had a pound for every guy that's threatened to kill me…"

Seeing that threats were no use, Bujar started to blab, telling her a dozen things she already knew, and several things she didn't. In time, she would learn everything she needed to punish everyone who was even within spitting distance of Howard's murder. Eventually, the police would take notice, when Albanian criminals started dropping like flies, but for a while they would likely chalk each death down to gang warfare. It gave Sarah a little time. Time to continue her work at the Institute, chasing after killers and babysitting her lunatic of a partner.

"Plenty of work ahead of me," she said, "but I'm afraid it's *mirupafshim* for you, my friend."

She shoved a plastic bag over Bujar's head and gaffer-taped it closed around his neck. He struggled and fought, but eventually he wore out and stopped struggling. Then, Sarah sat cross-legged on the floor and watched him slowly suffocate to death, gasping, and sucking in the bag that was too thick to break with his teeth.

"It'll all be over soon," she soothed, "and then you'll go to the place where all monsters go. Maybe I'll see you there one day."

She waited for almost an hour, enjoying the crisp night air and the silvery glow of the full moon. Then she went home to her room in Tithby Hall and slept deeply for ten hours straight.

It was a monster's sleep. A monster who was well fed.

Don't miss out on your FREE Iain Rob Wright horror pack. Six terrifying books sent straight to your inbox.

No strings attached & signing up is a doddle.

Just click here

PLEA FROM THE AUTHOR

Hey, Reader. So you got to the end of my book. I hope that means you enjoyed it. Whether or not you did, I would just like to thank you for giving me your valuable time to try and entertain you. I am truly blessed to have such a fulfilling job, but I only have that job because of people like you; people kind enough to give my books a chance and spend their hard-earned money buying them. For that I am eternally grateful.

If you would like to find out more about my other books then please visit my website for full details. You can find it at:

www.iainrobwright.com.

Also feel free to contact me on Facebook, Twitter, or email (all details on the website), as I would love to hear from you.

If you enjoyed this book and would like to help, then you could think about leaving a review on Amazon, Goodreads, or anywhere else that readers visit. The most important part of how well a book sells is how many positive reviews it has, so if you leave me one then you are directly helping me to continue on this journey as a full time writer. Thanks in advance to anyone who does. It means a lot.

ALSO BY IAIN ROB WRIGHT

Animal Kingdom
AZ of Horror
2389
Holes in the Ground (with J.A.Konrath)
Sam
ASBO
The Final Winter
The Housemates
Sea Sick, Ravage, Savage
The Picture Frame
Wings of Sorrow
Hell on Earth (6 books)
TAR
House Beneath the Bridge
The Peeling
Blood on the bar
Escape!
Dark Ride
12 Steps
The Room Upstairs
Soft Target, Hot Zone, End Play, Terminal
The Spread (6 books)
Witch
Zombie
Hell Train
Maniac Menagerie
Ghosts
Bad Luck
Flesh Bargain

Iain Rob Wright is one of the UK's most successful horror and suspense writers, with novels including the critically acclaimed, THE FINAL WINTER; the disturbing bestseller, ASBO; and the wicked screamfest, THE HOUSEMATES.

His work is currently being adapted for graphic novels, audio books, and foreign audiences. He is an active member of the Horror Writer Association and a massive animal lover.

www.iainrobwright.com
FEAR ON EVERY PAGE

For more information
www.iainrobwright.com
iain.robert.wright@hotmail.co.uk

f 𝕏

Copyright © 2024 by Iain Rob Wright

Artwork provided by Carl Graves

Editing provided by Richard Sheehan

All rights reserved.

No part of this book may be reproduced in any form or by any electronic or mechanical means, including information storage and retrieval systems, without written permission from the author, except for the use of brief quotations in a book review.

❦ Created with Vellum

Printed in Dunstable, United Kingdom